FLASH MOB

MIDLIFE IN AURA COVE BOOK 2

BLAIR BRYAN

READ MORE BY THIS AUTHOR

Use the QR code below to access my current catalogue. **Teal Butterfly Press is the only place to purchase autographed paperbacks and get early access.** Buying direct means you are supporting an artist instead of big business. I appreciate you.

https://tealbutterflypress.com/pages/books

Also available at Barnes and Noble, Kobo, Apple books, Amazon, and many other international book sellers.

Find My Books at your Favorite Bookseller Below.

Books by Ninya

Books By Blair Bryan

To all of the women I know who embrace aging gracefully:

You already understand your greatest treasure is your heart, soul, and mind.

To the women who are fighting it every step of the way:

It's going to be okay if your forehead moves and your lips don't become flotation devices.

Promise.

ONE

Katie sped to the pin Marisa sent in the text, drumming her fingers on the steering wheel to dispel her nervous energy. She was glad she'd been summoned in the clear light of day. In the dark, the neighborhood currently surrounding her would feel infinitely more menacing. She parked behind an old neighborhood pharmacy sandwiched between several other bodegas, restaurants, and check-cashing establishments. Her fingers flew over the keys as she fired off a text that simply stated, *Here. Green Beetle.* Glued to her phone, she watched the status change from delivered to read.

"C'mon, c'mon," she mumbled into the air, unable to contain the excitement bubbling inside her. "What a rush." Every sense was heightened and alive, and pangs of guilt tingled among the giddy frisson of her newfound purpose. "Relax, Jack. This isn't a Lifetime original movie, it's Marisa's real life," she mumbled under her breath in an attempt to quell her excitement.

Katie took a few deep breaths to calm her jumpy heart.

2 BLAIR BRYAN

"I wonder if this is how Yuli feels when she conspires with Karma," she mused aloud as she glanced around, eager to see Marisa's face. Each second ticked by slowly, ratcheting up her anxiety. Her eyes focused on the burgundy metal back door of the grocery store, waiting for Marisa to burst through it. She hummed as energy raced through her in a flurry of restlessness. To diffuse it, she organized the coins in her console, then glanced down impatiently at her watch. "Where the heck is she?"

Finally, the door flung open, and Marisa hurried through it. She paused briefly, her eyes darting around and her face pale. Seeing no immediate threat, she raced over to Katie's Beetle. She opened the door and sat down, ushering in a wave of jasmine, ylang-ylang, and fresh anxiety that dizzied Katie.

"Give me your phone," Katie demanded with her hand out, palm up.

"Why?"

"It's a tracking device. Haven't you watched Law and Order SVU?" Katie asked. "Dun-dun," she chimed with the distinctive sounds the show had made famous.

Marisa's expression was blank and confused by the reference, but she obediently handed over the phone, anyway.

"Never mind." Katie popped out the SIM card and opened the car door.

"Wait! What about yours?" Marisa asked, interrupting her dash to the dumpster, causing Katie to rethink her plan.

"Good point." Katie's cheeks pinked up, and her bubble of false confidence burst. She pulled her SIM card out, then ran over to deposit them both quickly in the dumpster before racing back and starting the car.

"Lie back," Katie instructed, and Marisa yanked the lever on the seat, lowering her out of view through the windows. Her skin was pasty and her hands trembled.

Katie raced back to her home and didn't utter a word until she shut the garage door firmly behind them.

"We're safe here. You can sit up."

With a sigh and a yank on the lever, Marisa lurched up in the seat. "What am I going to do? It's only a matter of time before Rocco figures out I'm not coming home."

Unsure how to answer her and wanting to bring the terrified girl some comfort, Katie defaulted to the question she always asked when a guest was a visitor in her home.

"Are you hungry?"

"Constantly, now that I'm pregnant," she admitted. "I can't stop eating, but I've been afraid to overdo it since Rocco weighs me every day. I'm allowed to fluctuate five pounds."

Katie reeled back at the admission like she'd been slapped. "Allowed? You've got to be kidding me. We'll deal with that misogyny in a minute." The admission incensed her. "You see how toxic and controlling his behavior is, don't you?"

"I know," Marisa admitted, her voice barely audible in shame. "I haven't told him yet about the baby. He doesn't know I'm pregnant."

"What were you going to do in another couple of months when you started to show?" Katie asked.

"That's why I'm here," she admitted.

Katie thought it over. "Have you been to a doctor and started prenatal vitamins?"

"No," she answered, then burst into tears. "I guess I

was hoping that, if I ignored it, it would go away and I wouldn't have to deal with it."

"Is that what you want? For it to go away?" Katie asked, forcing herself to keep her tone even and the judgment out of it. Though she'd never wanted to terminate a pregnancy herself, she deeply believed in the mother's right to choose.

"I don't know what I want," Marisa whispered, clearly overwhelmed as fresh tears spilled down her cheeks. Katie reached out to squeeze her hand.

"How about we get you inside where you can rest? I could run you a nice warm bath and then I'll have to make a run to the pharmacy and grocery store to get some supplies. Is there anything in particular you're craving?"

"Chocolate milk?" Marisa said wistfully, more like she was asking a question. "And some green olives?"

"You got it." She led the exhausted woman through the door of the garage and walked her into the bright kitchen. "Don't worry, we're alone here."

Arlo barked to make his presence known. "Well, except for my doggo, Arlo."

Marisa bent down with a smile on her face, and Arlo ran over to her, his tail wagging with glee in the presence of a friendly unknown visitor. She scratched the patch of fur under his chin and he licked her face.

"Are you cheating on me already, boy?" Katie joked. Arlo howled and then walked away to his post under the kitchen table. "I've got to run some errands, buddy. You keep an eye on our guest. This is Ms. Marisa." She turned back to Marisa and added, "I have some clothing that will fit, but it won't be as glamorous as what you're used to, I'm afraid."

"Beggars can't be choosers. If it's clean, I'll take it," Marisa said as she stood up quickly. Her skin turned green, and she covered her mouth with her hands, panic lighting up her eyes.

"In there," Katie pointed to the powder room down the hall, and Marisa hurried to the toilet, where Katie heard her retching for the next several minutes. "Poor kid." She walked to the pantry and pulled out a sleeve of saltines and two glasses, filling one with orange juice and the other with water. While she waited for Marisa to return, she set them on a tray.

"I'm sorry," Marisa said. Her hair hung in greasy strings, and she wiped her mouth with the back of her hand.

"You never have to apologize to me. I swear when I was pregnant with my youngest, Callie, I was so sick there were mornings I thought I would puke my baby right out." Katie laughed at the memory now. "You have my full support and sympathy. Pregnancy isn't always the walk in the park the movies portray it to be." She gathered up the tray. "Let's get you set up in the guest suite. It has its own bathroom and you'll have more privacy. I want you to feel at home here. Help yourself to anything in the refrigerator or pantry."

"Thank you," Marisa replied. She crept up the stairs, following Katie to the guest suite, where Katie set the tray down, pulled back the comforter, and patted the bed. "You look exhausted. Why don't you take a little nap and I'll run the errands, and then we can figure out what's next?"

Marisa climbed into the bed, and Katie pulled the comforter over her. The nurturing action made the young woman burst into tears.

"Oh no, are you hurt? Did I...?"

Marisa reached out and squeezed her hand. A faint flash of light blinded Katie and she reeled back from a blow. Inside her head, she heard a scream and the sound of metal scraping against the wall. The flash wasn't strong enough for her to receive any coherent visual messages, and it left Katie frustrated.

"I can't remember the last time someone was this kind to me," Marisa explained. "I'm sorry, it's probably the hormones. They are surging through me right now. Last week, an ASPCA commercial made me sob for an hour." She closed her eyes and relaxed into the pillow.

Katie nodded. "I get it. Just rest." She didn't even finish the sentence before she heard Marisa snoring softly.

———

Two hours later, Katie pulled the green Beetle into the garage and parked. Getting out of the car, she stood frozen for a moment, confused by the faint sound of Arlo's incessant barking.

"I didn't leave him outside, did I?" she asked herself. Whenever she ran errands, Arlo had the run of the house and usually spent the time curled up in a ball on the sofa now that Jeff was gone. But now, his barks continued on repeat, louder and louder.

"What in the world is going on with him?" She quickly grabbed two sacks of groceries and hurried into the house.

As she made her way down the hallway, the barking stopped. Seeing a light on, she rounded the corner into the kitchen. "Oh, good, Marisa, you're awake! I picked up your prenatal vitamins at the drugstore and some mandarin oranges. Also, dill pickle potato chips. Now I know that sounds disgusting, but when I was pregnant with Callie…" Katie stopped cold. The bags fell from her hands and the carton of eggs hit the ground, sending eggshells and yolks splattering across the floor. The brown glass jar of prenatal vitamins hit the ground with a clink, but thankfully stayed intact and rolled away.

Katie let out a whimper when she saw Marisa tied to a chair with a bloodstained gag placed over her mouth. Two kitchen stools lay on their sides and Marisa's eyes were wild. She muttered into the gag, but it muffled every syllable. Jerking her head repeatedly, Marisa lurched and tugged at the restraints. The chair they had secured her to squealed across the travertine as she struggled to wrench herself free.

To her left, Arlo was outside on the deck, growling and clawing at the patio door, and jumping up and flinging his furry body against it in vain. The glass was covered with paw prints and smears from his nose. He was baring his teeth, charging the door repeatedly, desperate to break through. When his eyes landed on Katie, his snarls became more viscous and demanding.

Her skin prickled with knowing a split second before she felt his forearm crush against her body and pull her feet off the ground. Katie made a split-second decision and reared her head back and head-butted him. His nose made a satisfying crunch as blood poured out of it and spread across a face she recognized instantly.

Rocco dropped her to the ground, yelped in pain, and covered his nose with his hand. Seeing crimson blood covering his hands he roared in fury, and Katie witnessed his aura shift from red to black before he delivered a fierce backhand that sent Katie reeling. She saw stars and points of light and suffered an instant headache when she hit the ground.

A second man in the room laughed at his pain. "Bested by a woman? You *are* a pussy."

"Shut up, Carmine! That bitch broke my nose."

"Wait until Big Tony hears about this."

The comment only seemed to incense Rocco further. Katie tucked her knees into her chest as Rocco kicked her in the stomach and lower back. Carmine's razzing fueled the attack as Marissa wailed into the gag. Katie's gaze focused on Marisa, huffing hard against the fabric to breathe, her nostrils flaring. It sucked in and out of her mouth in time with her panicked gasps. Her feet flailed, desperate to find leverage, bucking against the chair now in a burst of survival-fueled energy.

Carmine held Katie face down on the floor and then forced her arms behind her back and fastened them together with a zip-tie. He found his feet and yanked up, dragging her across the room, then jammed her down on the chair next to Marisa.

Rocco came into view, then Katie's vision clouded. She struggled to see through the black smudged aura covering his body. He picked up the bottle of prenatal vitamins from the floor.

"We're having a baby?" Katie saw the black haze that engulfed his being morph into red the closer he strode to Marisa. "Amorino?" He untied the gag and Marisa spit in his face, then howled.

"I hate you!" she screamed. "*We* are not having anything." Her voice was rough and strangled from terror.

"You will not take my child from me," he shot back.

Grabbing a handful of her hair, he yanked her head back and she yelped in pain.

"Who said I am carrying *your* child?"

Carmine chuckled again from the shadows.

"Maybe it's Carmine's," she dared and turned toward the other man. "I know you watch me in the shower, you pig!"

"Whoa! Wait a minute." Carmine held both his hands up and backed away. Rocco crossed the room in two strides and socked him in the gut, sending him to the ground with one punch before he could even dispute her story.

"Maybe I liked it," Marisa purred. "I did. I *did* like it." She ground her teeth together and made a passionate moaning sound that seemed to level Rocco. "Carmine especially loved when I called him daddy and let him take me in our bed."

Rocco's palm rocketed forward and struck Marisa's cheek with such force her head whipped back and then lolled to the side. A cut on her jaw dripped blood down the front of her shirt.

"Stop hurting her. She's carrying your child. You are putting stress on her *and* the baby."

"Who the hell are you?" Rocco crouched down in an effort to intimidate Katie. "You look familiar." His face was inches from hers, and she felt his hot breath on her cheeks.

"I'm nobody," Katie offered, hoping to distract him.

"Is that right?" Rocco stood up and walked over to the bookshelf where a photograph of Katie's children was proudly displayed in a gold leaf frame. He plucked it off the shelf and brought it closer to Katie's face. Seeing the faces of her children in his meaty hand made her stomach flip.

"Children are a gift from God, are they not?" He studied the portrait for a long minute. "They are also a person's biggest weakness. Beautiful. It would be a shame if a razor transformed the porcelain skin of this beauty." He turned the frame to her, pointing at a beaming Callie. "I could wipe that smile off her face with the blade of my knife." He dragged his index finger up in a line on each cheek, leaving a trail of blood in its wake. "You've inserted yourself into my life where you don't belong, and I am feeling the need to return the favor."

"Please," Katie begged, "leave my family out of it."

Rocco laughed and glanced around her home. "I'm sure your kids had idyllic childhoods growing up here, spending their weekends playing soccer and surfing. They probably thought nothing bad would ever happen to them in Aura Cove." He clicked his tongue. "Children are so naïve, aren't they? Random acts of violence can happen to anyone, anywhere."

"Please, I'll give you anything you want. Just leave my children alone."

He made a tsk-tsk noise. "Isn't that interesting?" He bent back down, inches away from her face. "Tell me why I should extend you a courtesy that you had no intention of extending to me?"

Tears washed down Katie's cheeks. She'd put them all in danger and was out of her depth. Who did she think she was? Just because she saw a few flashes and had Karma on her side, did she think she was powerful enough to take on a full-fledged member of the mob?

"You should have known to stay in your own lane.

Marisa is mine. And now that I know she is carrying my baby, there is nothing I won't destroy to keep my family intact. I'm sure you can relate."

Katie nodded as her eyes filled with tears.

"This is an impressive house and I have a new mouth to feed. Seems like a lottery ticket fell into my lap just when I needed it." He turned toward the other man. "Carmine, I'm going to ransack the house quickly and grab valuables. You put the mouthy bitch in the back of the van with Marisa and we'll go."

"Are you too afraid she'll nail you again?" Carmine laughed, poking the bear. "That's right, you need to hire a real man for the job." He paused long enough to produce a couple of body builder poses and then kiss his own biceps.

While he was distracted, Katie twisted her wrists together and then tried to wiggle her wrists out, but the zip-tie cut into the skin and drew blood. After several long moments of struggling, she felt a surge of hope when she pulled her hands free. With her heart thundering in her ears, she waited for her opportunity. Rocco was upstairs ransacking the house when Carmine bent down within her grasp. Katie sprang into action, clawing at his face with her fingernails until she drew blood. She ripped at his hair, pulling out a small chunk of it with her fist. Carmine lurched back, and she landed a solid punch to his solar plexus that took the wind out of him and sent him reeling. Adrenaline coursed through her, and she kicked free, running to the door as he stumbled to follow. She grabbed a cook book and flung it at him, darting away to the door. Like a caged animal, she was frantic, hearing Arlo howl on the deck in unison.

At the front door, her hands landed on the deadbolt to

unlock it. So close to freedom, just beyond the door were streets filled with neighbors who could help. One more second and she'd be free. Her heart soared as she pulled the heavy door open. She screamed, "FIRE!" that was cut off before the door was abruptly rammed shut by a powerful arm just behind her.

Rocco shoved her and pinned her to the wall with his body. His heavy palm pressed the back of her head into the hard wall. She writhed around and struggled to fight herself free, tasting the copper in her mouth. She spit on the walls and rubbed her bloodied hands against them, leaving clues behind of a struggle. Rocco yanked her up, and she fought him off. Her foot kicked at a vase full of peonies, and it crashed to the ground. He forced her down, and she felt the shattered crystal from the vase dig into her neck and back, making her whimper in defeat.

An early nineties episode of *Oprah* flashed into her mind. "Never let them take you to a second location. Fight with all your might. It's your only chance to survive." Katie gave one more valiant effort, summoning every ounce of strength and power within herself. She kicked and screamed, clawing and writhing against her attacker. She bucked and yanked him around the room, her desperation to survive lighting her on fire. Rocco wrestled with her, and she crashed down onto a coffee table that shattered under their combined weight. Her head felt light, and a trickle of blood obscured her vision. Dazed, she tried to gather her thoughts together, pinned under the weight of Rocco.

She bit his neck, tasting sweat and bile. A second later, she felt a rough rag cover her face and her eyelids become heavy. Refusing to inhale, her mind raced, a tightness spread from her chest to her limbs and, after a long minute, desperate for air, she took in her first deep breath. She fought against a heavy gray wave. Her eyes latched onto the portrait of her children, upside down on the ground a foot away from her. She forced herself to keep her eyes glued to their faces. Another smaller breath later, and she succumbed to the gray. Beckett, Callie, and Lauren's faces drifted by like a grainy movie, and she followed them into the abyss.

Two

Frankie lived just twenty minutes away in St. Pete's Beach. She was a native Floridian and could remember a time when you could fish off the piers without a license or easily park at the beach without a permit. She longed for the Florida she remembered as a child. Over the last twenty years, greedy developers had restricted public access to the water, slicing up her hometown's coastline, putting up fences, no trespassing notices, and private property signs. She resented the businessmen who cut off her easy access to the beaches and ocean and only allowed the wealthy to fully enjoy it.

She'd met Katie at an Aquacise class ages ago when Frankie had been ordered by her doctor to get more cardio or face giving up the junk food she craved. She'd worked her way unsuccessfully through almost every class offered at the YMCA, and her last hope was Aquacise. Wearing her bright red one-piece bathing suit she'd impulse purchased after watching re-runs of *Baywatch*, she dropped her bag and towel on the bench and entered the water where small groups of white-haired octogenarians were conversing about adding more fiber to their diets and whether Medicare A or B was the better option.

Bored to tears, Frankie dog-paddled past them and was relieved to find a woman who appeared closer to her age hiding out in the back, who seemed to have less coordination than she did. After class, Frankie offered to buy her a freshly-squeezed carrot juice at the smoothie bar across the street. It was a timid offer that Katie politely declined, then surprised Frankie by grabbing her hand and asking, "How about a margarita and some queso instead? I've had a day." That's when Frankie knew she'd found her person.

Over the next nine years, despite Jefferson's obvious disdain for Frankie, they were joined at the hip. Her mouth usually got her in trouble as Frankie lacked a filter and, for the most part, she loved and accepted that about herself. Over the years, she found keeping female friends as an adult required a level of pretending she wasn't built to maintain. Luckily, Frankie never had to pretend with Katie. Sustaining a friendship with her was easy from the get-go. It was never work. Katie was one of the warmest, most unassuming women she'd ever met. When you get to fifty and you find a gem like that? You hold on tight with both hands.

Even when Katie outgrew her and climbed into a much higher tax bracket that came with a beach house, she remained the same. She didn't put on airs and become an entitled jerk now that she had an ocean view. Jefferson's success afforded Katie's family a move into the tiny beachfront gem of a town called Aura Cove. It was an affluent zip code that attracted wealthy socialites and tanned retirees who'd won at the financial game of life. Yet, somehow, Katie was still the same woman she'd met at the YMCA.

Frankie remembered seeing Katie's new ocean front digs for the first time. Her jaw dropped as she drove through the ornate gates of Aura Cove in her sixteen-year-old Honda Civic. It leaked oil in a steady dribble creating permanent stains on her own driveway. Seeing the pristine concrete that made up Katie's new parking pad, she opted to park on the street, but Katie's new driveway was lengthy and she'd had to walk two city blocks in the sweltering Florida sun to arrive at the front door. When she finally rang the bell, she was drenched in sweat and a hot mess.

"Water! I need water," she'd demanded, clinging to the door frame to hold her parched body upright. Her t-shirt was stuck to her back, and a wet patch of sweat was starting its pilgrimage across the fabric covering her belly.

Confused by her dramatics, Katie searched the driveway for Frankie's car, then asked, "Did you walk here? Where's your beautiful beast?"

Frankie's cheeks reddened, and she sheepishly looked down at her feet. "It's too fancy. I couldn't take the risk of Esmerelda puking her black gold all over your fresh concrete."

"Frank, it's just a driveway. Next time, park in it." Katie pulled her by the arm into the showplace beach house, enjoying Frankie's dumbstruck amazement at her first glimpse of it. "That's exactly the look I had on my face when I saw this place for the first time." She smiled at her friend. "Relax, the only thing that's changed is my address." And it had been true. Katie didn't take on the same insufferable 'better than' attitude that Jefferson employed. She was a true ride-or-die friend.

That's why Frankie was deeply concerned earlier that Saturday morning when Katie was unresponsive. Frankie rolled out of bed and was drinking coffee, trying to wake up as she normally did, scrolling through her socials in search of memes that she knew would make coffee shoot out of her best friend's nose. She texted two hilarious contenders to Katie and waited. Checking her phone frequently for new notifications and the hit of dopamine they would deliver, she became antsy when they never arrived.

It wasn't like Katie not to respond with at least an emoji. Twenty minutes later, she looked at her phone again in dismay. Still nothing. Ill at ease, she scrolled up to see when Katie had last responded to a text message. It was at 4:17 pm the *previous* afternoon. Even when she wasn't up for company, Katie *always* responded, and the fact that she hadn't for hours ushered in the first burst of irrational fear.

"Something is wrong," Frankie said to herself in her own smaller kitchen miles away. It was an outdated space lit by overhead fluorescent lighting. Her home was a quintessential Florida ranch with dark, cramped rooms. It had large awnings and shutters on the windows to keep the punishing Florida sun from destroying everything in it and provide protection during hurricanes. There was a slight twinge of mildew in the air that was only chased away by fabric softener sheets on laundry days, and her lanai was being invaded by neon green lizards.

After downing a second strong cup of coffee, and still getting no response from a flurry of several more texts, she dialed her best friend's phone number and waited. Frankie hated to talk on the phone, and making calls was reserved for emergencies only. She was certain this brazen act would grab Katie's attention and force a response. It rang four times and then went to voicemail. Frustrated, she barked out a demanding voicemail message. "I'm giving you five minutes to send me proof of life or I'm jumping in Esme and heading your way. You know how much I detest talking on the phone. That's how worried I am! Call me."

She quickly dressed and grabbed her purse. On her feet were her trusty Birkenstocks, and she tugged on a ruffled aqua top and a pair of cut-off shorts she'd salvaged from her favorite pair of jeans. Frankie was a champion thrifter and spent hours searching for treasures at "Seconds" the little vintage shop on the corner of the town square, catty-corner from Kandied Karma. Aura Cove was a thrifter's wet dream. The castoffs of the wealthy were stellar, and Frankie spent many hours unabashedly picking through them.

One more quick glance at her watch indicated six minutes had elapsed, so she jumped in the car and headed straight to Katie's house. The difference between the dingier streets of her neighborhood was night and day compared to the immaculate ones of Aura Cove. The main entrance into the town was gated, with a heavy wrought-iron gate and palm trees flanking both sides, giving Beverly Hills a run for its money. Even the shoulders in Aura Cove were meticulously landscaped with flowering trees and bushes. As Frankie sped down the quiet streets of Aura Cove toward Katie's house, she cranked up the stereo. *Dua Lipa's IDGAF* (her current theme song) spooled out and filled her foot with lead, the way a great song always did. She had more than a few speeding tickets tucked into her glove box to prove it. Frankie sang the lyrics woefully off-key, though in her head they sounded worthy of an *American Idol* run, or at the very least would encourage Adam Levine to swing his chair.

Worried about her friend, she finally pulled into Katie's driveway and eased up to the garage. When she clicked the remote Katie had given her to open the garage door, the first tingles of panic crawled down her spine. Seeing Katie's car parked there was deeply unsettling. Sweating already, she quickly grabbed a hair tie and pulled her wild red hair into a haphazard ponytail at the base of her neck as she stepped out of the Civic.

At the door, she tapped in the security code to let herself inside Katie's house and walked down the hallway.

"Hey, babe, you scare me when you're incommunicado! Now that you're a free woman, let's go..." Frankie stopped mid-sentence, standing in the great room flooded by bright morning light. Under her feet, glass crunched against the soles of her shoes and ground into the travertine. The phone she'd clutched in her hand clattered to the ground and hit the floor with an ominous crack as she absorbed the disheveled state of Katie's beautiful beach house. A strangled cry escaped her lips, and her heart started to drum in her chest. Rattled, she cataloged a faint barking sound, and she turned to locate its source when, through the glass of the patio door, she saw Arlo leaping up and scratching his claws against it. When his eyes met hers, he stilled, sat on his haunches by the door, and howled.

"Katie!" she hollered out, already knowing she wouldn't get an answer. She crouched down to grab the phone and quickly dialed 911. Having watched enough *CSI: Miami*, purely to poke fun at David Caruso's one-liners while he whipped his sunglasses on and off, she knew enough not to touch anything. Her chest tightened, and it was difficult to inhale a full breath. She pinched the bridge of her nose to staunch the tension headache that was forming behind her pupils. Afraid to move, she stood paralyzed, waiting for the authorities to arrive. Minutes stretched into what felt like hours as time slowed down and she glanced around the great room. Her stomach flipped when it registered what looked like splattered blood on two walls. A bouquet of flowers was strewn all over the kitchen floor, and the vase smashed into a million pieces. The coffee table was destroyed. Something—or someone heavy—had crashed through it and shattered it.

"Come on. Come on," she said to herself, willing the police to arrive. It was obvious Katie had been engaged in the fight of her life, and she wrapped her arms around herself as shock numbed all her senses.

At last, there was a firm knock on the front door, and Frankie picked her way over to answer it. Outside, two muscular policemen stood wearing mirrored sunglasses to deflect the overpowering morning sun. She opened the door, grateful to hand her fears over to someone in authority because, on her own, they were proving too much to bear.

"I'm so glad you're here!" she cried. "Something terrible happened here and my best friend is missing."

"Ma'am." The older officer stepped by her and into the living room. Seeing the upended furniture, the shattered coffee table, and a blood-like substance on the walls, he pulled out and distributed gloves and booties to his partner.

"I'm Officer Longmont and this is my partner, Officer Willey."

The other officer was taller and lanky and, under different circumstances, Frankie would have embraced opportunities to squeeze his impressive biceps, but not today. Today, it barely registered that his freshly shaven face held a wisp of a five o'clock shadow and the cleft in his chin was a feature that gave her butterflies being a life-long John Travolta fan.

"Longmont and Willey?" Frankie repeated. Normally, this would be the place where she would gleefully thank the universe for this auspicious comedic gift and spend the next several minutes engaged in a tirade of inappropriate sexual innuendo. But not today. Katie was gone, and if she wasn't around to appreciate it, then… Frankie broke down in tears, the first she would cry. Crumbling to pieces in fear, her eyes darted around the room that was now a crime scene instead of her best friend's kitchen.

"I'm sorry, ma'am," Officer Willey apologized and cleared his throat, clearly uncomfortable in the presence of intense female emotion.

"Please call me Frankie," she said.

"Okay, Frankie, can we ask you some questions? It's best to do it now while the information is fresh." He pulled a small notebook from the pocket on his chest, and the radio on his shoulder squawked to life. "We have a 10-32 in progress. All available units be advised the suspect is armed." He waited until the alert was over to continue speaking. "Why don't you step over here with me while Officer Longmont secures the scene?"

"The scene…" she squeaked out. "…of the crime. Oh my God. Katie." Frankie was frozen in place.

He removed his glasses, and Frankie searched his eyes. They were neutral and calculating.

"Officer Willey, is that really your name?" she asked, eager for a distraction that would keep the truth from seeping in.

The corners of his mouth tilted down. "If I had a dollar for every time I've been asked that question." He sighed. "Yes, ma'am, it's my real surname. It's not exactly one you'd choose for yourself, if you know what I mean."

"Righto," she said awkwardly, grateful for his candor.

"Let's start with an easy one. Can you give me her full name?"

"Katie Beaumont." She answered and watched as he spelled it out in capital letters on the top line of his notebook.

"Have you touched anything?" Officer Willey asked.

"Just the garage door to type in the code to unlock it. I walked into the great room and then called you immediately."

"Does anyone else that you're aware of have the security code?"

"Katie's kids," she said, "and Yuli, her grandmother. And the housekeeper and the gardener." Frankie's voice tightened in a panic. "God, she gave it out like chlamydia during Fleet Week. I told her that was a bad idea, but she has always been too trusting." She burst into fresh tears.

"Do you need a minute?" the officer asked.

"Oh, God!" Frankie cried. "The kids!" She wrapped her arms around herself for comfort. "What am I going to tell her kids?"

The officer's eyes darted around. "Are there minor children in the home?"

"Oh God, no!" Frankie said. "They are all adults and out of the house. She lives alone."

"Does Mrs. Beaumont have any enemies?"

"Ms. Beaumont," Frankie corrected. "She just got rid of one. Divorce," she mentioned, and the officer scribbled more notes in his notebook.

"But everyone loves Katie. I can't believe anyone would want to hurt her."

Wait.

Frankie bit back the question that surged forward.

Was this the work of Zoya?

Katie hadn't given her any more information since the night they'd had too much tequila. She'd refused to even acknowledge it happened, which made Frankie start to doubt if the confession transpired at all. Frankie ran over plausible theories in her head while she tried to answer the officer's questions.

"When did you last see Ms. Beaumont?" Officer Willey asked. In shock, Frankie tried to piece the previous week back together. To help her focus, he gently tugged her arm and led her to the office out of the main traffic pattern. Her eyes locked on a crew of three that arrived in coats labeled Pinellas County Crime Scene Investigation. They fanned out into the great room, operating with well-rehearsed precision. A woman pulled out a camera and photographed the area. The brightness of the flash forced Frankie to blink. She saw the wall light up, illuminating blood splatter, and had to turn away as the images seared into her brain. It was definitely blood. Possibly Katie's blood.

"Frankie," Officer Willey murmured. "I need you to

stay with me." Frankie nodded, feeling the blood drain from her face. "When did you last see Katie?"

"A few days ago. On Thursday. Her divorce was final. She was finally free of that scumbag and we were going to celebrate."

"Was the divorce amicable?"

"Is any divorce really amicable?' Frankie interjected. "He's a big hotshot lawyer in St. Pete's Beach. Jefferson Beaumont." The word sounded more like law-yer coming from Frankie.

"The defense attorney?" His hawkish eyes narrowed, and he scribbled a few more notes.

"The very same," Frankie confirmed, then asked, "Why? Do you think he had something to do with this?"

"I can't speculate, but we'll see if he has an alibi. Spending thirty years with victims on the worst days of their lives has taught me this—anyone is capable of anything if the circumstances are right."

Frankie's eyes widened. "What can I do? We have to find her." She pointed at the wall. "She's hurt."

"She may be, but I will tell you there isn't enough blood here for you to worry. The first seventy-two hours are the most critical. I understand you are upset, but the more questions you can answer right now, the more light you can shed on Katie's life and help us bring her home safe."

Frankie gulped and nodded.

"Has she been acting strangely or doing anything out of the ordinary?"

It was a loaded question. Frankie was torn between divulging all of Katie's secrets in an effort to find her friend and concealing her new magical abilities. She didn't know who to trust.

Yuli. She would talk to Yuli and then decide if she should report anything further to law enforcement. Besides, if she started shooting her mouth off about her best friend's supernatural powers, they would probably think she was a nutcase and throw her in the looney bin.

Yes, officer, why don't we ask her dog what happened? He can speak, you know. Although I'm not sure if he can talk to Ordins. That's you and me. It's what the magical people call us ordinary folks.

Yeah, that explanation would go over like a lead balloon. Frankie bit back the story. No. It wasn't the time to bring it up. She'd talk to Yuli and then decide.

"We're going to need to fingerprint you and collect a DNA sample to rule you out as a suspect."

"No problem. It's probably a good idea. I'm over here several days a week, so my DNA is all over the place."

"Are there any surveillance cameras on the property?"

"Not anymore. She cut back her security system when she changed the locks. Said she always hated it when Jeff sent her camera footage of herself, when she'd forget to close the garage door, or when he monitored her interactions with the Amazon delivery drivers. She didn't want that kind of negativity around anymore. Dammit, Katie!" Frankie broke down.

"That's unfortunate." The officer said. "We'll canvas the neighborhood and see if anyone saw anything. Chances are pretty solid in an affluent neighborhood like Aura Cove that one of the nearby neighbors has footage."

He pulled a business card out of his breast pocket and handed it to her.

"That's all my questions for now. Thanks, Frankie."

She glanced down at the card in her hand. It had a gold shield that glinted in the morning light, but it was the name engraved on it in bold capital letters that caught all of her attention.

OFFICER HARRISON WILLEY.

Frankie's eyebrows shot to the ceiling and then she shook with repressed laughter before breaking into a heart-wrenching sob. Like a pendulum, she swung from one extreme emotion to the other, and the officer was clearly concerned.

"Are you okay? Is there anyone I can call for you?" He studied her. Frankie was certain he was looking for evidence of a psychotic break.

"No," she answered sadly. "Just find my best friend." He nodded and took a step back. Putting physical space between her messy, seesawing emotions and himself. She brushed her tears away and looked down at the card one more time before tucking it inside her pocket.

There she was, standing in front of an officer of the law named Harry Willey, and the worst part was she couldn't even tell her best friend about it.

THREE

cross the street, Katie's nosy neighbors eyed the police cruisers parked in the circular drive. Was it a domestic? Curtains swiped to the side as bespectacled residents peeked out their windows, then became bolder and spilled out onto the sidewalks and streets wrapped in bathrobes and slippers. Taking longer to drag their garbage cans to the street and retrieve newspapers at the end of their drives than was necessary.

It was the curse of the retired, to suddenly have so much extra time on their hands, but no tasks to fill it. You either found a hobby or you ate yourself to death in two years. There didn't seem to be much middle ground.

It appeared that Aura Cove's five-year streak of being St. Pete's Beach's Safest Place to Retire was in jeopardy, and the rare sight of a police presence on one of their unblemished streets fired the rumor mill up into a frenzy. Even though all the retired residents' yards were meticulously maintained by gardeners, that day, under the guise of 'gardening', her meddlesome neighbors dug their shears out of the garage as an excuse to get them closer to the action. Hoping to hear a juicy little tidbit of gossip they could share at the Aura Cove Golf Club. When the crime scene investigation unit from nearby St. Pete's Beach pulled into Katie's drive, it only added fuel to the fire.

Her closest neighbor, Sam Oslo, (who insisted people call him Oz) prized himself an amateur internet crime sleuth and had started a true crime podcast out of his soundproof walk-in closet a year ago. The show only had a handful of listeners so far, which was fine with Oz. He wasn't chasing fame. While searching for his purpose in retirement, he discovered a newfound love for solving mysteries thanks to documentaries like *Don't F*ck with Cats* and *Making of a Murderer*. Now, Oz's days were consumed with interacting with a like-minded community in internet chat rooms and combing through grainy video footage for clues. It was a hobby that kept his seventy-two-year-old mind limber.

He was against the idea of buying an oceanfront home in Aura Cove initially. "We can't take it with us," His wife, Betty, reasoned when she first broached the subject of moving to the affluent community. He had put in almost forty years at the Post Office and had a decent pension, and Betty retired from a highly lucrative career at an investment firm. Their frugal habits without the financial drag of children had given them options. Options they'd waited too long to exercise while Oz hemmed and hawed.

"Come on, honey," she'd begged. "We can afford it. I don't know how many years we have left together, but I know I want to spend them all with you at the beach. Think about it, sweetheart. It will help us stay active. Imagine taking sunrise walks every day, hand-in-hand in the sugary sand." She was swooning that day, and it erased years from her features.

"We can take long walks on the beach *without* the additional tax burden, not to mention the work of boarding up during hurricane season. Getting on ladders at our age is how you break a hip," he'd argued, and now he wished he hadn't. Oz was more grounded and pragmatic, while Betty's head was always in the clouds. That was the one thing he missed about his wife the most. There was a constant stream of everyday magic she brought into his life that he hadn't given her credit for until she was gone.

She'd slipped away. Here one day in perfect health, and then gone the next. He'd crawled into bed next to her that last night, and in the morning, his eyes opened but hers never did. It was the way she'd always said she wanted to go, but he was ill-prepared and inconsolable.

It would have been easy to just give up. He'd lived a great life with the love of his life by his side for five decades. Their lives were so intertwined, Oz didn't know how to go on without her. His first trip to the grocery store where he dropped two navel oranges into a plastic bag and spun it closed had gutted him when he realized he didn't need two now that she was gone. He'd wallowed for two months, every day bleak and gray, before Betty came to him in a dream.

She was lying down on the bed next to him, face to face. Her soft hand brushed his cheek, and a sweet smile bloomed on hers.

"Live your life, sweetheart. If you waste away in that bed, I'll come back there and kill you myself."

He'd woken with tears on his cheeks, and that morning, he called a real estate agent. The same morning, another gift he was convinced was from Betty landed on his doorstep. He found a golden Pomeranian puppy scratching on the back door of their modest home. Shaking and wet, she barely weighed five pounds. He'd nailed flyers to telephone poles and shared it on Facebook, but when no one claimed the dog, he decided he was as good a person as any to take care of her. Oz named her Shasta, after his favorite childhood soda. He needed someone to come home to, something to fill the silence that was suffocating, and thanks to Betty, Shasta appeared.

Three years ago, Oz moved into the house next to Katie. It was Oz's biggest regret in life and a bittersweet moment to buy their dream home without the woman who had dreamed about living in it with him. After moving to Aura Cove, Betty's prophecy was fulfilled. With a dog to walk daily and nothing but the ocean behind him, he'd dropped twenty pounds.

Avoiding the rubberneckers out front, from his back patio, Oz glanced over at Katie's house. The night before, he'd heard Arlo barking for hours and kicked himself for not listening to his intuition and calling the police.

Katie was a sweetheart, bringing over food for him and treats for Shasta every once in a while, and had made him feel welcome when he'd moved in. Now he hated himself for waiting. After a string of phone calls to the police to report suspicious lurkers, the Aura Cove Police Department didn't take him seriously anymore. When they found out he had a true crime podcast, he became an even bigger joke to law enforcement. In their eyes, he was the old man who'd cried wolf one too many times.

He sipped his coffee and wished he'd made the call

anyway, willing Katie to come out onto the patio and wave him over to ask for tips to keep her bougainvillea alive.

Across the backyard on Katie's pool deck, an emotionally dazed Frankie was relieved when the officer finally allowed her out onto the lanai to comfort Arlo. He was exhausted and agitated after spending hours running up and down the stairs and over to the door. While the crime scene investigators processed the scene, he whined and clawed at the glass, utterly inconsolable. After they cleared a walkway, Frankie brought out his dishes. He lapped up an entire bowl of water so quickly she thought he'd throw up, but he didn't even sniff the food dish.

Frankie bent down and sat on a chaise by the pool. She stroked his ears like she'd watched Katie do a million times before, and it seemed to calm him down. Cupping her hands around his face, she looked deeply into his woebegone eyes. She patted her lap, and he jumped up into it, trembling. Frankie continued to comfort the shaking dog, brushing her hands from his head down his back in long, rhythmic strokes. When he finally curled up into an awkward oversized ball on her lap, she made a few phone calls.

The first was to Kristina. Frankie often stepped up to help Katie's parents in a pinch, and they'd adopted her. With both her parents gone for years, she thought of them as family. She pulled her phone from her pocket and scrolled through the contacts, exhaling a long breath before tapping Kristina's name to begin the call. This was the hardest phone call she'd ever had to make, and it filled her with dread. Kristina picked up on the first ring.

"Well, Frankie!" she answered, her voice sunny. "This is a pleasant surprise."

The sweetness in her statement tore at Frankie's heartstrings. Her mouth dried up, and she doubted she could put forced pleasantries into words.

"Frankie? Are you there?" Kristina asked.

In the silence, two heavy words tumbled out. "Katie's missing."

"What?" Kristina's voice was muddled with confusion. Frankie gulped down the fear and continued.

"Katie's gone. I'm at her house with the police right now. I wanted to make sure you didn't hear about it on the news." Frankie heard the phone hit something, and she stifled a choked sob in her throat. She swallowed hard, gripping the phone with her hand and petting Arlo with the other, not sure who was comforting who.

"David!" she heard Kristina shout, her voice pitchy and strained. "Katie's missing!"

"What?" she heard him ask.

"She's disappeared!" Kristina cried. "The police are involved."

There was a scratching noise in the background that Frankie couldn't make out and, a second later, she heard, "David, here. Tell me what's going on."

Frankie was in shock at hearing his voice on the other end. Katie used to joke that he wanted to be kept in the loop, but only if that didn't require his active participation. Hearing him overcome their shared aversion to speaking on the phone indicated her best friend was in real danger.

"We're coming over," he demanded.

"I don't think that's a good idea right now. They are processing the scene for evidence. But could you do me a huge favor and tell the kids? I want to make sure they hear it from a loved one, not some random story on the six o'clock news or, God forbid, pull up here for a visit."

"Yes, of course." He sounded uncertain and smaller somehow than the man who'd wrestled the phone away from his wife for the first time in years. "What do I tell them?" he asked.

"I'm afraid I don't have very many details yet," Frankie began. "I'm going to take Arlo over to Kandied Karma until we figure out what's happening. I'll call when I hear anything else. Promise."

"How do they know she didn't just go out for ice cream and forget to take her phone? She does that sometimes, you know. Last week, she was MIA for almost an entire day." His voice was filled with a delusional longing that broke Frankie's heart.

Frankie paused, unsure what to say next. She didn't want to lie, but she knew the shocking news of the foul play, home invasion, and kidnapping of his only child might send a father with a weak heart over the edge. Instead, she tried to vaguely reassure him.

"They know." Frankie's voice was low. "There is evidence of a struggle at the house."

She couldn't get the spray of blood spatter on the walls out of her head. Frankie didn't want him to have to carry that burden.

"I have to go. I will call you when I have more information."

"Thank you, Frankie," he said.

"They are going to find her," she reassured him. He cleared his throat, and then ended the call. After enlisting the help of Officer Willey, she gathered Arlo's leash. She clipped it on his collar, picked up his dishes, and carried him over to the front door, afraid a piece of glass would cut into one of his paws. When she got outside, she set him down, and she started walking to the car, but Arlo dug in and refused to follow. He sat down in defiance, yanking at the leash.

"Dude, we don't have time for this right now," Frankie said as she tugged the obstinate dog, hoping he'd finally stand and walk. He did not. Instead, he laid down and made little distressed yipping noises deep in his throat.

Frankie knelt down on the grass. "What did you see, boy?" She stroked his fluffy head, and he closed his eyes. "You saw it all, didn't you?" She commiserated, "Katie says you can talk. I've never seen you do it, but if you can, now is the time."

He swiped his paws in front of his eyes and burrowed his head into her hand.

A flash of inspiration zipped through Frankie's mind. Yuli. Take the dog to Yuli. She's the dog whisperer. She'll get to the bottom of this.

Four

Frankie drove down the freshly swept streets of Aura Cove to the bustling downtown area where glassed storefronts housed a myriad of luxurious boutiques. It reminded her of the time she'd shopped downtown with Katie. The posh shops catered to a higher caliber of customers, and Frankie stuck out like a sore thumb dressed in her thrift store garb. That day, they'd stood on the sidewalk outside staring up at the gold-leafed hand-carved sign that read "From the Vine."

"Ooo! Wine! Big fan!" Frankie reached out a hand to pull open the door with a grin.

Katie winced as she delivered the bad news. "Actually, it's a vinegar emporium."

In disbelief, Frankie entered the boutique. Seeing the walls ringed with golden vats of vinegar, she asked, "Who needs all these flavors?" She walked down the row, reading aloud a few of the handwritten signs. "Truffle… Madagascar vanilla… raspberry." Next to each golden dispenser was a stack of tiny plastic cups to sample the vinegar before making a selection.

"Are we supposed to drink it?" Frankie wrinkled up her nose, finding the suggestion revolting. "You know I'm always a fan of doing shots, but yuck. Rich people are weird."

Katie laughed. "You're just supposed to take a little sip to get the essence of the flavor."

"I'm good," Frankie said, holding one hand up.

"Quit being a baby and help me pick a couple," Katie told her. "Just dip your pinky in it."

"So I know if it's a good marinade for human flesh?" Frankie joked. "When did you become a cannibal?"

Katie laughed. "You're ridiculous."

The clerk came over and, much to Frankie's chagrin, rattled off a thirty-minute presentation about the types and qualities of fine vinegar and its historic rise as the world's premiere condiment. It was the kind of yawn-worthy yarn Frankie couldn't stand. She entertained herself by asking bold, snarky questions, taking little sips of the acidic liquid with her pinky finger extended, and making inappropriate moans of false pleasure. When he turned his back, she bobbed her head to mock him, pretending to be taking tea with the Queen.

To help him save face, Katie offered the man a huge winning grin and said, "We're in a bit of a hurry. Can you get us a bottle of the pomegranate garlic and the passion fruit balsamic to go?"

When they walked out of the store and out of earshot of the clerk, Frankie groaned. "Sweet Jesus! That little TED Talk on the finer points of artisanal vinegar just shaved three years off my life that I can never get back."

Katie laughed. "You're such a drama queen! He was a nice guy who found something he was passionate about. Isn't that the holy grail? We're all just trying to find something that starts a fire in our soul."

Frankie snorted. "The fire in *my* soul is stoked by a chiseled jaw or a pair of muscular hands. Sorry, babe, but vinegar just ain't gonna cut it."

The memory of that average day hanging out with her best friend, tasting gourmet vinegars against her will made tears gather again at her lashes. She parked the car and turned to Arlo. "Come on, boy. Let's go see Yuli." She clipped on his leash as a precaution. The last thing she needed was for Katie's dog to run away.

Arlo crossed the console, jumped down onto the ground, and followed closely behind Frankie. On the front door was a closed sign, and the shop inside was darkened. She pressed her face to the glass, but there was no movement inside. Frankie almost turned around to head back to the car when she decided to test the door and gave it a push. Her heart leapt when it opened and she heard the familiar jingle. Frankie entered with Arlo, then locked it closed behind her. Inside, the store was deathly silent. The absence of the daily bustle was off-putting and eerie. It was usually such a festive place and one reason Frankie loved to visit. That and the free truffles Yuli sent her way that didn't meet her strict quality controls. Frankie gulped and walked back toward the kitchen, Arlo's tags jangling together as he trailed behind her.

Yuli was seated at a stool, and in front of her sat a plate of strange-looking truffles. Having worked her way through the entire menu at Kandied Karma, Frankie knew it by heart, but these she had never seen before. She loved every flavor of every truffle she'd ever tried, but these were furry and unappealing as she glanced down at them on the plate. Yuli's bright white hair was covered in a black headscarf that was tied under her sagging neck. She waved Frankie closer. Yuli muttered words Frankie couldn't understand that didn't sound like English.

"Our girl is gone," Frankie finally voiced.

Yuli nodded. "I know."

In the presence of Yuli's calm confidence, Frankie let herself relax for the first time since her impromptu visit to Katie's house. She'd been unhinged holding it alone, and the responsibility had tested her mettle. Now that she had deposited it in Yuli's capable hands, she found she could finally breathe again. No one was better at getting shit done than Yuli.

"You know?" Frankie asked, "How?"

"I can see," Yuli answered.

"What did you see?"

"A future," Yuli muttered. "Many of them."

"Then where is she?" Frankie asked, thrilled that they had magic on their side, certain it would hold all the answers and bring Katie home immediately.

"That's not how it works, Frankie. The easiest way to explain is…" Her voice trailed off for a long moment, then she snapped her fingers, finding the perfect analogy. "When Katia was in middle school, she was always reading those choose-your-own-adventure stories."

"I loved those books, too!" Frankie enthused.

"The concept is very similar," Yuli explained.

"God, I *wish* it were that easy to undo poor decisions in your life! That all you had to do was go back a few pages and make a different choice."

"You can," Yuli said simply. "Life *can* be a choose-your-own-adventure story if you let it."

"Let me guess, next you are going to tell me I should meditate?" Frankie asked. "Because I tried it a few times, but I think that switch is broken. I'd think about pizza, and that I forgot to pay a parking ticket, and then the clicking noise from the ceiling fan would start to drive me insane. I'd end up curled into a ball, rocking myself in the corner. See? Squirrel!" Frankie took a deep breath and tried to re-center herself the way Katie always did. "Focus, Frankie," she said to herself, then continued in a much more serious tone, "We have to find her. Time is ticking and the first seventy-two hours are the most crucial in any missing person's case. And I was figuring, since... you know..." She couldn't bring herself to use the word magic in a sentence.

Yuli began to explain, "It's not that simple. Free will impacts every decision a person makes. I cannot accurately forecast future events, but I can see a vast array of outcomes. It's a moving target. To hone in with greater accuracy requires a sacrifice that would leave me weakened. It's a monumental decision that could have adverse effects."

She pulled out a stick of incense and lit the end. She waved the billowing smoke toward her face with her thick hands and inhaled its deep patchouli scent.

"It smells like dirty hippies in here," Frankie commented, and Yuli snorted with a dry laugh.

"You know, I've always appreciated your candor and sense of humor." Yuli closed her eyes. "But now, if you can be quiet, I must focus." Next to her, Arlo sat at attention and whined.

"That's not usually my strong suit," Frankie admitted, unable to stop herself.

Yuli snapped her fingers, and Arlo lay at her feet. He growled and panted, side-eyeing the pair, his anxious energy palpable. Frankie took a seat across from Yuli and got the first whiff of the truffles. They were skunky and earthy, and the scent of rotting garbage was so thick she gagged and had to turn her face away.

Yuli unwrapped one truffle and devoured it quickly, swallowing it without chewing. Her body shook, then settled back in the chair as her eyes lightened to a bright silvery gray. She snapped them shut and began chanting something Frankie didn't understand, and when they reopened, Yuli's knowing eyes were glowing.

Terrified, Frankie popped up, her eyes wide. "This is some freaky shit."

"Sit down." Yuli barked the order, and Frankie knew enough not to back talk. She leaned as far away from the pungent truffles as she could. A second later, Yuli snapped her fingers, rendering Frankie limp and unconscious as she flopped back on the chair, snoring with her mouth open.

"Don't get me wrong, I love Frankie, but I also love when Frankie is quiet," Arlo said, then shook his coat and sat on his haunches.

"Alright, old friend, tell me what you saw."

"Katie picked up a woman named Marisa and brought her back to the house. She's blonde, has a nice rack, and cries all the time."

Yuli considered the ramifications of this information. "She's so far out of her depth. This is very troubling because Marisa is with child."

"How did you know?" Arlo asked.

"They were in the shop last week when Katia received her first flashes from a stranger." Yuli exhaled and declared, "And the worst part, Marisa is a Gabriano," Yuli uttered.

Arlo howled in pain. "Oh no. This is not good."

"Not at all," Yuli agreed. "After what happened with Sally, Zoya's been jonesing for an opportunity to bring the full brunt of retribution down on the Gabrianos, but payback now could get Katia killed. Zoya has a one-track mind when it comes to revenge."

Arlo whimpered and Yuli banged her hand on the table in frustration. "I made a terrible mistake. I underestimated Katia's confidence to step into her birthright. I thought we had more time. I thought she would seek me out for guidance and we would find a solution together." Yuli stood and paced the back room. "If I'd known she was going to try to intervene by herself…" Yuli circled the tables in the kitchen, her arms wrapped behind her.

Arlo followed behind her, deep in thought. "Katie's different. I don't know if it's the awakening or the divorce, but she's not the weak-minded, wait-and-see person she's been in the past. She's evolving."

Yuli grimaced. "That's what I was afraid of. She used to be so timid. I don't even recognize her anymore."

"The awakening changed her," Arlo declared. "It made her more decisive and bold."

"Possibly, but also when a woman matures, she discovers the only person she can count on is herself. She learns all the self-limiting beliefs she clung to don't serve her anymore, and she lets them go. It's a beautiful thing to see a woman step into the strength of her own power and let all the naysayers and societal norms fall away. I didn't think it would happen so fast. She's a quick study." Yuli continued to pace and think.

She heaved a heavy sigh. "I'm thrilled to see her take chances and believe in herself, but you always have to have a back-up plan." She crouched down and asked, "What else did you see? You must have more information. Tell me every detail, no matter how small."

"There were two men. First they subdued Marisa, and then when Katie came home from running errands, they ambushed her. She fought like hell, and even head-butted one of them," Arlo said with pride. "But I'm afraid that's all I can report. It was hard to hear anything useful through the triple-paned glass." He flopped down onto the floor and pouted.

"You were *outside* while Katia was fighting for her life?" Yuli was stunned by this new development. "You were supposed to keep her safe! Zoya will not be happy if she hears about the lack of verifiable intelligence you can provide. She'll likely add more time to your sentence."

"That's unfair. Marisa let me out. You know I have the bladder of an infant!"

"It's not for me to decide."

"I can't go against my instincts any more than you can go against Katie's free will. You open a door and I will run through it. You leave food on the counter, I will find a way to snatch it. You put a stuffed animal on the floor, I'm going to make it my mission to rip its head off and leave chunks of stuffing all over the house as evidence of my skills in battle. You can't fight your nature."

Yuli reached out and rubbed the dog's ear. Scrambling to shift some of the blame from his shoulders, he continued, "You are just as much to blame for this setback as I am. We both missed opportunities to intervene."

"You're right," Yuli admitted. "We both failed Katia, but now we've got to work together to bring her home."

"Don't you think we need to come clean? Maybe joining forces with Zoya right now could bring Katie home alive."

Yuli shook her head violently. "No way. I don't trust her. Maybe this is all an elaborate scheme she's orchestrated to maintain her role as the most powerful witch in our bloodline. She might view Katia as a threat."

"But the triad?" Arlo asked. "Wouldn't hurting Katie ultimately make her weaker?"

"Technically, but desperation drives people to do foolish things," Yuli explained. Getting more resolute, she continued to explain, "Zoya is a loose cannon. I am not willing to risk Katia's life in the hope that her motives are above board. We must find her ourselves."

"Okay. What can I do to help?" Arlo asked.

"We're going to have to keep Zoya in the dark," Yuli said. "If she checks in with you, do your best to be as vague as possible."

Arlo quickly nodded.

"We have to find her before Zoya knows she's missing, or it won't bode well for either of us."

FIVE

Katie's eyelids were heavy, and she opened them slowly in the darkened room. Disoriented and with a pounding headache, she swallowed the urge to vomit. The tension built in her eye sockets, an ominous precursor for a migraine. Her mouth was bare, but she didn't scream, somehow deducing it was futile and a waste of precious resources. Her shoulder ached from extended contact with the cold cement of the floor she was lying on, and she struggled to pull her body into a seated position and looked around the room, trying to piece together her muddled thoughts.

"Save your energy," she murmured to herself. Tucking her feet under her, she pushed up to a shaky standing position. Taking a coltish step, Katie stumbled to the wall and broke her fall with her hands. She pressed her body into the blocks and leaned her forehead against the cool surface, taking in several long gulps of air. The cottony landscape of her mouth combined with an unquenchable thirst made it hard to swallow. As her eyes finally acclimated to the dark, she glanced around and first noticed the high windows that let shafts of moonlight into the room. They were far too high overhead and completely out of reach. Without a ladder, they were a useless avenue of escape whose mere existence mocked her.

She walked the perimeter of the dark room, searching for clues, dragging her forearm against the walls to hold her shaky body steady. The walls were concrete block and spongy in places from moisture, and the scent of mildew lingered in the air. As far as she could tell, she was in an abandoned warehouse, but where? She hadn't been awake during their transport and could have been unconscious for twenty minutes or eight hours.

"Marisa?" she whispered into the darkness, and it did not surprise her when there was no response. The first drums of panic beat in her chest as the events all came rushing back in a torrent. From the bits and pieces of cases Jeff bragged about over the years, she knew the Gabrianos had a way of making their problems disappear, and without thinking the consequences of her actions through, she'd just become Rocco Gabriano's biggest problem. The first regrets started to pile up, and she beat herself up in the darkness for acting too swiftly.

"Oh, Yuli," she said aloud in the darkness. "What was I thinking? I should have waited."

She closed her eyes, and the faces of her children appeared. A few tears broke free and traced down her face. She sniffled in the darkness as sorrow washed over her.

Was their recent dinner together the last time she'd see their beautiful faces? The thought crushed her, and the tears came faster. The panic of never seeing them again sucked the air from her lungs.

"How could I have been so stupid? I put you all at risk," she whispered into the darkness. Katie hated herself for the tunnel vision she'd had about her new purpose in life without weighing the costs. The terror swallowed her, and as she ruminated on the actual possibility of dying, it caused her to hyperventilate.

"If I die here, at least they know I love them," she whispered to console herself as reality set in. "No!" she chastised herself, knowing keeping her mindset positive in adverse conditions could be the difference between life and death. "I *am* going to walk out of here, and I *am* going to hug my kids again." It would have been easy to let defeat settle in and curl up in the fetal position, but she refused.

"Get it together, woman," she mumbled under her breath, giving herself another pep talk, and focused on slowing down her breathing. In for four seconds, hold for four, out for four. Finally, her breathing slowed, her mind was clearer, and she could focus.

She circled the confines of the room again, looking at it with fresh eyes, stretching her arms overhead and reaching back to rub her shoulders. There was an old industrial sink on one wall. She stopped at it and turned the crank in vain, desperate for the flow of water. The ancient knob cut into her hand, refusing to surrender one precious millimeter. It was rusted closed and a dead end. She forced herself to continue her evaluation of the warehouse. The room was composed of crumbling concrete and unforgiving metal. Still searching for something she could wield as a weapon, she walked the perimeter again. Finding nothing, she felt hope dissipate and slid down the wall, landing on the floor, where she hugged her knees to her chest.

"What if they never find me?" She shivered at the truth and, desperately having to urinate, made a brass decision. Katie walked to the corner, pulled down her yoga pants, pressed her back against the wall, and peed. She marked all the corners of the room, wrinkling her nose at the strong ammonia smell. Katie wasn't ashamed. She was proactively spreading her DNA all over the room, so if it became a crime scene, there would be no way to deny she had been imprisoned there.

"Think!" she said to herself, her eyes darting around the room. Moonlight spilled from the windows at an angle that glinted across a metallic object near the ground. She walked over to it and pulled at a metal Allen wrench that was wedged between the floor and the wall. It was a rusted "L" shaped tool, only about four inches long. Not much, but it was something. She stared at it, resting in her palm before she chose a spot that wasn't visible from the door and, using the Allen wrench, started carving into the wall. The concrete was soft, and the tool crushed it into a fine powder that fell to the ground and made Katie sneeze. One line at a time, she pressed her fingers hard against the wrench until they turned red. The effort made her sweat and her stomach rumble. She'd scratched out a K-A-T and then had to take a break. Her fingers ached from the strain of pressing the tool against the blocks.

"I need help, Yuli," she cried, hugging her legs to her chest and rocking herself forward and backward. She envisioned Yuli in the shop at Kandied Karma. By now, surely, her family would know she was missing. "Help me, Yuli.

Send me a sign. Please help me survive this," she begged into the night air.

Her stomach rumbled. The hunger was annoying, but the thirst was impossible to ignore. She needed water soon and did not know how she was going to get it. "Zoya," she cried out into the darkness as despair filled her entire being. "Help me. I'm alone and afraid, and I don't know what to do. I know you would." She leaned against the wall again and waited. The heaviness of regret hung on her heart.

"Arlo!" she cried, thinking about her poor pup and how he'd fought in vain through the glass. Who would take care of him if she didn't make it out of here? She shook her head to clear it. "Stop it! That kind of thinking will not save you. What would Yuli do?" she asked herself and stood to pace the dark room. Walking always helped her when she was wrestling with a decision or formulating a plan, and she'd never needed one more.

"A weapon. I need to find a weapon," she mumbled to herself. Scanning the room again, her gaze landed on the industrial sink. She walked over to it and knelt down. The pipes were corroded and rusted. It was a cast iron relic that was probably over a hundred years old. Katie tugged on the pipes one at a time, looking for weaknesses. Under the pressure, one long length of pipe wiggled.

Over the next hour, she yanked on the pipe, rocking it forward and back, hoping to loosen it enough to break it free. At the end of the hour, she had nothing tangible to show for her efforts and leaned against the wall for support. She was exhausted, and a film of cold sweat made her forehead clammy. Her hands were filthy, covered in chipped pieces of the cast-iron pipe and greasy black residue.

That's when absolute terror set in and she sobbed. The tears kept coming, and she briefly thought she should force herself to stop. She was dehydrated, and they were a luxury she couldn't afford, but she couldn't stop them from coming. Katie was terrified and in need of a miracle.

Six

Yellow crime scene tape crisscrossed the front door of Katie's home and flapped in the sea breeze. News vans with skeleton crews of teams of two were parked haphazardly wherever they could find a spot on the normally silent street. Violence had blemished Aura Cove's perfect reputation, and it was the talk of the town.

"This is a nightmare!" Callie cried, looking out of the window of the backseat of Lauren's car. "To see that yellow tape wrapped around stakes in Mom's yard, it gives me chills."

"We couldn't go inside if we wanted to," Lauren filled them in. "The police haven't released it yet." She shivered. "Seriously, how messed up is it to call Mom's house a crime scene?"

Beckett's eyes were red and his jaw tightened as he glowered at the news vans that filled the streets. The muscles in his jaw rippled with tension. "Are you getting harassed by the media, too?"

"Yeah, it's been constant phone calls and emails," Lauren answered.

"Bottom feeders, making a living off the misery of others. It's disgusting," he growled as he witnessed a bold reporter turn their way with a cameraman in tow.

"Let's get out of here and go see Yuli," Lauren offered and started the car, driving off as a horde of photographers rushed closer, snapping photos of their grief. From the back seat, Callie gave them the finger as Lauren sped away.

She pulled into the back parking lot of Kandied Karma, and a few moments later, Yuli opened the door to let them in, then promptly locked it behind them when she'd noticed they'd been followed by two news vans.

Beckett's eyes widened. Seeing David and Kristina already seated on stools reinforced the seriousness of the situation. His grandparents were exhausted. A despondent Kristina stirred the espresso in front of her with a spoon, and David's skin took on a sickly gray pallor. It had only been twenty-four hours since their entire world was torn apart.

"Any news?" Beckett asked David.

"No, grandson."

"We have to *do* something," Beckett demanded. "We can't just sit around here waiting when Mom's out there somewhere."

"He's right," David agreed and got to his feet, holding his cane.

Kristina was tearing a tissue in her hands into long strips. "Who would do this to our Katie?" She burst into tears. "I just don't understand it at all."

"Let's print up some flyers with her picture and start

canvassing the neighborhood," Callie offered. "Someone knows something. She couldn't have just disappeared without a trace."

"Maybe we should get some friends together and start a search party?" Beckett offered. "We could start at her house and branch out from there."

"What about using the media to our advantage?" Lauren offered. "We need as many eyeballs out there searching for Mom as we can get. They are going to be skulking around, anyway. Let's use them to help us. I'll call to see if we can get them to do a story."

"That's a good idea, honey," Kristina said, turning toward Yuli. "Mom?"

Yuli was quiet and seemed distracted, but nodded in agreement. "Those are all good plans." She puttered around, dispelling the nervous energy that consumed her.

Kristina continued, "You've always been the closest to Katie. Do you have any idea who would have wanted to hurt her?"

Yuli shook her head no. She lied to her family, trying to protect them, because she knew the truth was more terrifying than they could handle.

———

A few hours later, Katie's smiling face was staring back at them from the stack of flyers that remained on the cafe table inside the shop. They'd canvassed the entire downtown of Aura Cove, handing out flyers and taping them to windows inside businesses on Main Street. Completely spent, they returned to Kandied Karma where Yuli had sandwiches delivered to keep the volunteers' strength up.

She knew all the efforts were futile, but she also knew staying busy helped her family work through the fear that overwhelmed them when there was nothing to do but wait.

At Kandied Karma, thanks to Beckett's pleas on social media, a group was gathering to begin a search party. The shop had been transformed into a makeshift volunteer resource center, and Yuli was shocked to see many of her loyal customers stop by and offer to join the search efforts.

At a table in the corner, Beckett poured over enormous printed maps of Aura Cove, dividing the search area into quadrants. When a group of his friends from college walked in the door, he had to fight back tears. He clapped them on the back and divided the volunteers into teams of two, handing them the map of their search quadrant.

Oz walked in the door next and beelined over to Yuli, who poured him a cup of coffee and sat down in the seat across from him. She watched her great-grandchildren organize the growing group of people that flooded into the store with Frankie, who bent down to unclip Arlo from his leash. The dog hobbled over to their table without his usual exuberance.

"Looks like that one is miserable without Katie," Oz remarked when Arlo whined and flopped down on the ground next to him. Arlo was becoming despondent in the absence of his favorite human. The usual bounding energy he had in droves was lethargic and weakened. He lay in the corner, refusing to make eye contact, his despair evident in the tuck of his tail, and his refusal to even sit up when a new visitor came into the store.

"We all are," Yuli stated.

Oz reached down to stroke his curly fur. "Have the police interviewed Jeff?" Oz asked. "In cases like this, it's almost always the husband who has the biggest ax to grind."

"He just got demoted to ex-husband," Yuli informed him. "But, yes, they did interview Jeff. According to the police, he's got a rock-solid alibi and has been ruled out as a suspect." The doorbell jingled and Yuli muttered, "Well, speak of the devil."

Jeff walked into the store, and Yuli's eyes focused on him. He was dressed plainly in a powder blue button-down oxford and dress pants. More withdrawn than she'd ever seen him, it was the way he carried himself that struck her. He walked through the crowded shop, hesitant and often stepping aside to give another man the right of way. In the past, he'd been more of a peacock strutting around, his feathers on full obnoxious display, but now, he was more reserved and diminished. There was a softness to him that didn't exist previously.

At her side, she heard Oz continue, and it shifted her focus away from Katia's ex-husband. "I gave the police the footage from my security cameras, but there wasn't much there. Just a car and some headlights. The license plates were too dark and pixelated to read. I wish we could press a magic easy button to enhance the footage and render it crystal clear, like they do on all the TV crime shows." He sighed.

Preoccupied, Yuli nodded, deep in thought. She didn't need to identify a getaway car. She already knew who was responsible; she just didn't know how to find Katia. "Will you excuse me?" Yuli asked Oz, who nodded. She got to her feet and busied herself refilling the coffee pot, waiting for Jeff to make his rounds to the kids. Finally, he was alone, and she shuffled toward him.

"Can we speak privately?" Yuli asked in a low voice. He didn't make eye contact at all but nodded and followed her into the kitchen where she buttered him up. "It's good of you to come here to support the kids." She began looking for common ground. "To be honest, it surprised me to see you walk in."

"Well, thanks, I guess," he said evenly, the usual bravado of his cultivated courtroom voice dimmed to a conversational level.

"I need to ask you something, but I need you to keep it to yourself."

"Okay."

"I have reason to believe the Gabrianos have Katia."

"That's absurd." Jefferson was shocked and pursed his lips, shaking his head no. "What leads you to believe that?"

"Rocco Gabriano was here last week with his wife. Katia seems to have taken a shine to the young woman."

"That makes absolutely no sense at all," he dismissed.

Frustrated, Yuli continued, "Since you've been working with them for years, I was wondering if you could do some digging, maybe provide a list of their real estate holdings?"

"That's unethical, not to mention a breach of privilege," he answered. "I could lose my license."

Yuli shrugged his concerns off. "We're talking about Katia, the *mother* of your children. If that's not a good enough reason to break privilege, I don't know what is."

He shook his head. "They'd have my head on a spike." Jefferson shuddered. "They are not the kind of people who take kindly to betrayal. I'm sorry, I wish I could help, but maybe you should take your suspicions to the authorities."

Yuli sighed, frustrated at reaching another dead end. Done with the weak man, she left him there.

Later that evening, the search party returned to the shop without success. Yuli wiped down the chairs and the tables quietly. She was bone tired. With the store finally emptied, she flipped the sign to closed and locked the front door.

"Mom?" Kristina was the first to notice. "You look exhausted. Why don't you head home and rest for a bit? We can hold down the fort here tomorrow. Right, kids?"

Callie and Beckett nodded. Yuli tried to protest.

"You can't be of any help if you don't take care of yourself first," Kristina said as tears dusted her eyelashes. Yuli opened her arms and gathered her daughter's broken heart into them.

"Sounds like good advice you should take yourself," Yuli said softly.

Lauren nodded. "We've got the store. Why don't you both take a break tomorrow?"

"If you're sure," Yuli said.

"We are." Lauren nodded with a tight smile.

Yuli gathered up Arlo and drove Kristina home. She was running out of time. Every hour that passed brought her closer to Zoya discovering the truth.

Yuli knew from experience, Zoya could go scorched earth in a millisecond. Who knew what she was capable of when her powers were threatened? Katia's existence and supernatural abilities were tightly intertwined with them both. If Katia died, it would destroy the triad. It would be a setback that would weaken their bloodline for generations, and there was no way Zoya would allow that to happen.

SEVEN

At the compound, Zoya's eyes acclimated to the darkened room, and a curious sound wave hit her. It was an off-putting auditory stimulation from a tuning fork that resonated into the air. "Help me." The muttered words tumbled into her ears along with the cacophony of piercing, hypnotic noise, and goosebumps broke out on her arms. At her side, her chocolate lab Terrance barked and growled, a sound that, when coupled with the tuning fork, was driving Zoya out of her mind.

"Hush!" Zoya commanded.

He whined and then circled and sat down at her feet. She promoted Terrance after she'd freed Magnum from his servitude, and while he was doing his best, he still had a long way to go. Another wave of vibration crashed over her, and she covered both her ears. She felt the sensation of being tugged toward her expansive closet, and she gave into it, following the signal with Terrance nipping at her heels.

Inside her jewelry wardrobe, an amulet she'd long

forgotten about was glowing with intense purple light, and like a moth to a flame, she was drawn to it. Zoya reached out to touch the gem, and the metal that wrapped around the crystal was warm to the touch. Picking it up, she fastened it onto her neck and centered the crystal face. It was heavy in her hand, and the glow intensified the longer she held onto it. She felt her skin flush with unexpected warmth.

The amulet was a connection to the past and her supernatural lineage and had been included with the deed to the island so many years ago. She'd thought it was just a beautiful bauble and tucked it away. Now she recognized it held a much more important purpose. She followed the intuitive urge to her pantry where she gathered salt. Then she walked to the sea and poured the salt into a sacred circle on the white sand. When the circle was completed around her, she closed her eyes and chanted. With one hand, she clasped the amulet and meditated, humming and chanting, using vocal incantations to go deeper inside herself.

It took several deep breaths and her iron will to peel away the annoying sound layers to the quiet center of her soul. Eventually, she felt the distinct shift and harnessing of energy, and it pulled her away from the sand and surf, into the air, carrying her on a breeze. A few moments later, she tumbled to the ground, landing on a prairie filled with grasses glowing during golden hour, the most magical hour of the day.

Finding her feet, she was tugged toward a tree where a dark-haired little girl was swinging on a tire swing. She grinned from ear to ear as the warm glow from the remains of the sunlight shone bright in her green eyes. Swinging back and forth, her musical laughter filled the air as she pumped her chubby legs to gain momentum.

The setting sun backlit the figure of a man, and Zoya gasped. She'd memorized the lines of that familiar form decades ago. Her heart leapt, and she raced over to him and threw herself into his arms, reveling in the comfort she found there. He pulled back and offered her a devilish grin.

"You're sure a sight for sore eyes," he drawled, and she melted.

"Sally." She sighed his nickname into the warm crease of his neck, relaxing into his embrace. His lips brushed against hers softly and her heart burst. It was a sensation she'd longed for every day since she'd lost him decades ago.

The amulet at her neck became warmer, and it singed her skin. "Ow," she cried out and used her fingers to hold it away from her collarbone. It seared her thumb and she reflexively let it go to settle back onto her chest, where it tingled. "Why haven't you ever come to me before?" Zoya asked when she found her voice, the pain grounding her.

"It's not up to me, doll-face. You know I'd be in your arms every day if I could," he said with a grin, and he was just as handsome as she remembered.

"Where have you been?"

"I ended up in the same place most gangsters do, with the demons in hell, but lucky for me, Lilith took a shine to me."

"Lilith?" Zoya's eyes widened in shock. There weren't many women that struck wonder and awe in her, but Lilith was the rare exception. Lilith was the female embodiment of everything Zoya believed in. Thought to be the true first wife of Adam, she refused to submit to him sexually and declared her equality. She was the mother of the reverse cowgirl, and the kind of brash, confident woman whose pure, adulterated, feminine power inspired and energized Zoya.

"The Dark Goddess has enslaved me and I exist purely to do her bidding, but I made a deal with her to come to you." His expression turned somber. Sally pulled back and caressed her cheek with his hand, and she closed her eyes and squeezed his wrist, getting lost in the moment. "You must listen." His tone was grave, and she locked her eyes on him.

Taking a step away, he returned to the little girl in the swing. He pushed little Katia's back, sending the girl higher. Her laughter echoed out into the field and bounced back under the canopy of the massive oak tree.

"She's such a beauty, your great-great-granddaughter," he said as they watched the little girl ricochet back and forth from the sky to the ground. "She favors you," he said, pointing at Katia. "The adorable apple didn't fall too far away from the gorgeous tree." He pushed once more, and she shot up to the sky with a giggle and a swoosh of her pink cotton dress.

He flickered, and fear coursed through her. Panicked she would lose him again, Zoya reached out for him with both arms, pitching forward when they didn't connect to anything solid. She cried out when she landed hard on her knees as her eyes locked on his.

"I don't know how much time we have." He reached down to offer her a hand to pull her up. She grasped at it, making two failed attempts before she connected with the warm skin of his hand. He pulled her to her feet and wrapped her in his arms, and her heart swelled. She was ensnared in the web of feelings he'd always been able to bring out of her on contact, and she closed her eyes to revel in them.

He glitched and disappeared, then returned instantly. "Doll-face, listen to me. I have a very important message. It's about Katia."

At the mention of Katia's name, her eyes snapped open, and she regained her focus. "What about Katia?" she asked.

"She's in great danger," he warned, his expression grim. "The answers are in the archives. The bad blood, it goes all the way back to us."

The words had barely left his lips when she felt him stumble back. Then his form tugged away and turned into a black shadow. He rocketed up into a sky where ominous clouds were collecting, pregnant with rain. The physical separation from him was so painful, she shrieked as the agony of loss rushed back in. Zoya was drowning in a cocktail of despair and desperation, and she sobbed inconsolably, reaching for him with fingers that clawed at the air.

"Sally!" Zoya whimpered. His presence was gone, and the silence was deafening. She heard the creak of the tree swing, and her focus shifted back to the child on the black tire. Behind Katia, a pair of arms connected to a black shadow pushed and sent her higher into the warm breeze. Her laughter bubbled up and echoed across the field.

"Again, again," the little girl cried, and the shadowed figure grew taller and pushed her higher.

Zoya's heart ached from the memory of pushing Nadia in a swing she'd made from two long lengths of rope and a branch she'd tied for a makeshift seat so many years ago.

Those emotional darts to the heart that surfaced without warning were the price she'd paid for loving her daughter and losing her.

"Again!" Little Katia sang. "Higher!"

Zoya was so close she could almost touch Katia. She could reach out and run a finger down her widow's peak and the white streak of hair that shot out of it. To console herself, she reached out with a melancholy smile to touch the child. In an instant, the shadowy figure doubled in size, continuing to grow larger until it completely eclipsed the child and the swing.

The sun disappeared behind a cloud. In seconds, a fierce wall of storm clouds gathered in the sky with their ominous heaviness, and she heard the first rumble of thunder in the distance. The wind gusts intensified, and the shadow's hands brushed the child's back. Hearing a deep, maniacal laugh reverberate across the blustery prairie, bolts of terror surged through Zoya's center. The little girl was undeterred by the change in weather and hollered in her singsong voice, "Push me higher!"

With one more massive push from the enormous black-ened hands, Katia sailed up to the sky with a giggle. Then the swing broke away from the tree. It sent the little girl flying away higher into the black clouds until they completely devoured her.

"No!" Zoya shrieked, landing hard on the grass when the first bolt of lightning zinged across the sky and struck what was left of the tree. It disintegrated into ash in the wind as the storm began to howl. Rain pelted down in sheets, and she shrieked in tandem with the wind.

Her throat closed, and she struggled to swallow back tears. They streamed down her face as she cast her gaze up to where Sally had disappeared, squinting her eyes as the rain pelted her face and washed away her tears. The drops were cold and unrelenting, and she shivered as goose-bumps broke out on her arms. Zoya was alone. She wailed into the wind and the storm clouds that engulfed her and finally closed her eyes, submitting to their relentless power.

When she opened her eyes, she had returned to the beach. On her hands and knees and gasping for air, it took several long moments before the panic in her heart subsided enough for her to process the message Salvatore had tried to send her. At her throat, the amulet burned and she could smell searing flesh. With one hand, she yanked it off her neck, grimacing when the amulet seared her palm. She'd lied to herself for years and buried her grief over Salvatore's death, but it had resurfaced, relentless in its pursuit.

Pushing the loss away again, she composed herself and weighed her options. She'd waited for decades to claim the full force of her ancestral power. There was no way anyone would take it from her now.

Time was ticking by, and she needed to act. There wasn't a second to delay.

———

An hour later, Zoya disembarked from the aircraft and sped over to Katia's house. Seeing the yellow crime scene tape surrounding her home and floating in the breeze confirmed her deepest fears. She wasn't used to feeling anything but the lofty superiority she thrived on, but reconnecting with Sally reopened old wounds, and all the weakness that accompanied them took her breath away.

Katia's home was dark. Confused, she slipped through the gate, past the gurgling fountain in the pool, and walked up the back stairs to the patio slider. She cupped her hands around her face and pressed her nose against the window to peek in, hoping to see Arlo come running to the door, but he was gone, too. She tried to focus, to hone in on him and conjure the dog in her mind, but she was too distracted.

"Dammit!" She balled up her fist and struck the glass in frustration. She let out a hot exhale between her teeth and considered her next move. Feeling eyes boring into her back, she whirled around. Across the way, on his own patio, Oz gave her a friendly wave. She rolled her eyes when, a few minutes later, he walked down his steps, heading toward her.

"Here we go," she said under her breath and pasted on a huge smile. The brown wig she had donned as a disguise itched, and she couldn't wait to tear it off.

"Hello there!" he shouted out as he neared. "Can I help you?"

"I highly doubt that," she rebuffed him. Ordins were so simpleminded and tedious, conversing with them often tested the limits of Zoya's minuscule patience.

"Have you got any news to report?" he asked. There was a pathetic hopefulness in his question.

"About?"

"Katie," he offered, but then his forehead crinkled in confusion and he took a step back. "Her disappearance."

"Her what?" Zoya's voice rose in fear.

"Who are you again?" He was getting suspicious, his eagle eyes narrowed as he took her in.

"The dog walker," Zoya answered, quick on her feet, and it seemed to convince him enough to continue the conversation.

"Oh. Okay. You probably don't watch the news."

"Do you mean Manipulation Daily? Or A Sheeple's Guide to Politics?"

He laughed. "You might have a point there," Oz admitted. "Katie is missing, and the police suspect foul play."

"Oh my God, that is terrible!" Zoya offered, thinking it was an appropriate response for a dog walker and not wanting to rouse suspicion.

"It is. Katie is the sweetest woman." He nodded. "She kind of took me under her wing when I first moved to Aura Cove."

"Can't say I'm surprised," Zoya answered. Though it wasn't her way to latch on to people and help every bleeding heart she came into contact with, she knew Katia was different.

"I pride myself on being somewhat of an amateur sleuth." He shrugged his shoulders in a self-deprecating way. "I started a podcast last year."

Her eyebrows shot up. "You?"

He laughed again. "I know. I'm an old dog learning a new trick over here. But really, I'm just trying to create new connections for my dendrites and keep the Alzheimer's at bay."

"Fascinating," she said, her sarcasm thick. "Well, Sherlock, what do *you* think happened to Katia?"

"Usually, in these types of situations, it's the husband. Or ex-husband, I should say," he divulged.

Zoya considered his answer and discounted it immediately. "I doubt he has the balls." She was tickled at her own joke and had to stifle the glee that wanted to spread across her face. Technically, he *had* the balls, but that was all. "It's not him," she declared.

"You're right. They ruled him out as a suspect. Apparently, he's got an irrefutable alibi," Oz offered. "Not to mention, the way Arlo was barking his head off, it had to be stranger danger. I knew something wasn't right. Wish I'd called it in." He took off his glasses and rubbed one beleaguered hand across his wrinkled face, clearly distressed at the missed opportunity. "He's with Frankie now."

"Jefferson?" she asked.

His forehead wrinkled again. "No, Arlo."

"Of course." She deflected with a quick smile, trying to put the old man at ease. Zoya cataloged that tidbit away for future reference and drew the conversation to a close. "Well, I better be going. I have a Shih Tzu to walk in an hour." She strode away, unwilling to waste one more precious moment with Katia's ancient neighbor.

"It was nice to meet you," he hollered to her back as she quickly descended the stairs, heading to her car. She waved one hand over her shoulder at him in response, then disappeared.

No wonder her connection to Katia was broken, Zoya thought as she hurried back to the car. She *was* in danger. Sally's warning was dead on.

"Take me to the airstrip," she barked at Higgins, her driver, who sped back to the hangar.

Arlo was the key. She had to find the dog. He was the only witness, and he'd have answers. She leaned her head back into the seat and closed her eyes, impatient with how long it was taking her powers to return to full strength after her showdown with Jefferson.

Sally drifted back into her thoughts. He was trying to warn her about Katia. What was he trying to say? The bad blood, what did he mean? With dread, she realized she would have to go back to the archives and open the boxes that held the most pain. It would not be a simple journey, and she tried to give herself a pep talk as the town car pulled up to the hangar. She'd always trusted Sally, and if he said she had to go back, then she would, no matter how much it hurt, because if something happened to Katia and destroyed the legacy she'd labored to build, heads were going to roll.

EIGHT

The next morning, Lauren tugged at her suit jacket and pulled down the visor to check her makeup. In the back seat, Callie said, "You look great. I don't know how you can even put two thoughts together right now."

Lauren stifled a yawn with a balled fist. "I don't either, but it's important. We need everyone in the Tampa Bay Area out looking for Mom," she said. "I figured we'd use the bottom feeders to our advantage. Did you email the photos of Mom to the newsroom?"

"Yep," Callie responded.

Lauren exhaled and pasted on a smile, then opened the car door to a sea of flash bulbs. Gathered in the streets of the cul-de-sac were news vans from all the surrounding counties. She boldly walked up to the Bay News 9 truck where a cameraman was seated in the driver's seat, wolfing down a breakfast burrito.

"Sorry." He stood and shoved the remnants of it back into a brown bag and brushed his hands together. The door popped open, and a blonde with razor-straight, flat-ironed hair and eyebrows so perfect they were almost cartoonish said, "You must be Lauren Beaumont. I'm Grace Bellows." She held out a small hand, offering a firm handshake before continuing. "Thank you for agreeing to speak with us."

"Of course," Lauren said. "Anything to help bring my mom home."

The cameraman placed wireless microphones on Lauren and Grace. Her mouth was dry, and she swallowed, listening to Grace give out last-minute instructions. "Don't think of it as an interview on the most-watched newscast in the Bay area. Just think of it as a discussion between two best friends in your living room."

Lauren had to fight not to roll her eyes. Was this woman serious? But she forced on a tight smile and agreed. "I'll try."

A few minutes later, after the cameraman counted them in, Grace's voice deepened to a rehearsed, nasal, authoritarian tone. "I'm standing here in Aura Cove with Lauren Beaumont. Her mother, Katie, was the victim of a home invasion in this sleepy seaside borough and disappeared without a trace. Her abduction is sending shockwaves through the close-knit community. Aura Cove was voted St. Pete's Beach's safest place to live for the last five years running, but it looks like their luck has just run out."

Lauren stilled her breathing and inhaled through her nose, perfectly poised thanks to her years of litigating cases in the courtroom. On air, her nerves were electric as she understood these stakes were higher. She spoke from the heart, desperate to connect with the viewers in hopes it would bring her mother home. "Thank you for having me."

"Can you tell us more about your mother?"

Lauren knew she must humanize her, in case her kidnappers were watching. Looking right into the camera, without flinching, she said, "Our mother, Katie, is a magnificent, vibrant woman and a tremendous asset to her community. She's the most generous and giving person I have ever known, and frankly, she is my hero."

"She sounds like a remarkable woman." Grace's voice morphed into a practiced compassionate tone that didn't fool Lauren.

Lauren paused for a breath and continued, "You might recognize her if you have visited Kandied Karma lately. It's my great-grandmother's artisanal chocolate shop on Main Street in Aura Cove. She's worked there for years."

"Kandied Karma is an Aura Cove institution," Grace said with a tight nod. "Can you tell us what happened?"

"We've been told she was the victim of a home invasion. We haven't gotten a call from the kidnappers or any message indicating their motive."

Grace nodded, her thin lips straightened into a line, then she continued, "Do they have any suspects?"

"The police are following up with leads and canvassing the neighborhood, but my mother, Katie Beaumont, seems to have disappeared into thin air. We need the public's help to locate her as soon as possible. We know she's being held against her will as there were definite signs of a struggle inside her home."

"Isn't it true she was recently divorced?"

Lauren bristled at the question. "Yes, but…"

"Isn't it also true that in most of these kinds of cases, the first suspect is often the husband?"

"He's the *ex-husband* and my father had nothing to do with this. He's been cleared by the police as a person of interest and is united with us in his desire to have Mom returned home safely."

"What do *you* think happened to her?"

"We're dumbfounded. Everyone loves our mom. When the officer asked us about her enemies, I didn't know what to say. To my knowledge, she simply doesn't have any."

"If you could speak to her captor right now, what would you say?"

Lauren gulped and looked directly into the camera lens. "My mother has three children who can't live without her. She's the heartbeat of our family. You have our word that when you return her to us unharmed, we will lobby for leniency with law enforcement." Lauren choked up and stilled her breathing for a long moment before continuing. "Please, if anyone watching this has noticed anything suspicious, or if you have seen a woman that matches Mom's description, please call the tip line today. These last few days have been a nightmare. We just want to hug our mother again."

Grace turned to the camera and swallowed it up with her presence. "A desperate plea from the family of Katie Beaumont, a beloved Aura Cove resident and mother of three who disappeared forty-eight hours ago. Thank you for joining us during this difficult time, Lauren, and we look forward to reporting her safe return. I'm Grace Bellows, Bay News 9, reporting from Aura Cove."

Lauren stood frozen in place until the cameraman gave

her the signal. Then she waited for him to unclip the microphone from her back.

"You did a great job," Grace complimented her. "Live television can be daunting and some guests freeze up. Not you. You handled that like a rock star."

"Thanks," Lauren muttered. The words were hollow.

"I've actually met your mother at Kandied Karma. She's a wonderful woman—the epitome of every mom," Grace offered. "That's why this story will resonate with our viewers. She's so relatable, and if it can happen in Aura Cove, it can happen anywhere." She leaned in closer and lowered her voice. "You're lucky. If she was a woman of color, her disappearance wouldn't be half as newsworthy."

Outraged by her brazenness, Lauren didn't know how to reply. She cleared her throat and felt dirty standing next to Grace. Unable to let the off-handed racist comment slide, she said, "I assure you, we don't feel lucky at all."

Grace shrugged off her response, and it infuriated Lauren.

"Furthermore, *any* family, regardless of race or socioeconomic background that goes through this harrowing experience, is newsworthy and deserves the same opportunities to use your resources to bring their loved ones home."

"I'm just telling you how the world works," she offered. "White, upper middle class, beloved mother? It's the trifecta. I wouldn't be surprised if all the major outlets pick up the story."

"Wow." Lauren said the only word that came to mind, then couldn't stop herself from adding, "You're what's wrong in the world today."

Grace's eyes flashed and she shook off the insult like a calloused professional. Then, without so much as a pause to take a breath, she rendered Lauren speechless when she was bold enough to ask, "Do you think your family would be open to an interview at Kandied Karma?" Her eyes glittered with transparent greed and the overambition of someone who routinely manipulated people's misery simply for ratings.

Exasperated, Lauren finally answered, "I'll have to speak to Yuli and let you know."

"Of course."

"We're finished?"

"Yep. It will air at six and nine pm tonight."

Lauren walked away, back to the car where Callie was waiting. "This world," she remarked, dumbfounded. "Sometimes I wonder if life is all just one long episode of *Punked*."

NINE

The short flight home allowed Sally's cryptic message opportunity to become an ear worm in Zoya's brain. On repeat and inescapable, it filled her with trepidation. She mentally shored up her resources to psych herself up for a task she knew would rip open decades of scar tissue.

Not wanting to waste another minute, she drove the golf cart to the archives and let herself inside with the skeleton key. Zoya felt the same sense of awe blooming in her chest she always felt when she entered the sacred space. Seeing the vast stores of her ancestral legacy carefully collected and preserved was comforting and yet required a significant store of self-control.

Over the years, during low moments, she often contemplated re-opening the sweetest ones, but she heeded the warning chiseled into the stone at the entrance. The price she'd have to pay, to lose those moments forever, was too steep. She traced her finger over the carving on the stone.

Painful days must be relived.

Zoya knew firsthand that past traumas were powerful teachers. She also knew if she could revisit the sweetness of her best moments as often as she desired, she would get lost in them. Much like a drug addict always reaching for comfort, the past would consume her present, weakening her and forcing her to become dependent. Two qualities found in most women that were abhorrent to her.

Zoya weaved her right hand in a tight figure-eight shape faster and faster, and the shelves of the ancestral archives sped up. They whirled past her so rapidly that they created a breeze that blew her hair back. Like a train on the tracks, they became a complete blur as they rushed by.

She was hyper-focused on the years she'd spent with Salvatore, and his advice was the soundtrack in her mind. "The bad blood, it begins with us." Reaching the correct decade, the track finally slowed down, then lurched to a complete stop. On the second shelf from the top, one music box glowed. It called to her, rattling on the shelf, inching toward her, magnetically drawing itself closer. Under its spell, she climbed the ladder and pulled it from its resting place. It was heavy in her hands and filled her heart with longing and dread.

Constructed of Italian olive, the box was dense and oiled, a beautiful golden brown with black streaks running through it. Painted on the top was a small Italian flag that had mellowed in color as it aged.

Conflicted, she studied the music box for a short time before deciding to open it up. She paced in between the shelves of the archives restlessly, weighing the pros and cons as the beautiful box sat there mocking her, glowing with the promise of answers but also the guarantee of pain. Zoya had kept the store of agonizing memories in the past locked for decades, but Sally's insistence forced her to confront the weaker woman she'd been when she'd met him. Long before her own awakening when she'd had to eke out her existence with little Yuli who was forever the albatross around her neck and a painful reminder of what she'd lost.

The woman she was now would be unrecognizable from the one she'd been back then. A woman is a chameleon, endlessly changing and adapting to the world around her, and Zoya had been forced to change more than most. It felt like she'd lived hundreds of lives and had become a hundred different women in order to survive.

Zoya recalled how difficult it was to lock the box closed the last time and she shivered. Subjecting herself to the box was masochistic in a sense as she knew the mere sight of Salvatore would awaken the sorrow in her heart. It weakened her to go inside the box and, as much as she dreaded it, she had to face the truth. She cracked her neck and circled her shoulders like a prizefighter psyching herself up for a title fight. Finally, she closed her eyes, exhaled a hot and heavy breath, and cranked the music box. The tune that spooled out of it was a jaunty jazz tune that took her right back to the moment she met him.

She tugged open the lid with focused effort and closed her eyes. Her stomach dropped in time with a slide whistle, and the sensation was like the first major drop of a roller coaster. Then she was drawn inside the box, pulled without warning, and flinched when she went skidding to the ground in a dirty alley. Finding her feet, she stood up and dusted herself off, looking around to get her bearings. It always amazed her the sheer amount of dust and dirt that swirled around in the early 1900s, gathering on every surface, and the constant underlying scent of horse droppings.

On the busy street in front of her, people rushed by on the recently paved roads. Horses and buggies trotted alongside the streetcars of the wealthy, who were making money hand over fist in a stock market craze that just kept rising. It was 1928 and the obscene bullishness and greed of Wall Street was reaching a fevered pitch. Optimism reigned supreme, and investors doubled down on their speculation, unaware that Black Monday was just around the corner. A cataclysmic once-in-a-lifetime event that would destroy their fortunes and send them reeling into the Great Depression.

Across from her vantage point in the alley, she saw a younger version of herself who was rail thin, sizing up the men on the streets, looking for easy marks. She remembered how the hunger was all-consuming, clawing at her insides, and watched herself sidle up to men she chose because they were well dressed. Zoya would bump into them and then force herself to flush with embarrassment while she apologized and her small hands darted inside their pockets for anything of value. She'd become very adept at it and rotated locations in order to avoid detection by the authorities. In those days, beauty was an effective defense, and she'd escaped detection, exploiting the common myth that beautiful women didn't commit crimes.

Knowing the events of this day already by heart, from the alley, Zoya's eyes darted down the street looking for him, finally locking onto the vision of a handsome Salva-

tore Lombardo strolling carefree toward her younger self.
The sight of him made her heart clench, and she gasped
and reached out, unable to stop herself. He cut an impressive figure, walking down the busy street where the crowd
parted around him, giving him a wide berth. He was
dressed to the nines in a three-piece black wool suit and
wearing a black fedora.

Seeing her younger self seize the opportunity, she
watched as she boldly stepped closer and bumped into him
on purpose. His hat flew off his head, and his hands
wrapped around her upper arms, keeping her from falling
to the ground. There was a fluttering in her belly that
corresponded with the way she remembered feeling when
he'd touched her the first time.

Her younger eyes locked on him. His wavy, dark hair
that had been coaxed back and locked in place with sticky
pomade now swooped in front of his eyes. His coal-black
mustache and beard were trimmed close to his face, but it
was his icy blue eyes that captivated her. Her distraction
by them caused the briefest hesitation that exposed her
misdeed. Zoya's hand grasped his leather pocketbook and
had just finished tucking it away when she felt his warm
hand cover hers. He yanked her closer to him, and she
gasped as she felt his warm breath on her face. Fine lines
gathered at the corners of his remarkable eyes that burned
into hers.

"It must be my lucky day to cross paths with a beautiful woman with such sticky hands." His eyes didn't look
angry; instead, they were amused, his full lips pressed
together like he was trying to suppress a grin. "Your little
helpless waif act won't work on me."

Thinking she could win him over like every other man

she'd encountered, she answered, "I was just being help-ful." She looked up at him with green doe eyes, batting her eyelashes innocently to distract him from the truth.

"So, I am to assume you were just holding my wallet for safekeeping?" His gaze lingered, then walked down to her cleavage. He licked his lips, a dastardly act that made her flinch.

Zoya pulled away and stood up, feeling shame crawl up her insides. "I suppose you are going to report me to the authorities?"

"Unless you have a better proposition," he offered with a smirk, and her heart dropped. Rage flickered in her eyes as she sized him up. Was he another entitled man who was intent on helping himself to her? His reactions were so unorthodox, she couldn't tell. Another enormous man stood behind him, waiting. He had gathered up the displaced Fedora and was holding it in his gloved hands, a bored look on his ruddy face while he watched their inter-action. Around them, the sea of people continued to weave by without so much as a sideward glance.

Resigned to end this impromptu meeting as quickly as possible, she pulled a pocketbook from the pockets of her dress that were already heavily laden with the valuables of other men and handed it over to him.

First, his forehead knotted up with confusion. She waved it at him, but he refused to take it. "That is not mine," he said as he took a step closer, his eyes twinkling with interest. She hastily tucked it back into her pocket and then pulled out another one.

"Nor is that." He was taken aback and laughed, an action that flushed her with anger.

"Just how many men have fallen victim to your damsel

in distress charade?" he asked, sizing her up. She stared him down for a long moment before answering.

"A few," she answered with a shrug, aware he'd caught her in the act and wondering what he was going to do about it.

"You aren't fooling me. I see the crow's feet gathered near your eyes. Aren't you a little long in the tooth for this tired masquerade?"

Her cheeks burned with hostility. "How dare you judge me!" Her nostrils flared as her eyes locked on his.

"Rage makes you even more lovely," he whispered, and his eyes flicked down to her pinked cleavage and drank her in again, inch by inch, making her fidget uncomfortably.

"A gentleman would do well to look a woman in her eyes!" she spat at him, and it made his grin widen.

"That may be true, however, I do not claim to be a gentleman," he boldly declared, and Zoya's brow knit in confusion. "But I do crave a worldly woman who knows her way around the bedroom. The young ones exhaust me and need too much training."

Zoya's hand itched to slap his face, and yet, she felt the stirrings of something more animalistic in her core. Love and hate were two sides of the same coin, split down the middle by lust.

"What's your name?"

She studied him, considering giving him an alias, but there was a magnetism to this man she couldn't deny, and she found herself answering truthfully, almost against her will. "Zoya."

"That's a beautiful name," he complimented, and she narrowed her eyes as he buttered her up. "I can't place your accent. Where are you from?" His hands still gripped her arms, and the warmth was not altogether unpleasant.

Although her years in America had softened it, since she'd lived in the States almost as long as she'd lived in Ukraine, her native tongue still lingered on certain syllables and in the choppy way she sometimes spoke. Embarrassed by this, Zoya often relied on her ability to intuitively read people instead of actively engaging in conversation.

She refused to answer his question and felt the fire of outrage build again in her belly. Her body was a flutter of contradictions. He was unsettling and magnetic, but at the same time uncouth and outrageous. She felt herself getting swept up in a tumultuous sea of emotion and yanked her arms back, desperate to put physical distance between them and break the spell he had on her. She took a step away, grateful that the surging attraction subsided when he was no longer touching her.

He held out his right hand, and after a long pause, she reached out and shook it. "Zoya, I am pleased to make your acquaintance. I'm Salvatore Lombardo, but my friends call me Sally." He bowed dramatically at the waist and then returned his twinkling eyes to hers with another playful grin.

"Likewise, *Mr.* Lombardo." She boldly refused the more intimate invitation as her defiant eyes flashed to him.

He pouted playfully. "I thought since you'd groped me mere minutes ago, we were closer acquaintances." His playful attitude was infectious, and against her will, her lips quirked. "It seems the dame is entertained," he declared, awash in confidence.

She pulled her hand back, afraid she'd be taken under

his spell again. With an exhale, Zoya smoothed the front of her dress that hung loosely on her frame. It was a pathetic costume of sorts, frayed at the cuffs and the fabric had faded over the last year. She tucked away the money she earned picking pockets in her room at the boarding house in an old coffee can. Zoya was going to use it to fund a closet full of dresses she planned to wear when she could level up to bigger and more lucrative cons. Picking pockets was a means to an end, and she had much bigger plans for her life.

In contrast, Salvatore was razor sharp and stylish with his pinstriped suit cut close to his body. The wide trouser legs were cuffed at the bottom, and the lapels of the suit were wide with a sunny yellow carnation pinned on the left-hand side. The flower intrigued her.

He opened his wallet, pulled out several bills, and held them out to her. It was more money than she'd brought in picking pockets in a month. Her eyes darkened with greed as she reached out to grab them, but he refused to let go. Defiant, her eyes met his. "One date," he said. "Think of this as a small investment for your time."

"You're reducing me to a common whore? Am I to be grateful, Mr. Lombardo?" Her eyes narrowed on his, and he squinted at her, inspecting her from head to toe.

"Everything is transactional, darling. You would do well to learn that." He leaned closer and his voice took on a harsher edge. "Or perhaps I should flag down the constable over there and fill him in on your activities." Her eyes flitted over to the officer on the street, wondering if he would make good on his threat.

"Then I accept." She changed her mind as he finally let go of the cash, and she quickly tucked it into the bodice of her dress. "Once I get past your offensive tone, I must admit I find your honesty refreshing."

"It comes with age," he said as he leaned in, and she felt his breath brush across her collarbone, making her shiver. Noticing his effect on her, he grinned. "You're like a fine wine. Flawless well into your thirties."

"I'm *forty,* Mr. Lombardo," Zoya corrected him.

"Even better." He brushed a tendril of hair from her cheek. "In the sexual prime of your womanhood."

"You're awfully forward," she said and took a small step back, desperate to break the spell again. Why was it so easy to want what was bad for you?

"I assure you, I am not awful at all," he whispered. "You'll be scratching your fingernails down my back in a fortnight."

Her eyes widened. "Never."

"Never say never, doll-face." He winked. "Would you care to make a wager?"

She narrowed her eyes again, and overconfident in her ability to control herself, proudly declared, "I will make that bet." She shook his hand with a grin, self-assured that she would emerge the winner. "What do I get if I win?"

"Ah, my dear, the real prize will be when you lose." He flashed her another impossible grin and his bravado never wavered. "Since I'm rather certain you'd prefer not to give me your address so I can call on you properly, be at the corner of 5th and Franklin tonight at eight."

She nodded, then turned and left. When she dared to look over her shoulder, she was shocked to see he remained in the thick of the crowd, watching her walk away with his arms folded across his chest and a smile on his gorgeous face.

———

At precisely eight pm, she stood waiting on the corner. Her shiny black hair was cropped into a short bob and had been coaxed into smooth finger waves that exposed her creamy neck. She'd dressed in a drop-waist, lacey red gown with an asymmetrical hem that exposed her stunning legs all the way down to her siren-red heels. Two long strings of pearls draped down her chest, and she'd taken the time to paint her face properly. Coal black mascara adorned her lashes, and the rouge on her cheeks made her skin glow.

A lamp cast warm yellow light on dingy, empty streets, since the shops were shuttered. She felt her edges sharpen as the minutes crawled by. She opened her clutch and looked down at a fine pocket watch she'd acquired a week prior with her sticky fingers. "I'll give him five more minutes," she said aloud and felt the rush of frustration well up inside her. Seconds before she was prepared to turn on her heel and leave, a showy car pulled up and the horn blasted a long *ah-oo-gaaa* as it rolled to the curb and stopped.

"Hey there, doll-face," he said with a grin from a rolled-down window. His voice was deep and playful inside the confines of the streetcar, and he had a carefree attitude she'd never possessed. "Well, don't you clean up well?" She felt his eyes as if they were fingers tickling down the length of her body, and she shivered in antic-ipation.

"You're late," she scolded him.

His eyes glittered with mirth and she felt herself tear in two. One part of her was supremely frustrated with his lack of respect for her time. The other was oddly drawn to him like a moth to a flame. He was the first man to have this effect on her in decades, and it was unnerving.

His driver spilled out of the parked car and rushed to open the door for her. She hesitated for the briefest second before climbing in beside him and sitting a respectful distance away.

"Don't be cross with me, darling," he murmured.

"I'm not your darling," she shot back and folded her arms across her chest.

Without hesitation, he reached his arm around her small waist and pulled her closer.

"That's very forward, Mr. Lombardo," Zoya chastised him, feeling the heat searing her hip and thigh where their bodies touched.

"You ain't seen nothin' yet," he offered with a smile as the driver pulled the car away from the curb and drove them toward an undisclosed location. When they arrived, the driver opened the door, and Salvatore slid out of the car before extending a hand back to Zoya, who took it. She couldn't help but be intrigued. He led her down a dark path, her hand gripping his strong biceps, warmed by his other hand tucked over the top. They walked down the sidewalk in companionable silence, then down a concrete staircase to a lower level where she could faintly make out the sound of orchestra music. When the door opened, the sound intensified and crashed over her in a wave. Jazz notes from a big band streamed out of the club. Bold trumpets and swoon-worthy big bass jutted into the air and made the atmosphere festive. Behind a dark walnut stand, a maître de stood.

"It's great to welcome you again to the Briar Club, Mr.

Lombardo," the man greeted with a smile, and Sally reached out and greased his palm with a folded-up bill.

They were promptly escorted to the best table in the joint. It was front and center in the club, directly in front of the house band. Fascinated at the ease with which he floated through life, she observed more cash exchange palms, and then a round of drinks magically appeared and he placed a gin martini in her hand.

Nervous, she gulped it down, and he quickly replaced it with another one. The booze smoothed her rough edges and melted her frustrations away. An enveloping warmth and fuzziness softened her self-protective impulses and encouraged her to lean closer to him. When her empty stomach growled audibly in between sets, he chuckled. Embarrassed by the overt display of weakness, she wrapped her hands around her stomach with a tight smile and leaned away.

"When was the last time you had a proper meal, doll-face?" His eyes probed deeper into hers and made her uncomfortably warm. "You're so thin," he whispered as he drew his index finger up the length of her forearm. The contact sparked on her skin as the warmth trailed up and set loose a flutter of butterfly wings in her center.

Proud, Zoya refused to answer the question. It had been a while, but she would not dare admit it. Undeterred, he signaled the waitstaff again, and twenty minutes later, a server brought two steaks seared to perfection to their table. A baked potato with a salted jacket and oozing with butter, and a basket of fresh baked rolls were added a moment later. The scent made Zoya's mouth water instantly, and she fought the urge to tear into the food in front of her and look overeager. Gifts from men always came with strings attached. He cut into his rare steak and popped a chunk into his mouth. His elbows leaned on the table, his hands still holding his knife and fork. Assessing her refusal to take a bite, he encouraged her softly, "Go on, eat."

Reluctantly, she gave in, unrolling the aubergine cotton napkin and pulling out her fork. She stabbed it into the grilled meat, slicing it with the steak knife, and had to fight a sigh from escaping her lips when it melted in her mouth. It took her back to her childhood, where she'd feasted nearly every night with her father and his friends. On her own, a luxury like steak wasn't something she could afford to indulge in. She made quick work of cutting the meat into cubes and thrusting them into her open mouth. Once she started, she couldn't stop herself until every bite in front of her had been devoured.

"I like a woman who doesn't shy away from pleasure," he admitted, his deep voice warming her from the inside out, and she felt her cheeks flush. "Do you know how many dames I've brought here that picked around their plates?"

"Hundreds?" she teased. "Or was it thousands?" The martinis made her warm and pliable, softening her wary thoughts. There was a reckless tingle of arousal gathering in her hips that emboldened her.

He grinned, and it made her stomach flip, but then fear clenched her fingers together under the table as she gripped the napkin in her lap into a tight ball.

"I can already tell you are going to break my heart," he declared, and the bold statement confused her.

"Is that right?" She gazed over the glass that held her third gin martini. "You must learn to control your impulses, Mr. Lombardo. I have a bet to win," she reminded him, delivering a well-timed, coquettish wink.

Another grin lit up his face. "Ah, I do seem to remember our little wager." His eyes swept down her face to land on her plump breasts spilling out of the top of the lace of her dress. She'd dusted them with the merest shimmer of translucent powder and reveled in the power over him she felt filling her. Satiated and in control, she leaned back in her chair and sized him up, considering his longer-term potential. She felt her resolve weakening and longed to return to an easier lifestyle, like the one she'd enjoyed in her childhood. The battle of survival she was currently engaged in was exhausting, and she was ready to move back to easy street. At that moment, she decided he would be as good a ticket as any. She leaned closer and offered him a winning smile and dared to reach out and place her hand in his. She lifted her glass once more and locked her eyes on him over the top of it.

Behind her, a rumbling of voices intensified. She heard the screeching sound of a woman's voice gaining considerable volume as it neared their table. Out of the corner of her eye, she saw a flash of movement, and a second later, her drink was yanked from her hand and thrown into Salvatore's face by a hostile yet gorgeous woman. Stunned, Zoya stood and addressed her.

"Who are you?" Zoya asked, the anger forcing her accent to be more prominent. "You had no right!" All the heads in the club swung toward the women, engrossed in their heated exchange.

"I have *every* right." The woman had platinum blonde waves with bold red lips and was beautifully adorned in a black lace flapper dress. She stood tall with her hands on her hips, facing Zoya.

"Let me guess. Sally conveniently left out the fact that he was married."

Salvatore stood. "Calm down, Greta. You always seem to get your knickers in a twist."

"Calm down? I'm sitting at home taking care of your son while you parade around town with this... this..." She waved her hand at Zoya, seeming to struggle with finding the right word, "Russian whore!" The music screeched to a halt, and the club was silent. The hum of conversation quieted abruptly, and you could hear a pin drop as the sudden focus of derogatory attention welled shame in Zoya's gut.

"I'm from Ukraine," Zoya demanded. She gathered up her clutch, getting ready to walk out of there with her head held high. She was seeing red.

Frustrated, Greta screamed at Salvatore and lunged at his face. Salvatore's bodyguard rushed to his side and tore her away, kicking and screaming, and dragged her off. Her protests died as he rushed her out of the club.

Dumbstruck, Zoya's eyes met Salvatore's. He swept his fingers through his unkempt hair and straightened his jacket, then offered her an apologetic smile that infuriated her. She reached up and delivered a sharp slap to the side of his face while the crowd gasped, astonished at the spectacle. Then Zoya turned on her heel and strode out of the club, leaving Salvatore behind.

"Bet you didn't think you'd be enjoying dinner *and* a show tonight!" She heard him crack a joke as she quickened her pace, eager to put space between them. The crowd chuckled, and the band started playing again. The last few mortifying moments of Zoya's walk of shame were swallowed whole by a blaring trumpet and thumping drums.

Zoya raced away from Salvatore, angry with herself. She'd almost let her guard down and let a man in. She ran back up the steps and then out onto the streets, where the lights illuminated her path. To quicken her pace, she pulled the heels off and walked home furiously on bare feet. Thoughts raced through her mind and out her mouth in a flood of obscenities. Men were always such a disappointment.

———

She was tugged out of the alley and felt her skin tingle as she reappeared inside the archives. Exhausted from the transformation, she closed the box with extreme effort. In her long life, there had been many crossroads, but this was the one that had sent her on an agonizing trajectory she never saw coming.

If only. If only she'd never met Salvatore Lombardo. If only she'd never chosen to entwine her life with his. With the passage of time comes clarity and understanding. Meeting Salvatore had been the most pivotal moment of her entire life. He was trouble; she knew it that very first night. Disappointment swelled as she realized the music box didn't hold any of the answers she was searching for and she would have to keep going.

"The answers are in the archives," she heard Sally whisper again in her ear. "The bad blood, it begins with us."

"Where?" she asked aloud. Her question broke the

silence. On the shelves, a black box that was riddled with bullet holes began to quiver. The rattling sound was ominous and overbearing. She resisted the sensation at first, unable to face the pain that was waiting inside.

"I can't," she whimpered. The thought of reliving the most painful day of her life was terrifying. Going inside the box would test her and weaken her further. She needed to shore up her resources to undergo the arduous journey. Exhausted, she climbed on the golf cart and headed back to the main house. She would regroup and then face the next box, refreshed and ready to tackle the trouble she was certain waited within.

She sunk to the floor in her meditation space and closed her eyes, but even in the darkness, Sally's pursuit never faltered. Again and again, his instructions were intrusive and unrelenting. She sighed and grasped the warmed amulet at her throat that she'd taken to wearing daily, hoping it was the gateway to Sally. Her future was at stake, her lineage was in danger, and she was its guardian. Knowing she must stay the course, the first slivers of apprehension seeped in. The problem with danger was, when you invited it in, sometimes it stayed.

TEN

Three days after Katie's home invasion, Frankie was exhausted and desperate for answers. After another long night spent tossing and turning, Frankie knew the best way to get those answers was to just show up at the station, so she grabbed two cups of strong coffee in a carrier and a dozen donuts and headed into the Aura Cove Police Department. At the front desk, a bald man who had the flabby jowls of a bulldog was manning a telephone that never seemed to stop ringing.

"Can I speak to Officer Willey?" Frankie inquired, her voice low, not wanting to interrupt the clearly overworked man. He nodded and pointed to an empty seat several feet away in the middle of a small concrete-block room filled with two rows of desks. One was manned by an officer sitting at his computer, staring at the screen. Another officer was relaxing with his feet up on the desk, seeing a civilian he promptly pulled them down and sat up, pretending to work.

Scanning the room quickly, her eyes landed on a black

name placard that had the words Officer Harrison Willey engraved in bold white lettering. She settled herself in the chair next to his desk and waited. To pass the time, she inventoried the items in front of her. There was a framed snapshot of him with his arm around a man, both of them beaming at the camera on top of a rock formation. She pulled it closer to study it.

The absolute joy on his face and relaxed intimacy confused her. Usually, her gaydar was infallible, but in her drained and discombobulated state, the photo niggled a few doubts to the surface. Frankie pulled out her phone and started tapping out a text message about this new development to Katie without even thinking, then shut it down when the truth flooded back in and tucked it sadly back into her purse.

Jittery, she reached out to grab the photo with her hands, pulled out her readers, and scrutinized it more closely. Behind the bold orange glasses perched at the end of her nose, her calculating eyes analyzed his expression. In the photo, he was lit up. But why? Was it from the exertion it took to climb up the mountain or the man he wrapped his arm around? She considered both options carefully.

Behind her, Officer Willey rounded the corner, and the timbre of his deep voice startled a jumpy Frankie, causing her to drop the frame in her lap.

"That's from Pike's Peak last year," he offered in explanation as he strode closer. "My best friend and I are working our way through the Thrillist's Ten Most Awe-Inspiring Mountains You Can Actually Climb."

I knew it! My gaydar can still claim 100% accuracy.

With a little perverse pride, she quickly returned the

frame to his desk and passed one coffee over to him as he took a seat. His uniform hugged all the right places, and the authority he commanded wearing it did not go unnoticed by Frankie. At his hip, a handgun was holstered. It was the closest she'd been to a firearm in ages, and its presence was sobering.

"Thank you," he said, taking a sip. "You have no idea how much I needed caffeine right now." She opened the box of donuts, and the scent of sugary grease wafted to her nostrils and made her stomach growl. "And donuts too? Are you trying to turn me into a walking cliche?" He gave her a winning grin. There was a lightness to him she'd never encountered before in other members of law enforcement. The man was straight-up likable.

Frankie hung her head, and her lips tightened in a grimace. "Oh, man, I didn't even think about it. I'm so sorry. My brain doesn't function very well on only two hours of sleep."

"It's a joke," he said. "I love donuts, always have, and I thank you kindly." To prove the point, he rubbed his hands together in anticipation, opened the box, pulled out a maple-iced long john, and sunk his teeth into it.

"That's my favorite kind, too," Frankie mentioned, discreetly observing the absence of a wedding ring on his fourth finger and then hating herself for being distracted from what was important.

"It is? I'm sorry." He put it back down on the box and opened one of his desk drawers and rifled through it. "Why don't I cut it in half? I'm happy to share."

"That's sweet of you to offer, but no, you go ahead." Frankie said, "I wanted to check in and see if you can give me an update on Katie's case."

"Of course." He licked icing off his index finger, logged onto his computer, and looked at the file on his desk for a few minutes, giving Frankie's exhausted brain time to catalog his intelligent brown eyes and freshly shaven jawline. Attractive details she would kill to be giving Katie over a glass of wine on her patio. Kill... the thought made her tear up, and she shook it off with a deep breath and was happy when he finally spoke and quieted her busy brain. "The crime scene has been officially released, so you are free to enter Ms. Beaumont's home. We conducted a canvas of the neighborhood, but there wasn't much to report there."

His eyes slid over to hers, and his lips puckered as he bit the inside of his cheek. His silence made Frankie nervous.

"What aren't you telling me?" Frankie asked.

"The case got kicked upstairs to major crimes, and Detective Ludlow was assigned. He will be the one to keep you abreast of future developments in the case moving forward."

"But wait." She leaned toward him, afraid she was going to lose her only ally. "Isn't there something *you* can do? Katie's my best friend. I don't want any leads to get lost in the cracks."

"I'm a beat cop, Ms. Stapleton," he admitted.

"Frankie," she insisted.

"Frankie, it's out of my hands." He pursed his lips with obvious regret. "I'm sorry."

She burst into tears. Her only lifeline was floating away, and she was desperate to stop it and peppered him with questions. "Who is this Detective Ludlow? Have you brought him up to speed on the case? Do you trust him?"

His brief hesitation spoke volumes, and Frankie's eyebrows shot up. "What am I missing here?" Her suspicions were on high alert.

"Nothing, Frankie." His eyes darted around the room, and Frankie had a feeling he was keeping his mouth closed on purpose.

"As I said, the investigation is ongoing and they are still trying to narrow down a motive. It's in the early stages, and I'm afraid there isn't any new information to share yet, but I need you to understand all further official communication and updates should be conducted through Ludlow. I'm sorry." His apology was convincing, but Frankie felt the bottom dropping out from under her and panic consumed her.

Frankie looked down at her watch. "But the first forty-eight hours are over, and the chance of finding her alive has already been cut by half!" She cried, "The longer this continues…" She dropped off, unable to complete the chilling thought.

He nodded. "I understand you are terrified, but try to look on the bright side. There's *still* a fifty percent chance we'll be successful. Keep the faith. We *are* going to find her and bring her home."

Frankie knew he was leaving something out. The word 'alive' was what she longed to hear. But Officer Willey didn't seem like a liar, and she'd watched enough *Dateline* to understand he couldn't make that promise.

"What about Jefferson? I know he's been ruled out as a suspect, but did you interview him? He's been elbow to elbow with criminals for years, *and* he's the lead counsel for the Gabriano family," Frankie offered, scrambling for motives, desperate to keep Officer Willey's attention on

Katie's case. "It can't be a coincidence that Rocco and Marisa Gabriano visited Kandied Karma, where they were witnessed interacting with Katie just a few days before her disappearance."

The name stopped him cold, and he set down the remainder of the donut and brushed his hands together, then steepled his fingers and leaned forward. "We did, but he wouldn't go on the record because of privilege."

"Can't say I'm surprised," Frankie muttered. "Katie always joked that half of her life was subsidized by the Gabrianos' billable hours." She looked over her shoulder like saying the name out loud in a police station would get her whacked.

The officer thought through her revelation. "Wouldn't they have a bigger ax to grind with Jeff? Especially after their divorce was final, why would they wait to hurt his ex-wife *after* he was out of their home? It doesn't add up."

"I don't know," cried an exasperated Frankie.

"It just doesn't ring true." He leaned back and polished off the long john, engrossed in thought. "We need more than a weak connection between her ex and the Gabrianos to bring them in for questioning. Let's wait and see what the fingerprint results are."

"How long will that take?"

"Three to five days."

Frankie huffed, "It might as well be thirty-five days!" She cried, standing up, "I can't just sit here and twiddle my thumbs. We have to *do* something!"

"Trust the process," he offered.

Exasperated, she jumped to her feet and shouted out, "NTM!" Then she stormed out, leaving the officer wondering what the heck she was talking about.

Frustrated, Frankie drove to Katie's house, desperate to clean up the crime scene before the kids saw it. It would crush them to see their mother's home in disarray, not to mention the blood stains Frankie had cataloged on the walls.

With a heavy sigh, she sliced through the evidence seal on the front of the door and swung it open in total silence. Knowing where Katie kept all the cleaning supplies, she got right to work. Frankie swept up all the glass and then vacuumed the travertine floors twice, knowing Katie's penchant for walking around barefoot and her desire to keep Arlo from an injury to one of his paws. She wanted to create a safe place for Katie to return.

The dead peonies were scattered on the ground in the great room. Frankie bent down to pick up the stems, and the lifeless petals fluttered to the floor, which required another sweep and vacuum.

Seeing the outer skin of the drywall removed from the wall in more than one place, it was obvious when Katie was home she was going to need a drywall expert to patch the affected areas. Frankie pulled out two magic erasers, dampened them, and scrubbed the rest of the wall clean until the blood spatter was gone and the erasers had disintegrated in her hands. Her fingers were sore from the effort, and she broke out in a sweat, but she was glad to have something to do, a task that would make the waiting Officer Willey asked her to do less unbearable.

She gathered up the sharp remnants of the destroyed coffee table and hauled them into the garage to drag out to the curb on garbage day. On the ground, she picked up the framed photo of the kids. She used a razor blade to remove a dried substance she couldn't bear to admit to herself was blood on both of Callie's cheeks. The sight of it made her shudder.

After two hours of scrubbing and cleaning, the house looked like it always did, clean and organized. She glanced over at the front door, desperate for the sight of her best friend walking through it.

"Where are you, Katie?" Her question pierced through the silence. Exhausted, she sank to the ground while tears coursed down her face. "Come home, please," she begged, unable to comprehend living her life without her best friend.

ELEVEN

The waxing moon was luscious in the clear sky, surrounded by a sea of flickering stars. The blue light it cast illuminated the surrounding darkness and Yuli stood in Katia's driveway for a long moment, taking it all in. She looked up to the heavens, reveling in the swell of energy. There was an undeniable magnetic pull she always felt from a full moon as it conspired with the tides at the edge of the sea.

At Katia's front door, Yuli punched in the code to let herself inside. The lemon scent of furniture cleaner tickled her nostrils as she turned on the lights and walked into Katia's spotless kitchen. She was searching for a talisman, an object to hold in her hands to bring her intuition into stronger focus. An item that Katia cherished would provide the strongest physical and psychic connection with her granddaughter, and she was on a mission to find it.

Yuli explored the kitchen, lingering at the collection of framed photos on the wall, where a smiling Katia was sandwiched between Beckett and Lauren. She brushed one finger across her granddaughter's cheek and nodded with fresh purpose, getting right back to her task at hand. She reached down and pulled open the junk drawer, rifling through its odd cornucopia of useless and broken items for a few minutes. Nestled inside, under the mass of USB cords and old pens, was a purple crystal she'd never seen before. She pulled it out and held it in her hands. Closing her eyes, she conjured Katia's face in her mind's eye. She brushed her worn thumb over the smooth face of it and concentrated. Nothing.

Returning it to the drawer, she closed her eyes and listened intently, waiting to receive a message. A few moments later, she was led to Katia's closet. Tucked into one of the velvet-lined drawers was the string of pearls she had given Katia on her wedding day, the ones she had worn at her own wedding. Yuli pulled out the familiar crimson case and it creaked as she pried it open. Inside, the pearls emitted a soft glow. She pressed her fingers to them and felt a slight vibration. Yes. This would help.

From Katia's ensuite bathroom, she pulled out a hair brush that still had long black hairs wrapped around it and Katia's toothbrush. The latent DNA on both of the items made it easier to establish a connection. Gathering them in her hands, she placed them on the patio table near the pool. She lit a clump of sage and started to chant, making figure eights in the air for the first few minutes. Then she let it continue to smoke in the saucer next to her. She removed the string of pearls from the case and fastened them around her neck. Their glow intensified, and the vibration increased as they settled into place at the hollow of her throat. Holding the toothbrush and hairbrush in her hands, she closed her eyes and focused. A surge of electricity crackled, and she saw the first streaming image light up in her mind.

Yuli gasped for breath as the sensation of being trapped inside a dark room magnified. In the center of the room, bathed in the cool moonlight, Yuli recognized a face. It was a terrified Marisa, and she was wielding a gun pointed at Rocco, who was using Katia as a human shield. His veiny forearm was clenched tight against her windpipe, and her teary eyes were filled with fear. Yuli watched Katia raise her foot and bring it down hard on Rocco's, then deliver a quick elbow to his gut. It was a perfectly executed surprise attack forcing him to release his choke-hold on Katia who dropped to the floor.

"Now!" Katia screamed, and Marisa closed her eyes and squeezed the trigger. A shot rang out, and the bullet casing clinked as it ricocheted on the concrete. Marisa opened her eyes, trembling with fear, then locked on Katie, who lay on the concrete wearing a stunned expression on her face and clearly in shock. She pressed her hands to her belly, where a pool of red was bleeding through her clothing and spilling onto her fingers. She writhed on the ground, moaning in agony. Her face was pale and her eyes wild.

Marisa screamed and raced over to Katia and knelt down. She pressed her hands on Katia's to staunch the flow of blood, but it was coming too fast.

"Call an ambulance! She's going to die here," Marisa pleaded.

Rocco pulled Marisa to a standing position by her hair. His breath was warm in her ear. "Maybe you should have considered that possibility before you shot me," he snarled. Marisa yanked free and knelt down at Katia's side again.

Sobbing, she keened, "I'm sorry. Oh, God! No! No! NO!" Katia gasped and then let out one long exhale before her eyes went vacant. Desperate, and knowing she only had seconds to collect useful information about their surroundings before she was pulled out of the vision, Yuli's eyes scanned the room. It was dark, and the walls were concrete. Then the image flickered away before she could gather any more details.

The second stream flickered and sent her reeling, the speed of the vision quickening and unfolding in double-time. Her heart raced as she observed Katia wielding a gun, gripping the pistol in her hands, her aim shaky, her feet jutting straight out from her hips. She hesitated for a moment before lowering her aim and squeezing the trigger. The bullet casing hit the wall, and Rocco let out a roar before dropping to the ground. His thigh bled through his jeans, creating a ferocious black stain as blood flooded out of the gunshot wound.

"You hit my femoral artery, you bitch."

Terrified, the gun clattered from Katia's hands to the ground, and she rushed over to the corner where Marisa was wailing. She wrapped her arms around the young woman and squeezed her eyes shut. As he bled out on the ground, Rocco reached out one bloodied hand to Marisa. His eyes begging for her, she took a tentative step toward him, but it was too late. He shuddered once, then his body went slack. In the warehouse, Katia shrilled as the weight of taking a life settled on her soul. Then Yuli's vision grayed.

The third visual stream Yuli received sped by in triple-time. In a whirl, she saw a mirror image of herself entering a warehouse. Then walking down a hallway to a set of double doors that were chained together. The doors flew open and, inside, she saw Katia and Marisa handcuffed to each other, both with their eyes closed. She shook Katia's shoulder to wake her up, and they both fell sideways, landing on the cold concrete floor. Yuli whirled around, looking for clues. In the distance, she heard a train rumbling on the tracks, and then the darkness enveloped her.

The fourth stream spooled by at super warp speed. Rocco pushed Marisa to the ground as he tried to fight off Katia. On the ground, Marisa gripped her belly, and she cried out in pain. Between her legs, blood dripped down and pooled at her feet. Seeing the blood on her hands, Marisa cried out, then her screams intensified as Yuli was once again cast into the darkness.

The fifth stream passed in a blink of distorted imagery. She saw Zoya whisk Katia away, giving Yuli a death stare that rendered her immobile like a statue. Zoya's loud, self-satisfied laugh rang in her ears, and she felt Katia's psyche rip away from her and disappear forever.

Back on Katia's patio, Yuli's consciousness tumbled back to her body that went slack in the chair. The brushes in her hands clattered to the ground as she struggled to inhale air that was thick and oppressive. The effort to connect to Katia in the future had taken its toll, and she wasn't sure she was any closer to finding out where her granddaughter was located. She labored to reconcile the images and piece together the clues she'd collected from each version of the alternate realities she experienced. Unable to move and exhausted from the effort, she drifted into a deep sleep. Hours later, the sky began to lighten with a new dawn.

"Yuli?" Oz's concerned voice jolted her out of her slumber. With great effort, she opened her eyes and turned toward him. "Are you okay?"

"Under the circumstances, I'm afraid sleep has been elusive, and you caught me trying to catch up," she offered, giving him the easiest explanation she could, not wanting to rouse his suspicions. She sat up with a blustering exhale and offered him a weak smile.

"A woman came by the other day, said she was the dog walker," Oz offered, and Yuli felt the hairs on the back of her neck stand up.

"The dog walker?" Yuli's eyes narrowed. Katia didn't have a dog walker. "What did she look like?"

He held a hand up a little higher than himself. "About yay high, beautiful green eyes. But the strangest thing, she was wearing a brown wig to cover up her white hair. Who wears a wig to walk dogs on the beach?" he mused.

Zoya. That's who. A twinge of dread accompanied the revelation. "Who knows why anyone does anything?" she responded with a shrug.

"Ain't that the truth!" Oz nodded, then leaned in and said in a low voice, "Between you and me, she was a touch condescending, far from the typical animal lover type who walks dogs for a living. It's strange that I've never seen her before, though, right?" He looked deep into Yuli's eyes. "Do you think I should report the incident to the police?"

"I'm planning a visit there myself. I will mention it, and if they need more details, I'll have them talk to you."

"Sounds good." He sighed. "Anything I say tends to go in one ear and out the other at the precinct." He glanced over to his own porch where a content Shasta was sunning herself in the morning sun. "Well, I better take the little miss out on her walk. We both need to get our steps in. You take care and get some rest."

"Will do," Yuli said as she watched him walk down the steps the way he came and then over to his own property.

Zoya knows.

The revelation filled her with dread.

TWELVE

In the darkness, Katie waited and listened. Her ears strained for sounds that could give her clues about her surroundings. She broke up the hours she spent awake by yanking back and forth on the loose pipe under the sink until her muscles were trembling, and she carved more of her name on the wall. Hidden from view, an I and an E joined the K-A-T she'd chiseled into the ancient blocks. Water had done most of the work for her over the years, softening the mortar to powder in places, and she was gratified when, within an hour, she had made significant progress. Being productive gave her a way to chip away at the time and stopped her fears from spiraling.

Katie licked her dry lips. She was desperate for water, almost delirious for it, and consumed with need when she thought she heard a key rattle in the lock. She tossed the Allen wrench under the sink, scrambled to the other side of the room, and slid down the wall, quickly landing on the ground when she heard the industrial metal door slide open on its tracks.

From the doorway, she heard an object rolling toward her on the concrete and was delighted when it turned out to be a large water bottle. She picked it up, twisted the top open, and sucked it down so eagerly the sides of the bottle squealed in protest when they touched each other. It was room temperature, but as far as Katie was concerned, it tasted better than the Fuji she'd gotten used to having on hand when she was married.

"Thank you," she said to the figure, who was standing silhouetted in the doorway, still unable to tell who it was. "Do you have any food?"

The blackened hulk that filled the door frame emitted a familiar guttural chuckle. "So, you think I'm here to take your sandwich order?" It was Carmine.

"No, of course not," Katie stammered. She racked her brain, searching for something to say to appeal to his humanity. "Do you have any children? I have three: a son and two daughters. My youngest though, is such a softie. She's probably going out of her mind right now with worry."

"Shut up," Carmine said, and she knew she'd hit a nerve.

"How's Marisa?" Katie asked.

"None of your goddamn business," he muttered as he entered the room.

"She needs access to water and food. If she doesn't eat or drink, it will put stress on the baby, and I know Rocco doesn't want to put the life of his son at risk." Katie exploited Rocco's desire to carry on his family name, a weakness of most alpha males.

Carmine grunted, acknowledging her words, but said nothing else.

Katie was desperate to keep him talking, so she dared to add, "If you kill me, your boss is going to have to find a new lawyer, because it will be a definite conflict of interest with Rocco's current representation."

"What do you mean?"

"I'm Katie Beaumont. Jefferson Beaumont's ex-wife." It was the only card she had, so she played it.

He emitted a low, grumbling noise and then exited the room and roughly yanked the door closed behind him. It groaned, then acquiesced along the metal track, a melancholy tone Katie was deeply in tune with. She listened as his footfalls became quieter and then silenced altogether. Her skin crawled and felt grimy. Black dirt was trapped under her fingernails, and she was desperate for a shower. She rubbed her chapped lips together. Though she was grateful for the bottle of water, the dehydration had taken a serious toll. She tipped the bottle to her lips one more time and let the last remaining drops drip onto her tongue.

"I should have saved some of it," she said aloud, already becoming thirsty again and not knowing where the next bottle would come from. Her eyes grew weary as the darkness enveloped her. Katie surrendered as mental and physical exhaustion weighed her limbs down and finally fell into a deep, fitful sleep.

An hour later, she stirred and was jolted wide awake with a gasp. "Help us." She'd been sleeping so soundly when the faint cry startled her awake. The words were clear as day, like someone had whispered them in her ear. She listened intently again. For a long breath, she strained to listen, then she heard another whisper. The voice was boyish and childlike like Beckett's had been when he was a toddler. "Help us." She struggled to make out the words against a fresh backdrop of thumping noises. They sped up and then slowed down. She stood and walked the perimeter of the room, her hands pressed against her ears to dampen the thumping noise. It was a continual, unceasing *thump-thump-thump*. A pounding that synced with her own heartbeat.

"Wait. Is that?" she asked aloud, unsure. "The baby?" Katie walked to the metal door and banged on it. The thumping in her ears intensified to a fevered pitch, and she crushed her hands tighter around her ears to stop the sound before it drove her mad. "Marisa!" she shouted, hoping to make contact with the other woman. There was no response, but the sound she now believed was the baby's heartbeat intensified and thumped harder. She squeezed her eyes shut, focusing on the voice, willing it to speak to her again. Katie's ears were bleeding as she was overtaken by a sea of audio sensations that enveloped her. She heard her breath rattle in her chest and a loud, hot exhale. In the distance, she heard a man whistling a tune she recognized but couldn't place. She focused on the sound and heard it again, finally recalling the song.

"The Itsy Bitsy Spider."

The whistled notes were haunting as he grew closer. Frightened, she bolted to the other side of the room. She heard footsteps getting increasingly louder as she cringed, anticipating the screech of metal on metal as the heavy door slid open to reveal Carmine. His arm gripped a familiar figure behind him, and Katie rejoiced. Being trapped alone in total isolation was wearing Katie's defenses down.

He shoved Marisa roughly into the center of the room, and Katie's heart leapt to see the young woman was alive.

"There. You got what you asked for, now eat," he demanded as he placed two bags on the ground. He then brought in three orange buckets nested in each other and yanked the door closed.

Dazed, Katie heard the lock snap into place once again. She got to her feet but felt woozy, so she leaned against the wall for a second, gathering her bearings. Then Katie rushed over to Marisa and wrapped her arms around her. She heard two staccato heartbeats, strong and unwavering. Relieved, she pulled back to look into Marisa's wide, fearful eyes. "Are you okay?"

"I think so," she said. "I'm so sorry I got you mixed up in my mess." She crumpled. "I never thought he'd take it this far."

"No apologies," Katie told her. "I made the decision to help you and I would do it again."

The sentiment made Marisa tear up.

"Why did he move you here?" Katie asked.

"I went on a hunger strike," Marisa answered.

"You did?" Katie was stunned.

"It was the only power I had."

"That was very brave," Katie said to Marisa. "I don't know if I would have been strong enough to do the same in your shoes." She offered Marisa a weak smile. "At least we're together now."

She walked over to the bags and took inventory. "There are bottles of water, sandwiches, and prenatal vitamins."

"I'm not taking them just because he wants me to." Marisa was defiant.

"I understand why you feel that way, but for now, we both have to focus on keeping our strength up, so when the opportunity to escape presents itself, we are strong enough to take advantage of it. Let's have something to eat. It will help our brains function better." Katie pulled out two bottles of water and two sandwiches, offering one to Marisa. Katie gobbled hers down quickly, but Marisa took tiny bites, belching in between.

"Are you nauseous?" Katie asked, concerned when she saw Marisa blanch.

"A little," Marisa admitted. "Mostly, I'm exhausted."

"I bet," Katie commiserated. "I remember how worn out I was with all my pregnancies and the heartburn was brutal."

Marisa nodded then burst into tears, and Katie nestled a comforting arm across her shoulders. "We're going to get out of here. I'll figure out something." She offered as she smoothed Marisa's blonde hair away from her reddened eyes. "Now that we're together, two heads are always better than one." The food and water hit her bloodstream and brought her usual sunny disposition roaring back. "Let's get some rest, and then we can figure out what to do next."

"I'm only valuable to Rocco as long as I'm pregnant," Marisa admitted as she covered her belly protectively with her hand, rubbing it in a counterclockwise direction.

"That's true, and that is a powerful tool we can use as leverage," Katie revealed. "Look at what you've accomplished already. You forced Rocco to put us together. There is strength in numbers." She brushed the tears away from Marisa's face. She was so much like Callie, and it made Katie's heart flutter. "Rest now. Everything will look more manageable after a few hours of sleep. I'll keep a lookout."

Marisa yawned and lay down on the floor, curling herself up in the fetal position.

"Can I ask you something?" Katie said.

Through another yawn, Marisa nodded and choked out, "Of course."

"Did you really have a thing with Carmine?" she asked, thinking it might give her some insight into his soft spots. If he had any feelings for Marisa at all, she could use them to influence his treatment of them.

Marisa made a face, obviously repulsed by the idea. "No way. I just said that to push Rocco's buttons."

Katie laughed. "You're much more of a badass than you give yourself credit for." Seconds later, she heard a soft snore coming from Marisa. She leaned her head against the wall and counted her blessings. The situation wasn't as dire as it had been even an hour before.

THIRTEEN

The next day, Frankie was walking Arlo down the street in her neighborhood. It was a gorgeous November day, and with Thanksgiving only a few weeks away, the fear of missing out on their holiday traditions made tears well up in Frankie's eyes. For the last several years, Frankie had a standing invitation to Thanksgiving dinner with the Beaumonts. After contributing an inedible carrot and onion casserole the first year that was still crunchy despite the hour it spent in the oven, Frankie was only allowed to bring the wine. She was an awful cook, but Katie viewed the holiday as her culinary Super Bowl, spending weeks planning the perfect Thanksgiving feast, brining the turkey and mixing up her own puff pastry from scratch.

Frankie gathered around the table with Katie's family as an honorary aunt, and every year they would eat until they almost burst. Then, after the dishes were washed, Katie and Frankie would scour the ad circulars and websites, spending hours creating their yearly Black Friday battle plan. Who else would get up at the ass crack of dawn with her to stand in the ridiculously long line at Best Buy for unprecedented savings on items she didn't really need? You never really notice how much another person has become a constant fixture in your life until they are gone. The thought crushed Frankie, and she was overcome with grief. Until that moment, she hadn't let herself think about a reality where Katie didn't come home, but now, five days after she'd disappeared, the idea of never seeing Katie again sucked all the air out of Frankie's lungs.

After Arlo stopped to cock his leg on the thirteenth tree they passed but only delivered two drops, Frankie said, "Seriously, dude, you have to be empty by now." She tugged on the leash, and he reluctantly followed, then raced ahead of her to lead the way.

She was rounding the corner to head back to her house when she saw a classic car she didn't recognize parked in her driveway. As she walked closer, she could see a man standing outside her front door. He knocked and waited. From across the street, she hollered out, "Can I help you?" then stopped abruptly when Officer Willey turned around and stood there in plain clothes.

"What are you doing here?" she couldn't help but ask, then her heart dropped, and she quickened her pace, rushing over in a panic, searching his face for clues.

"There's nothing to worry about," he assured quickly, holding up his hands, his voice calm and controlled. "I promised I'd keep you in the loop, and I wanted to give you an update."

Shocked to see him on her turf and in regular dress,

Frankie handed him the leash and pulled the keys from her pocket to unlock her front door. Mentally, she was trying to remember if all of her bras were still on the drying rack in the living room. She was pretty sure they remained haphazardly strewn from the last load of laundry she'd washed before Katie went missing. Her short-term memory was fuzzy, partially from the stress, but mostly because she'd only slept in small spurts, waking up in a panic with nightmares so real it took several long minutes in bed to calm her thundering heart to a normal range.

"Can you give me a second?" she asked, and he nodded. Frankie rushed in, swept the bras off the rack, and ran to her bedroom to shove them deep into the top of her dresser. Then she pulled the dirty dishes from the sink and shut them inside the oven, and shoved two bottles of liquor on top of the fridge into a hallway closet. "Good enough for who it's for," she said to herself and then rushed back to the door, took one quick centering breath, and opened it with a frantic smile.

"Come on in." She hadn't looked at her place with fresh eyes for a hot minute. She led him past the washer and dryer into the living room. Glancing back, she saw his eyes slide to the side table next to her recliner, where a tall stack of her newest smut books rested. On top, a dog-eared copy of *Morning Glory Milking Farm* sprawled open. His sharp eyes widened for the briefest of seconds, and his lips quirked up before he wiped the expression away, ever the professional. Then she watched him painstakingly catalog the rest of her home in one long calculated glance.

On the refrigerator, a photo of Katie and her kids was pinned to the front by an erotic magnetic bottle opener. It was a tiny carving of a well-endowed man intimately stroking himself she'd brought back as a souvenir from a trip to Jamaica she'd taken almost a decade ago. The first time she'd nonchalantly passed the bottle opener to Katie, she'd stared down at it in horror, frozen, her eyes wide. "Where am I supposed to put my fingers?" Katie had asked, and her awkwardness made Frankie laugh hysterically. The resurfacing of the memory now made Frankie grin and then tear up. She swiped the tears away and, slowly, her eyes drifted over to Harry's. His gaze lingered on the bottle opener, and she was surprised to see he was amused.

"What can I say? I let my freak flag fly." She shrugged her shoulders with an unapologetic grin. "I can make us some coffee," she offered. Then opened her refrigerator where half of an avocado was rotting in a plastic bag and a cardboard box containing two slices of dried-out pizza took up almost the entire top shelf.

"Do you have anything stronger?" he asked. "Maybe a beer?" The question caught her off guard. "Relax, I'm not on the clock." He swept a hand toward his jeans and polo shirt.

"Am I going to need one, too, in order to handle this conversation?" she asked, raking one hand through her hair to calm her anxiety. It was unnerving to see this version of him so informal and sitting in her home asking for a beer.

"You might," he admitted. "Besides, you don't seem like the type that would let a gentleman drink alone."

"Gentleman, huh? I think the jury is still out on that one." Frankie grinned, relishing the vision of the tips of his ears pinking up in embarrassment.

She walked over to the fridge and pulled out two green

bottles of Heineken, then held them close to the edge of the countertop and delivered one solid smack to pop the top off.

"Impressive," he said when she handed him one and took a long sip herself. "I'm sure you're wondering why I'm here and not relaying this information at the precinct."

"It has crossed my mind."

"There are a lot of ears at the station," he admitted. "When you don't know the character of the men they're attached to, it pays to be cautious."

"Men?" she asked, her eyebrows drifting up. "There aren't any women on the force?"

"No. I mean, yes. I mean, the *people* they're attached to," he stammered, trying to correct himself. He took another long guzzle of beer and wiped his mouth with the back of his hand before continuing.

"The fingerprints taken from the scene didn't get any hits from FALCON."

"What about the DNA or fiber evidence that was collected?"

"I have forwarded it to Detective Ludlow," he said. Frankie noticed his jaw tighten and his lips straighten into a harsh line.

"I got the impression you were less than thrilled he'd been assigned to Katie's case."

He heaved a heavy sigh and took another sip of his beer. "I shouldn't even be telling you this. I could lose my job," he admitted.

Intrigued, Frankie leaned closer. "But?" Her eyes locked on his.

"But...evidence has a way of disappearing or being

tampered with when he's around. He definitely falls into the morally gray category. There's a lot of chatter at the station behind his back about him being on the take by the Gabrianos. They are all unsubstantiated rumors, of course, but I just don't trust him."

"Can't you report him?"

"That's the thing, Frankie, there is nothing to report. He's slippery, somehow always comes out of incriminating situations smelling like a rose." He shook his head in disbelief. "It's like he's made of Teflon."

Frankie rubbed her hands over her weary face, frustrated by the lack of actual progress with the police. "So, what do we do now?"

"We continue to work the leads. I'm going to keep my ear to the ground at the precinct, and if I find anything promising, I'll run it down myself." His voice was steady.

"You will?" Frankie asked. "Why are you doing this for me?"

"I can tell Katie is pretty special by the way you and the other witnesses have spoken about her."

"She's one of a kind," Frankie admitted, then her voice cracked. "I hit the jackpot with her. She just got divorced, and I had so many plans for us now that she's free. What if…?" She trailed off, unable to finish the thought.

"Are you giving up on me already?" he asked, teasing her tears away.

"How do you do it?" She forced a smile on her face.

"Do what?"

"Stay positive in the face of so much trauma?"

He circled the almost empty bottle on the countertop for a long while, then answered, his voice smaller and softer, "My twin sister was abducted when we were seven. It destroyed my family, and I vowed I would commit my life to helping other families avoid that kind of devastation."

"Oh my God." Frankie's hand covered her mouth. "I'm so sorry."

"Thank you," he murmured, and then a long silence stretched out between them. Finally, he added, "Fonda's out there."

Frankie held up her hand. "Whoa. I'm sorry, but I have to stop you right there."

"What?" he asked and pressed his lips together, confusing Frankie.

"You're telling me your parents named your sister Fonda Willey?" She pressed her lips together to hold in an inappropriate giggle she was struggling to contain, but thankfully, he responded with a wink.

"Of course not. No one elects to name their daughter Fonda Willey," he teased. "I was just making sure you were still listening. Her name is Jessica," he answered as she punched him in the arm.

"You're terrible!" Frankie cried and laughed with him. "Fonda Willey! For crying out loud, you almost had me." She dissolved into another giggle fest, then halted herself. "I shouldn't be laughing. I feel guilty enjoying anything while Katie's gone."

"Oh, Frankie, you shouldn't. I had to learn that, no matter the outcome, life goes on. When you get a chance during a normal day to laugh or find joy in the mundane, you should grab onto it with both hands. Case in point, Fonda Willey."

Frankie sniggered, her shoulders shaking as she tried

to fight off the giggles. "I'm sorry, I have the sense of humor of a twelve-year-old boy." She looked at him and burst into a fresh round of uncontrollable chuckles that made her eyes water and her nostrils flare. "But your parents named *you* Harry Willey," she questioned, tittering, struggling to get herself under control. "How did that happen?"

"That's why I go by Harrison," he explained. "There's a longstanding tradition in our family to name the first son after his maternal grandfather. Add that fact to my mother's unfortunate romance with a man named Sam Willey, and you have the perfect storm." He shrugged his shoulders. "Trust me, I know how ridiculous it sounds. Middle school was brutal." He took a sip and then set the bottle down, peeling the label.

"I bet. Kids are jerks." She grimaced, imagining the ribbing he must have taken on the playground. "What was your sister like?" Frankie asked. "That is…if you feel up to telling me." There was a shy quality she heard in her own voice that was novel, and she felt her heart tug.

"It's funny how when you lose someone, people avoid saying their name at all. Like it will pop this bubble of happiness and denial you're living in, but nothing could be farther from the truth." He explained, "We were seven, so adjust your expectations, but there was a level of comfort, acceptance, and understanding without explanation that I miss." A soft smile settled on his lips and he continued, "You know that twin thing people talk about? Where you can finish each other's sentences, and when they feel pain, you do, too?"

"Yeah."

"It's true," he said. "That's how I know she's still alive.

Even after all this time, I know she is out there some-where. I can feel her."

"Wow."

He took another long drink from the bottle that was emptying quickly. "Did you know Elvis Presley and Liberace were twins?"

"Whoa! Really? I had no idea."

"They both lost their twin at birth. It's a phenomenon called being a twin-less twin. There's a whole Wikipedia rabbit's hole dedicated to it and I've gone down them all in search of answers," he said. "I will never stop looking for Jessica and never give up hope that someday I will find her."

"So, that's why you're here," Frankie whispered.

"Partially. It's definitely a factor, but I also want to make sure this case doesn't grow cold."

"I appreciate that," Frankie said.

"So, I've been wondering about something."

"What?"

"What did NTM mean?"

"Nothing," Frankie said and her cheeks pinked up.

"Come on." He gave her a smile that melted Frankie, and she felt herself soften. "I'm waiting." He smiled, and she buckled.

"Okay. It means never trust a man," she offered with a shrug of her shoulders.

"Wow. You must have met some real doozies." He stood up and walked over to her leaning tower of smut. He picked up a stack of them, the covers filled with bodice-ripping monster porn. "Especially if they left you running to get your jollies off reading *Morning Glory Milking Farm* and *Monster's Temptation*."

She flushed red, being called out like that, and raced over to pry the rest of the books from his judgmental hands. "Don't kink shame me. I'm *curious*," she emphasized, her face flushing crimson with heat. "I'm a *curious* person. There is nothing wrong with that."

He held up his hands with a smile and laughed open-mouthed, clearly enjoying her embarrassment. "You know, I thought *Monster's Temptation* was pretty hot, but *Monster's Obsession* took it to a whole 'nother level."

Her eyes threatened to pop out of her face. She burst out laughing so hard she snorted and then covered her mouth with her hand.

"You snorted!" He joked, joining in her laughter. "I made you snort." He was proud of himself, and a huge grin spread across his features, adding a boyish quality that made Frankie grin like an idiot.

"How could I not? I mean, come on! I'm standing in front of an officer of the law named Harry Willey who enjoys reading clit-erature." She cackled with delight, tears of joy streaming down her face. "It's a gift from heaven."

"Sometimes a man just needs to escape reality," he admitted. "What's the harm in that?"

"No harm at all." She snorted again and laughed out loud. "You have no idea how much I needed that," she said when she finally could speak. "Now we have to find Katie as soon as possible. This is too rich to keep to myself. I have to tell my best friend I met a unicorn."

He laughed at her and walked his empty bottle to the sink. "You have my card, right?"

"Yep," she confirmed, sorry to see him go.

"NTM, huh?" He pondered. "We'll see if I can't just change that about you."

He turned to leave, and Frankie watched him walk away. Admiring his trim waist and the way he filled out his jeans, she ogled him for a long moment, then felt guilt wash over her. With a little wave, he let himself out and her house was silent.

"Get home, woman!" she cried into the silence. "God, I have so much to tell you."

FOURTEEN

Yuli pulled into a parking spot at the station and then turned to face her daughter. Kristina's skin was ashen, and dark circles rested under her swollen eyes. She reached out and pulled Kristina's hand into hers.

"You need rest, dear. When was the last time you ate anything?"

She offered a weak shrug. "I'll eat when Katie comes home." Kristina's eyes took in the official building with a sigh, and then she climbed out of the car, waiting for David to join her on the sidewalk. Yuli regarded them both carefully, glad they had each other to lean on. David led the way into the station, leaning on his cane, and Yuli shuffled behind him, adopting the fragility and gait of a woman nearing a century. The ordins struggled to accept any aging reality that wasn't chronological, so in public, Yuli went to great lengths to reinforce their limiting beliefs.

A few moments later, Yuli sat stiffly in the vinyl chair,

her handbag perched in her lap, waiting for Detective Ludlow to grace them with his presence. Standing behind her, Kristina hovered, and David sat in the chair next to her, their clothing rumpled, neither looking like they'd slept a wink since Katia's abduction almost a week ago.

Yuli met David's concerned gaze, grateful when he pulled another chair closer to offer Kristina a seat and she collapsed into it. Her face was ghostly white, and her eyes darted around the room.

Around them, the normally calm Aura Cove Police Department was buzzing with activity. The ambient noise was humming with voices talking, phones ringing, and fingers flying on keyboards as they worked. All around her, oppressive energy surged. Yuli sensed a lingering darkness that swirled, concentrated in the building, and the rotten scent that accompanied it distracted her.

Finally, she locked eyes with a thin, bald man who was striding their way. As he closed in, she registered the fake smile he pasted on his face. A black aura smudged around the entire room, and she couldn't make the distinction whether it was the station or the man that inspired it.

"You're here about the Katie Beaumont case?" he asked as he sat down at the desk and logged onto his computer.

"Yes," she answered him, simply assessing the man in front of her. His tie was technically on, but off-kilter. She cataloged a stain on the cuff of his sport coat, and he reeked of cigarette smoke, as his beady eyes swept up and down, taking her in.

"And you are?"

"Yuli Davidovich, her grandmother," she answered, "And this is David and Kristina, her parents."

He reached out and patted her gloved hand, a gesture Yuli found so off-putting and pandering she had to pull her hand back. She only didn't call him out on it because she was desperate for information, and Frankie had informed Yuli he was the current gatekeeper of it.

"Can you give us an update on the investigation?" she asked.

"You know how these things are," he began, his voice a practiced condescending tone she often encountered now that she was almost a centurion. He spoke too slowly, and it grated on Yuli's nerves. She hated being talked down to and had to fight the urge to put the man in his place. Right now, he was the only ordin lifeline to her granddaughter, and she would not jeopardize it. "We're doing all the right things. We're waiting for results from the lab, and we've set up a tip line that has provided some new leads, but so far, there is nothing substantial to report."

Unable to contain himself anymore, David cried, "We can't afford to wait! Every day that goes by decreases the chances of…" Kristina cracked and let out a wail that made David's voice trail off.

Wanting to end her daughter's suffering, Yuli cleared her throat and began, "I believe her disappearance is connected with a visit we received at Kandied Karma last week. Marisa Gabriano came in with her husband and confided in Katia that she was pregnant and in fear for her life."

"Gabriano?" David repeated, leaning in. "Where do I know that name?" He focused his attention on it, trying to suss out the source.

Detective Ludlow leaned back. "That's a pretty bold accusation and a huge leap from an innocent visit to your chocolate shop to a home invasion and kidnapping." His tone was dismissive, and Yuli had to fight the urge to yank him across his tattered desk and talk some sense into him.

Pushing past her frustration, she continued, "Marisa was planning to leave her husband, and Katia was trying to offer her support," Yuli said.

"That sounds just like our Katie," Kristina offered. "Always looking for a way to help others in need."

"Rocco Gabriano!" David snapped his fingers and pointed at Ludlow, finally producing the name. "Katie's ex-husband has been his attorney for years. I knew that name sounded familiar! It's settled then. You'll bring him in for questioning?" David nodded, pleased to hear there was something more to do than wait.

"Let's not get too hasty." Ludlow held up both his hands, trying to minimize the information.

"I thought you had a duty to the public to follow all leads."

"We do," he said.

"He's got connections and real estate all over the Tampa Bay area. Can't you get a search warrant?" Yuli asked.

"I can't get a search warrant on the hunch of a little old lady."

Yuli's blood boiled, and she seethed with hatred as he tried to wrap up the conversation, placating them with a litany of words about police procedure he thought would deter and intimidate them. They didn't.

He was hiding something, Yuli could tell. She pulled off the short black glove that covered her right hand.

"Rocco Gabriano is behind Katia's disappearance. I'm

sure of it. He knows where she is. You must focus your attention there," she clearly stated, using short sentences as her last ditch effort to inspire Ludlow to act.

"I assure you, I will take this new information into consideration. Thank you for coming to the station. If there are any new developments in the case, I'll be in touch." He stood to signal the end of the meeting and put an arm around Yuli, trying to guide her to the door. A despondent Kristina and David trailed behind them. She reached out to pat Ludlow's hand, wincing when the first jolt hit her consciousness.

Images of Ludlow in a dark alley rocketed into her mind. A man handing him an envelope full of cash. Ludlow in the evidence room, moving sealed packets into different boxes and misfiling them. Eyes flitting around from side to side like the snake he was, then letting himself out of the room with his evidence badge.

The intensity of the sensation was overwhelming, and Yuli gasped.

"Are you okay?" he asked, his voice full of false concern. "You all must be under an immense amount of strain with Katie's disappearance." He turned to David. "You should head home and get some rest. Leave the police work to the professionals." At the door, they parted ways.

"Professionals?" Yuli harrumphed under her breath as she huffed and stepped further away from him, desperate to free herself from his grasp. He didn't have any intentions of helping her find Katia. In fact, she was now more certain than ever that he would throw up roadblocks to keep the fat envelopes of cash coming. She'd tried to go through the proper channels, but she could see she'd have to take matters into her own hands now. Katia was counting on her.

FIFTEEN

At Kandied Karma the next morning, the bell jingled as Frankie dropped Arlo off before she headed to work. She was running so late she didn't even get to stop for a cup of coffee. The dog raced back to Yuli, making whining noises, clearly distressed. He circled and circled her before shaking off the tension and settling down.

"Anything?" Arlo asked.

"Nothing concrete," Yuli replied. "We met the new officer assigned to her case, Detective Ludlow. It's obvious the ordins can't help us...or I should say *won't* help us," she corrected herself.

"We might have an ally in our midst. Officer Willey came by Frankie's, and he confirmed your suspicions of Ludlow."

"They aren't just suspicions," Yuli barked at him. "I took a reading, and he's definitely not the squeaky clean member of law enforcement he claims to be. The flashes revealed him to be a corrupt cop on the take. We can't trust him or the authorities."

Yuli sat down on a stool and stirred sugar into a cup of warm coffee.

"Maybe we need to involve…"

"Don't say it."

"She's going to find out anyway," he offered. "Don't you think it will be better if she hears it from us?"

"I believe she already knows." The confession made Arlo howl. "But, we don't need to involve her yet," Yuli stressed.

"Why?" Arlo asked. "She might be our only hope."

"Zoya can't be trusted," Yuli answered. "She would sacrifice anyone, including Katia, to keep her powers intact, and I am not willing to take that risk."

Arlo yowled in response and then plopped down on the floor with a dramatic sigh.

"I've got one more option to engage. If I don't get anywhere with it, then we'll have to join forces with her, but not before."

"What is it?" Arlo asked.

"I have to open a door from my past that I closed a million years ago." Yuli's eyes clouded, and she looked down at the cup of coffee in her hands before continuing. "When I was a child, Zoya fell in love with a man named Salvatore Lombardo. His only son, Dominic, and I grew up together in Chicago. He was the closest thing I had to a little brother, and we used to be very close."

Yuli took a long sip of coffee and set the cup back down. "When I was thirteen, his father was gunned down by the Gabrianos. After his death, we fled to the compound, but Dominic remained in Chicago and rose through the ranks. Now he is the don of the Lombardo family. If there is anyone that is looking for retribution against the Gabrianos, it will be him."

"Well, what are you waiting for?" Arlo asked, jumping to his feet, his tags jingling together, excited at the prospect of making real progress in finding his owner.

"I am reluctant to ask for the favor because, in that world, I will be indebted to him. I fought my way out of a life of fear, corruption, and control. If I ask this favor, I will be right back where I started, destroying people instead of helping them."

"I can understand that, Yuli, but this is Katia we are talking about."

"Don't you think I know that?" she snapped harshly at the impatient dog. "That's the only reason noble enough to reopen this wound." Yuli paced the room as Arlo whined, then circled and collapsed under a table.

She walked over to the window and stared out it down the main streets of Aura Cove. She'd been naïve enough to think they would be safe here, but that dream dissolved when Katia was taken. Glancing around the store, an hour before Beckett and Callie would arrive to man the counter, she strengthened her resolve. Kandied Karma was not the same without Katia—*life* was not the same without her granddaughter. Yuli bolstered her resources, preparing for battle. She was going to do whatever it took to see her sweet Katia come home and restore her to her rightful place, no matter what the sacrifice.

SIXTEEN

After unsuccessfully trying to reconnect with Salvatore in her meditation chamber, Zoya admitted defeat and forced herself back to the archives. This time, the black box riddled with bullet holes quivered the closer she crept toward it. She flinched before she reached out to touch it with one trembling hand, and when it didn't sting her, she steeled herself to pull it off the shelf. Once in her grasp, the music box pulsated and hummed, the energy spiking to a fevered pitch.

A few moments later, blood began to ooze out of the bullet holes onto her fingers. Shaking, she dropped the box, and it hit the ground with a loud crash. She rushed away from it like she'd been burned and haphazardly drove herself to the edge of the sea. Sobbing, she dropped to her knees in the sand and splashed water onto her hands, seeing the blood dilute and turn the water brown before washing away completely. She scrubbed until her fingers were sore. The sight of blood—Salvatore's blood—on her hands transported her right back to the night he died. She didn't know if she was strong enough to witness it again.

For the better part of an hour, she walked the shoreline, breathing in the scent of the sea and letting it calm the hammering of her heart. Zoya was unnerved by the swell of messy emotion that wouldn't leave her alone. It stalked her as she paced, refusing to relent. She thought she'd successfully left the pain in the past, but it lingered. Locked inside her heart, the route to it had been disconnected for almost a century, but in tandem with Katia's awakening, she sensed her own emotional reawakening taking place. The agony of losing her soulmate so long ago hadn't disappeared; it had simply laid in wait, and now she was a victim to it.

The aqua water of the ocean washed over her bare feet as waves crashed on the shore. Underfoot, the sand was satiny and warm and grounded her energy. She wiggled her toes in the sand, and the sugary grains clung to her perfect blood-red pedicure. The sun lowered on the horizon, kissed the sea goodnight, and then dropped out of sight. As darkness settled in, the sea became calm and she closed her eyes, trying to soothe the stormy sea of emotion within her.

In search of sustenance, Zoya drove herself back to the estate.

"How can I be of assistance, My Queen?" Terrance asked, his tail wagging, desperate to earn her approval and return to her good graces.

"I have a very arduous task ahead of me this evening," Zoya explained. "And my energy levels are bankrupt."

In his eagerness to fulfill her request, he zipped around the room frantically. Unable to contain his energy, he raced up onto the furniture and then jumped down again, his tail wagging as he compulsively circled the room four times. When he returned to Zoya, he was breathless and almost knocked her down when his clumsy paws landed on her chest.

Disgusted by his lack of control, she pushed him to the ground. "The zoomies, seriously?" Her question was cloaked in annoyance. "You need to do a better job controlling your basic instincts."

"My sincere apologies," he said, averting his eyes to the floor. "I will try harder."

"See that you do," she declared.

He cleared his throat and then said, "I've taken the liberty of having the chef prepare one of your favorite meals."

"Did you now?" she queried, tilting her head to the side. Food was a hedonistic pleasure that Zoya savored. It would restore her vitality, giving her the energy to continue her quest to find Katia. "This is exactly the kind of initiative I was hoping you would learn to practice." She delivered two quick pats to his velvety brown head.

He sat up straighter in the presence of Zoya's infrequent words of praise, but her glowing accolades didn't last long. "It was about damn time."

Terrance whined and lowered his head. "I hope it pleases your majesty." He bowed deeply, then continued, " Dinner will be served in twenty minutes in the formal dining room. First course is lobster bisque with seared leeks. Second course is seared scallops and a pecorino cheese risotto with smoked bacon. And last but not least, a dark chocolate souffle for dessert."

"Well, look at that. Even a blind dog can find a bone from time to time."

He bowed into a downward facing dog pose for several seconds and then scampered away before he could offend her again.

After a wonderful meal, she stood refreshed and ready to tackle the task in front of her. She climbed onto the golf cart and returned to the archives where the box waited for her on the floor where she'd dropped it. Taking a deep breath, she picked it up, relieved when there was no new appearance of blood on her fingers.

Holding it in one hand, she cranked the metal crank on the side, and notes from a melancholy cello seeped from the box. It was a glum soundtrack that set the woeful tone of the journey she was forcing herself to take. Gently, she pried the lid open, and red light bounced up from the box. It illuminated her features from below and distorted her face into a horrific mask. Zoya closed her eyes and felt the pressure build in her head and limbs. A tightness squeezed her body as she contracted into a ball and rolled out onto the ground at her destination.

She stood for a moment and shook her limbs, getting her bearings. Glancing around quickly, Zoya noticed she was on a deserted street late at night. Putting one foot in front of the other, she was tugged down the sidewalk where a street light illuminated a brick industrial building. Zoya was forced down the familiar path, unable to take a step in the opposite direction. She slipped inside the building and was enshrouded in the shadows as gruff unknown voices filtered through the door she hid behind. For several long moments, she listened intently as the past filtered back in familiar bits and pieces.

She heard a shotgun being cocked, and the metallic clink of bullets being loaded as the first prickle of fear pierced her heart.

"Sally has made a mockery of us, and it's time to teach him that the Gabriano family owns this town."

Zoya leaned around the corner, catching small glimpses of the gangsters who were gathered together loading weapons. A spindly boy, not even close to becoming a man, asked, "What did he do?"

"He's been overstepping his bounds and selling in our territory. Bootlegging cigarettes and liquor without cutting us in."

There was a hum of animalistic male energy as the group hollered and slammed their hands down on the wooden crates in consensus.

"The thing about a wise guy like Sally is he never learns," an intimidating man standing over six feet tall piped up, his voice rough and gravelly.

Another man spoke up. "Now he's going to feel the fury of the Gabrianos." In the circle, the men barked in agreement, riling each other up. Zoya could practically taste the testosterone.

"He's tied our hands," another man added. "It's time to make an example of him, so everyone in this town knows—you mess with the Gabrianos, you get whacked."

They passed around a flask, taking long guzzles of liquid courage from it and handing it off to the next person.

"The police are going to be otherwise engaged on the north side of town," a rotund man who leaned hard into the obese category bragged. "We've made prior arrangements." The rest of the group laughed, and their combined glee made Zoya shiver.

Abruptly, the music box pulled her out of the warehouse, and seconds later, Zoya tumbled onto the hard ground in front of the brick-faced townhouse she'd lived in with Sally, Yuli, and Dominic in 1938. Her eyes traced the graceful lines of the carved stone entry, remembering the first night they'd spent there when Salvatore demanded to carry her across the threshold. He'd swept her up in his arms like she was weightless while she protested, but secretly enjoyed it anyway.

Needing to hide, Zoya opened the door and crept up the steps and into the townhouse, darting into the hall closet. She cracked the door open to peer into the living room, where she watched Salvatore teach Dominic and Yuli how to play seven card stud. Yuli took to the game instantly, practically a poker savant. She had an impeccable memory and recalled with extreme accuracy what cards had already been laid. Her natural skill, understanding of the game, and her intuition of the other players amazed him. When she'd bested Sally six hands in a row, he handed her a twenty-dollar bill.

"Wow." She was awestruck. Holding the bill in her hands, she relished the possibilities it opened up for her. It was the first money Yuli had ever earned in her life, and she eyed the cash reverently, finally understanding why men were so driven to acquire it.

"What about me, Pop?" Dominic piped up.

"You gotta earn it on your own, boy," Sally said, patting him on the head. "Maybe Yuli can give you some pointers."

His expression soured being bested by a girl.

"Come on, Dom," Yuli encouraged. "I'll show you some of my tricks." They disappeared into the parlor. A few moments later, there was the incessant sound of a horn honking in the street below. In the bathroom, Sally lingered at the mirror. Running his fingers through his hair, he swiped it back from his forehead with a thick pomade that smelled like cedar. Striding confidently out, he walked to the bedroom where a much younger Zoya was lost in thought in front of the window, rubbing lotion into her skin. In the street below, the horns blasted louder.

"God, I hate this city," Zoya said under her breath.

Coming up behind her, Salvatore delivered a series of soft kisses to her neck and collarbone. Smiling, Zoya turned to face him and wrapped her arms around his shoulders. Her fingers rubbed the nape of his neck, and she leaned forward to brush her lips against his. He moaned in delight and pulled back.

"Keep that thought in mind, doll-face." He grinned. "I have to attend to some business, but when I return, I want to pick up where we left off." He kissed her deeply and then walked to the hall closet where Zoya hid. She quickly placed his overcoat and fedora in his hands and then silently followed him down the stairs of the townhouse, hovering close enough to breathe in the scent of his shaving cream.

At the landing, she ducked behind a potted tree when he reversed directions and ran back up the stairs.

"One more kiss for luck!" she heard him shout out playfully at her younger self. Taking the opportunity to hide, she raced down the stairs, out the door, and across the street.

From the distance, she watched the last few minutes of

his life play out in front of her. He ran down the stairs but, always slightly vain, stopped to preen in the mirror. The light from inside the townhouse illuminated his face, and Sally was so handsome he took her breath away. He took a long second to study his reflection, topping his hat on his head and straightening the yellow carnation in his lapel. Whistling, he opened the door with a huge smile and walked out onto the stoop when the first shots rang out.

Bang. Bang. Bang.

From her vantage point, Zoya recoiled as if she'd taken a bullet herself. Men poured out of the two streetcars and sprayed bullets over the entire block. Glass shattered as round after round rang out and decimated buildings, cutting through the carved stone like butter. In mere seconds, their average Chicago neighborhood was instantly transformed into a war zone as shell casings hit the concrete and potted plants exploded under the shower of gunfire.

Pop. Pop. Pop.

Across the street, Zoya clamped her hand over her mouth and stifled a sob as she gaped at Salvatore. The shots stupefied Sally at first, and time seemed to stand still. Then, in a blink, reality set in. He stiffened, then dropped to the ground face-down on the front steps, landing with a hard crack.

She heard herself scream and then watched her younger self yank open the front door as the group of men filed back into the two cars, burning rubber as they careened away from the curb and down the street.

Then total silence engulfed the scene. Above the destruction, lights flipped on, and windows opened while residents leaned out to ogle the gruesome spectacle below.

On the steps, a younger Zoya flipped Salvatore over onto his back. Blood covered his shirt and had already started to pool underneath him. She pressed her hands down, screaming at a teenage Yuli who appeared in the doorway, "Call an ambulance!"

Yuli was paralyzed with fear. Her eyes were wide and her creamy skin pale as a sheet. "Now, Yuli!" Zoya shouted at the child, who finally lurched into action and ran back up the stairs.

Across the street, Zoya hovered, cowering around the corner, her eyes glued to Sally's unmoving body. She watched herself tend to his wounds, almost in a trance as she floated closer. Soon, she was hovering behind the younger version of herself as tears flowed freely down her cheeks.

Her youthful hands were red with Sally's blood, and it stained the pale blue dress she'd been wearing. Blood spurted from his chest and from his mouth, reddening his teeth. Her chin dropped, and she cradled his head to her chest.

"Sally, stay here. Stay with me," Zoya begged, looking down at him.

"Doll-face," he whispered with a small smile as his eyes locked on hers. His hand reached up to touch her face. "I'm sorry," he apologized and then started to cough, choking on his own blood. Wetness shot out of his mouth and landed on her cheek.

"This is not the time for apologies," she dismissed as she smoothed the stubborn curl of his hair away from his face.

"I'm so cold," he told her.

"No, no, no!" Zoya shouted at him. "You promised you'd never leave me."

"I love you, doll." He coughed once more and then disappeared behind the veil. His warm brown eyes that always held such mischief and roguery were vacant. In the distance, she heard the whine of sirens from the approaching ambulance. Around her, a crowd gathered, drawn to the sound of gunfire. The air was infused with gunpowder and the metallic scent of blood. She clutched his body to hers, rocking him and humming the song he used to whistle while he stood at the sink shaving.

Behind the front door, Yuli witnessed his passing, barely thirteen years old and in the awkward stage right before womanhood. Dismayed by the scene on their front stoop, she stood frozen and was incapacitated by shock. She heard footsteps falling hard on the steps behind her and spun around to see Dominic racing toward her. When he reached the landing, she pushed him away from the window of the door. "Go back upstairs!" she demanded, trying to shield his twelve-year-old eyes from the carnage, not wanting his last visual memory of his father's face to be a bloody one. One look in her eyes, and he stumbled back, falling against the stair treads. Determined to know what happened, he scrambled to his feet again and tried to push her out of the way.

"No, Dom, go upstairs! You don't want to see this," Yuli begged him, and the intensity in her voice stopped him dead in his tracks.

When she heard the door to their townhouse close, little Yuli turned back toward Zoya, who hadn't moved from the sidewalk, still clinging to Sally's body. Her grandmother, the woman who always loomed larger than life in Yuli's mind, was shrinking before her eyes. The sensation was deeply unsettling, upending her entire world in a moment. The one person who had shown her kindness had been ripped away, and Yuli's eyes filled with tears, obscuring her vision completely.

Zoya watched the paramedics pry Sally's body from her younger hands. In shock, she didn't move. They checked his pulse, and the younger of the two men pulled down on Sally's eyelids to close his eyes.

"I'm sorry, ma'am. He's gone." The paramedic stood and turned to go back to the rig for a gurney.

"No!" she shouted, finding her voice and her feet at the same time. "Try again. You need to try harder."

"It's too late," he said as Zoya rushed toward him, her bloodied hands balled into tight fists that hung at her sides.

"Why did you take so long to get here?" she'd howled and battered his chest. In a defensive move, the paramedic gently clenched her wrists as the first wave of sorrow and rage engulfed her. It knocked the breath out of her younger self, and from her vantage point in the music box, mere steps away, Zoya also felt the brunt of it crash into her and pull her down violently into its undertow. She came up gasping for breath and drained from the effort. The paramedic said, "You're in shock. Is there someone I can call for you?"

She shook her head no, and her expression crumpled as she staggered to the steps of the brownstone. Completely traumatized and detached from reality, she noticed the pot full of yellow carnations next to her had been cracked in half from the gunfire. On the steps, the dirt poured out of it, mingling with Sally's crimson blood, becoming a sticky pool at her feet. She collapsed onto the stairs, her legs wobbly, and clutched her bloodied hands to her face, surveying the horrific scene in front of her in a daze.

On the sidewalk, the carnation that had been pinned to Sally's lapel had fallen off in the melee and was now wilted, red, and suffocating from the coagulating blood. In utter disbelief, a younger Zoya watched the paramedics load up Sally's lifeless body and drive away, while she remained on the blood-soaked landing, unable to move.

Hidden behind the bushes, she studied her former self for several long moments. She knew the rest of the story by heart. Eventually, Yuli would come out to drag her back inside. It would be Yuli who would help undress her and draw a bath, and Yuli who would put a nearly comatose woman to bed that night.

From her hiding place, she wiped the river of tears away. No matter how many times she would witness the events unfold, it was always like reliving them for the first time and never became easier. The same rush of adrenaline mixed with sorrow would overwhelm her. It was the reason she'd refused to enter the bullet-riddled music box for decades.

The cellos whined again, and she felt her form being tugged from the steps of the brownstone and lifted to a storm cloud that swallowed her whole. When she landed back at the compound inside the building amongst the archives, she lay on the cold ground for several seconds, disoriented and unable to move. The sorrow was so deeply palpable it trapped her inside her own mind. Tears raced down her cheeks and pooled in her snow-white hair spread out on the concrete. She lost track of time, staring at the ceiling. Exhausted, she closed her eyes and drifted to sleep on the hard ground, depleted from the journey.

Much later, she opened her eyes. Still fuzzy from the journey inside the music box, she gathered the strength to sit up and then summoned Terrance. He sent for her maid, and together they drove Zoya back to the main house and tucked her into her bed. He returned a few minutes later with the maid, who set a tray of refreshments on her bedside table.

"You must keep your strength up," Terrance murmured, concerned about the current state of his mistress. He nudged the tray closer to her with his nose. On it rested a mug of chamomile tea and honey-roasted peanuts. The maid had cut squares of gouda and peppery salami and added Zoya's favorite crispy crackers with caraway seeds.

"Please eat something, Your Highness," he begged when the tray had gone untouched for a quarter of an hour. Zoya was bereft and mumbling to herself in words he couldn't comprehend.

A little while later, Zoya finally forced herself to an upright position, picked up a slice of creamy cheese, and took a nibble. He was right, the food and drink would help replenish her energy, but there wasn't a morsel on the tray that could heal her broken heart.

SEVENTEEN

Frankie was hopping out of the shower before bed when she heard a knock at the door. She pulled on a robe and twisted her hair into a towel when a swift second knock rattled her nerves.

"Hold your horses. I'm coming!" She yanked open the door, ready to do battle with whoever was on the other side. Her first glimpse of the unexpected visitor made her clutch the lapels of her robe together to prevent herself from spilling out of it.

"Sorry," Officer Willey mumbled. He was standing under her front awning dressed in plain clothes, wearing a Wilson Phillips concert t-shirt and dad jeans. His eyes skirted around uncomfortably, looking for a safe place to land, drifting to the robe and down to her legs. Under his scrutiny, Frankie felt a rush of heat move from her core to her limbs.

"Dude, my eyes are up here," she joked, poking two fingers up to her eyes, clearly enjoying his discomfort.

The tips of his ears pinked up, and he winced while his

eyes darted away to perceived safety. "I should have called first."

"No, you should have held on for one more day," she quipped, rendering him speechless in confusion, but then she pointed at his shirt. He looked down and grinned back up at her, and it felt like stepping into the sun.

"Oh, yeah. I forgot I was wearing this shirt." He shrugged. "Can't help it. I have a soft spot for early nineties girl bands. You know, The Bangles, Wilson Phillips, TLC, and Salt-n-Pepa."

"Who doesn't?" Frankie grinned, happy to have an ally. Harry was the only bright spot in this horrific reality she was living. "Did you want to come in?" Frankie asked, jerking her head into the living room while holding her robe closed with both hands.

"I need to borrow your car," he blurted.

"What? Why?"

"I might have crossed a line," he admitted. Harry was wringing his hands together, clearly conflicted. Then he lowered his voice and muttered, "I put a tracker on Ludlow's car, hoping he'll lead us to a break in Katie's case."

"Isn't that illegal?" Frankie was taken aback. "Not that I have a problem with doing whatever it takes to bring Katie home safe."

He grimaced. "Well, technically, it's tracking without consent, a simple misdemeanor," he answered sheepishly. "But Ludlow was jumpy after Katie's parents and her grandmother came to the station yesterday. I overheard him make a couple of quick calls, and then he left for several hours. Now, I don't want to get your hopes up, because it could be a huge waste of time, but the investigation is stalling out. At the very least, this will put my suspicions about him to bed." He held out his hand. "So, can I borrow your car? I'd take mine, but when you drive a fully restored, cherry-red El Camino, it's hard to stay under the radar."

"Only if I can come with you," Frankie decided.

"No way."

"It's not up for discussion," Frankie countered, and seeing the firm set of her jaw, he gave in. "Just give me a few minutes to change and we'll go. Make yourself at home," she said over her shoulder as she ran back to the bedroom to throw on some clothes. It just felt good to be taking action. The waiting was killing her. Frankie pulled out a black t-shirt and a pair of worn athletic shorts, then pulled her wet hair into a ponytail at the crown of her head. She applied Chapstick and took two seconds to add a couple of swipes of mascara before heading back out to where Harry was seated in her living room.

"Where's the dog?" he asked. "Do we have to let him out?"

"He's with Yuli," Frankie offered, ticking off another invisible box of admirable qualities. Kind to animals and considerate. Check. "Are you ready?" she asked, and he nodded and held open the door for her. At the car, she tossed the keys in the air, and he caught them with one outstretched hand. After they were settled, he tapped on the tracker app on his phone, started the car, and navigated toward the blue dot.

He reached down to turn up the radio and hummed in tune with it, tapping his thumbs on the wheel. After a lengthy commercial break, the next song cued up. "Ooh! I love this one!" he enthused, reaching over to crank it up.

Queen's "Bohemian Rhapsody" began its six-minute auditory assault, and she was delighted to hear Harry's pitiful
attempt to hit the high falsetto notes. Even the hula dancer
mounted to the dashboard shimmied her hips in tune. Not
needing any encouragement, Frankie joined in to belt out
the chorus when Harry reached down and turned the music
down briefly.

"Whew! I was worried about you there for a minute."

"Why?"

"Bohemian Rhapsody" is a surprisingly accurate character barometer. You can't trust anyone who doesn't sing
along and at least attempt the falsetto."

She laughed and reached back down to turn it up.
Frankie stole glances over at him out of the corner of her
eye as they finished the song with gusto. There weren't
many men who were willing to make absolute fools of
themselves in front of others, and it was an endearing
quality that impressed Frankie.

Twenty minutes later, they turned onto the Gandy
Bridge and made the almost two-mile drive closer to Port
Tampa Bay swallowed in darkness.

"You know, ever since the Skyway Bridge collapsed
when I was seven, I get anxious when I'm driving over
water," Frankie shared, staring straight ahead as the headlights of the car illuminated the stretch of road in front of
them. The water was only visible in small snatches that
whipped by, but Frankie focused on a small chip in her
windshield. "I can't even look at it."

"You must know statistically the chances of another
tragedy like that happening are minuscule," he reasoned.

"I know. It's an irrational fear," she said, then asked,
"Don't you have any?"

"Clowns," he admitted. "They scare the hell out of me." Harry shivered. "John Wayne Gacy, Pennywise, Ronald McDonald? They all left their mark. There is something creepy about those huge red shoes and squeaky noses. It's not natural," he offered in explanation.

"Ronald McDonald?" She laughed. "You really think it's fair to lump him in with a serial killer?"

"It's an irrational fear." He shrugged. "By definition, it shouldn't make sense."

She held up her hands in defeat. "You got me there."

They rattled over railroad tracks, crossing over to the industrial park area. Frankie looked down at Harry's phone, noticing their car closing in proximity to the blue dot.

"That's him," Harry said, pointing at the car that was driving a block ahead of them. He hit the brakes to slow down to allow Ludlow more room. After a stop at a traffic light, Ludlow signaled a turn and then pulled into the parking lot in front of a nondescript industrial building.

"Dammit," Harry muttered under his breath as he drove past Ludlow's car and circled around the block. Finally, he eased the Honda into a parallel parking spot a block away from the building. He turned off the headlights and pulled a pair of travel binoculars from his pocket. Across the street, Ludlow sat in his car, waiting. The red brake lights on the back of his car were lit up, and exhaust was leaking from the tailpipe.

Two minutes later, a door on the building opened, and a burly man ran out with a thick envelope in his hands. Then another guy pushed through the open door with a dolly carrying two boxes. Ludlow got out of the car and popped the trunk for him, glancing around nervously while he chain-smoked a cigarette. Once the packages were safely inside, he slammed the trunk shut, dropped the butt to the ground, and crushed it with his boot.

Harry quickly dropped the binoculars into his lap and turned his face away as Frankie leaned into the door frame to hide from Ludlow, who was glancing around again. He lit another cigarette and took a long drag.

"He's an anxious one," Frankie declared. "People are only that suspicious when they're hiding something or breaking the law."

"I agree."

Through the windshield, they watched Ludlow return to the driver's seat, start the car, then pull out and ease down the isolated road. Instead of following him, Harry started Frankie's car and turned in the opposite direction, driving closer to the parking lot Ludlow just exited.

"You're losing him."

"Don't worry, we'll catch up later," he answered as he pulled closer to the building. ANO Delivery Service was spelled out on the metal sign fastened to the metal door.

"Have you heard of them?" Frankie asked as she tried to pull the business up on Google.

"No," he answered.

"There's no listing for them online," she confirmed.

"How about the address?" Harry asked. "711 Water-front Drive."

"Weird," Frankie said. "Nothing there either."

Just then, the back door to ANO Deliveries opened and the same stocky man walked out of it, rolling the dolly with two more boxes, heading toward their car.

"Oh, shit," Frankie said. "He thinks we're here for a pickup. We need to get out of here!"

"Maybe we should take the delivery and see what's in the boxes," he mused as the cart rolled closer.

"That's a terrible idea," Frankie rebutted. "Start the car!"

Conflicted, he cracked the window and shouted, "Sorry! Wrong turn!" as he cranked the ignition and whipped the car out of the parking lot. The confused delivery man abandoned the dolly and ran behind them. Frankie glanced through the rear window and saw him take out his cell phone from a pocket and make a call. Casting glances over her shoulder as Harry turned a corner, she was only able to relax when the threat was no longer visible. It took three miles of distance between them to calm her hammering heart.

"I don't know if I'm cut out for police work," she admitted. "To be honest, I thought we'd be spending a lot more time tonight eating sandwiches and peeing in bottles."

Harry laughed. "Is that what you think happens at a stakeout?"

"Maybe," she said with a shrug. He tapped on the app and eased back onto the freeway.

"We're headed back across the bridge," he warned.

"I know." She sighed and settled back into the seat, closing her eyes. "Just tell me when it's over."

Forty minutes later, they were driving down the streets of the bustling downtown of St. Pete's Beach. Harry eased the car into a spot a block down from Ludlow's car that was parked in front of an Italian Bakery that was closed for the night. Its windows were dark.

Ludlow jumped out of the car and was skittish again, scanning the area to make sure he wasn't being watched.

He tugged his pants up by his belt loops and lit another cigarette, taking several long drags before dropping it to knock on the door of the bakery. After a short wait, the door opened, and he went inside.

The scent of freshly baked bread wafted in the air. "My stomach is growling," Harry said as the door of the bakery opened and Ludlow walked out onto the street with a much larger man.

"Oh my God," Harry said as he stared at the pair through his travel binoculars. "Get down," he snapped at Frankie. "I don't want anyone to see you."

"What is it?" Frankie asked as she folded herself into the small space on the floorboard of her car among cheese-burger wrappers and empty soda cans. Her fearful eyes focused on Harry's concerned expression as he slid down in the seat further, hiding behind the dash. He was glued to the binoculars. "Another envelope just passed hands," he reported, focused on the exchange happening through the windshield.

"I'd bet my life the man he's speaking to right now is Rocco Gabriano."

"Holy shit." Frankie was stunned. "Yuli was right."

Harry ducked down in Frankie's seat.

"He's on the move again," Harry explained. His face was inches from hers and his intelligent eyes darted around the cramped space. She felt his breath warm on her cheek, and in other circumstances would have savored the sensa-tion, but now she was alarmed. After a long minute, his eyes darted to his phone, where the blue dot was on the move again. He sat up and turned on the ignition.

"We're not safe here," Harry confessed as he eased the car away from the curb and into the flow of traffic. His expression was pinched and the playfulness in his voice vanished. "I'm taking you home."

"Can I sit up now?" Frankie asked from the floorboard. Her back ached, and she needed to stretch out.

"Oh, sorry, of course," he said, and she pulled herself up into the seat and stretched her legs and arms.

"So, what do we do now?" Frankie asked. "There is a definite connection between Ludlow and Rocco."

He heaved a sigh. "I always had my suspicions about Ludlow. Now that they are confirmed, I need to gather enough evidence so I can convince Sarge or continue to track Ludlow and hope and pray that he leads us to Katie."

Impatient, Frankie cried, "Hope and pray? You've got to be kidding me."

"We don't have a choice," Harry said. "A beat cop accusing a detective without solid evidence is just going to get me fired. It will not get us any closer to finding Katie. I have to go through the appropriate channels."

"Ugh!" Frankie's frustration was evident.

"I have to play my cards right," Harry added. "Ludlow has deep connections that go all the way to the governor and many friends in the department. It's how he climbed the ranks so quickly."

Frankie pulled away from him, looking out the window as the streets sped by. She was disheartened by the lack of actual progress. Every day without her best friend was taking a toll. Hope and pray? Yeah, screw that.

EIGHTEEN

S un streamed into the windows of the warehouse when Katie awoke. Her eyes glanced around the room, and her heart eased when she saw Marisa still curled into a ball on the ground, sleeping. She was living a nightmare, but at least she wasn't alone. Together, they would find a way. She was sure of it.

Katie walked a bucket to the far end of the room and sat down to pee. Filled with renewed hope, she pulled a bottle of water out of the grocery bag and allowed herself to drink half of it. Then she nibbled at one of the four remaining peanut butter and jelly sandwiches while waiting for Marisa to awaken.

The air was already stale and heavy with humidity. A trickle of sweat ran down the side of her cheekbone when she heard Marisa murmur. She wiped it away with the back of her hand as Marisa's eyes fluttered open and she offered Katie a weak smile.

"I set up a prison bathroom over there for us." Katie pointed to the orange buckets, trying to keep her tone as light as possible. "I'll give you some privacy," she offered as she turned away.

When Marisa returned, she was green and gripping her stomach. "I'm so nauseous today."

"Try to eat little bites of one of the sandwiches," Katie instructed. "It's important to keep some food in your tummy all day long so it can help settle the acid." She passed an unopened sandwich over to Marisa, who took the tiniest bite. Then she opened the bottle of vitamins and pulled one out and handed it over to her. "You forget how huge these things are when you don't have to take them anymore." She tucked a chunk of hair behind her ear and wiped her sweaty forehead with the back of her hand.

"Is it me, or is the white streak in your hair thicker than it was yesterday?" Marisa mused. Katie pulled a face and reached to the crown of her head to pull a thick chunk of her hair down over her eyes. Shocked to see the brilliant white, she pulled another clump forward. It was true. The white streak had doubled in width overnight.

"It's definitely not you," Katie admitted.

"And your eyebrows are completely white. I never noticed that before."

"Hmm," Katie remarked, keeping her surprise to herself. Marisa never noticed because they had been mostly jet black. "Cool." She beamed a smile at Marisa, who was instantly confused.

"You mean you're not going to race to the salon when we get out of here?" Marisa asked.

"No way," Katie admitted. "I spent twenty years covering up my natural beauty to make other people more comfortable. It's time to embrace every aspect that makes me unique."

"Wow. You must be the healthiest middle-aged female I've ever met."

"Helen Mirren paved the way for all of us," Katie said. "I used to fight aging with every fiber of my being, but now I know growing old is beautiful and a privilege not given to everyone. Just because the male standard of beauty worships at the fountain of youth doesn't mean women need to."

Marisa looked down at her breasts with a groan. "Rocco insisted on the implants. But I have to tell you, a friend invited me to a Breast Implant Illness Facebook group, and it scared the hell out of me. If I survive this, I'm scheduling an explant and becoming a new card-carrying member of the Itty Bitty Titty Committee. "

"*When* you survive this," Katie corrected.

"When," Marisa repeated with a nod, and Katie offered her a dazzling smile. "How do you do it?"

"What?"

"Keep a smile on your face in the middle of this nightmare?"

"I learned a long time ago that controlling your reactions is the only true power you have in life. You can't control the outcome, or avoid the pain and trouble that shows up at your door. You can only control the way you respond to it."

"If you say so."

"Oh, I know so," Katie promised. "Even trapped in here, *we* get to choose how we feel."

Marisa shook her head and offered a weak smile. "You're special."

Katie returned the compliment. "So are you, my dear."

Marisa stood abruptly, clamping a hand over her mouth.

"The other corner, I set up a bucket for you!" Katie said and watched Marisa bolt over to the bucket to vomit.

A few minutes later, she returned, weakened by the effort. "That is getting old."

"Hang in there. It should dissipate as the day wears on. If men were the ones who had to have babies, the human species would face extinction," Katie mused.

Marisa returned a tight smile and took a few more bites and a small drink of water, working to keep it down.

"That's good, Marisa. Just breathe through the queasiness. You focus on cell division, and I'll work on getting us out of here."

"Why couldn't I have had a mother like Katie?"

Katie's eyes darted up in confusion and met Marisa's. She could almost swear she'd heard the words as if Marisa had spoken them aloud. It untethered her, blurring the line between fantasy and reality. Was she hearing Marisa's actual thoughts? Was this a new magical ability?

"If I had, I would have never ended up here."

The second intercepted thought was more difficult to ignore. Despite the unsettling way she gained the information, Katie's heart swelled and she couldn't stop herself from saying, "I might have to adopt you. One way or another, you're going to become part of my brood. I think you'll love my Callie."

"I always wondered what it would be like living in a normal family." Marisa's voice was tender and tinged with longing.

"There isn't such a thing," Katie said. "That's another bitter truth of motherhood. No matter how great your intentions are, you are going to screw it up." She laughed and continued, trying to explain, "You're only human. You're going to make mistakes. This little one inside you is going to drive you to the brink of exhaustion, and at your wit's end, you might snap at him. Or when he gets out of bed for the twelfth time in one night, you're going to lose your cool. We all do it."

"Him?" Marisa asked.

"That's my guess." Katie shrugged.

"It's too early to know, but I hope you're right." She rubbed her belly in a clockwise circle. "You make motherhood sound so incredible," Marisa deadpanned with such an overflowing amount of sarcasm, it made Katie chuckle.

"It's the most incredible part of your life, but also the most challenging and stressful. When you're a mom, you never stop worrying about them. You are bonded together with your children forever, even when they are adults. Motherhood is a thousand heartbreaking moments that you would never trade for the world."

The sentiment brought tears to Katie's eyes. "Your life is just getting started, kid. All we need to do now is stay strong and wait for our opportunity. When it comes, we need to be tough enough to rise to the challenge. We will not die here. I can promise you that."

Marisa took two bigger bites of the sandwich. "It *is* starting to settle my stomach," she said with a small smile.

"See?" Katie was relieved. She handed over the Allen wrench to Marisa. "We need weapons, and as you can see, we are pretty limited here. If you can continue to chip at the cement and free one of the blocks, I am going to work on loosening the pipe, but don't overdo it," she warned.

"Okay." She sat on the ground and began chipping at

the concrete, and Katie kneeled down in front of the old sink. She yanked back and forth on the loose pipe for almost twenty minutes. When it finally broke free in her hand, it sent her reeling back.

Laughing at herself, she stood up and brandished it like a sword. "Look at this! Our efforts are paying off!" The rusty wrought iron pipe in her hand was heavy. She swung it through the air, testing it to see if she could wield it at an attacker. The piece was about eighteen inches long and smelled like raw sewage, but to Katie, it smelled like freedom. A thrill of relief bubbled up in her, and the progress renewed her determination. She crouched down and hid the loose pipe along the wall under the sink, then walked over to Marisa, who was making significant progress in freeing one of the blocks.

"Nice job," Katie praised her. "Why don't I take over for a while and you drink some water and have another sandwich?"

Marisa groaned and rubbed her belly. "I had to eat too many peanut butter and jelly sandwiches growing up. When we get out of here, I'm never having another one again."

"Me neither!" Katie said.

Marisa handed over the Allen wrench and stood to stretch, propping her hands on her back and bending backward.

"When we get out of here, I'm going to make you anything you want to eat to celebrate," Katie offered and sat down on the ground to resume chipping at the mortar. She hummed to herself, getting lost in the physicality of it, and after a solid hour of focused work, tugged one solitary chunk of concrete free. She held it up in her hand. "Look at this! We did it!"

Marisa looked at Katie like she had three heads. "You are something else," she said with a smile.

"We have each other and *now* we have a way to defend ourselves. Things are definitely moving in the right direction." She walked over to Marisa who was still having trouble choking down the sandwich. "Let's close our eyes and pretend this is a Kobe filet mignon drizzled with creamy tarragon sauce alongside roasted fingerling potatoes with grilled onions."

Marisa laughed at the charade and then added, "Can we have crème brûlée for dessert?"

"Of course! And Chocolate Pots de Crème!" Katie enthused, joining in. "We will have whatever luscious French concoctions my pregnant friend desires!"

"We're friends?" Marisa asked, her voice tentative and with a childlike innocence that was endearing.

"Of course we are," Katie answered her, and Marisa yawned. Then in the silence, a solitary thought broke through the surface that humbled Katie.

"I can't remember the last time I had a friend."

It's definitely a new ability, Katie thought. *Now, I must find the best way to use it to our advantage.*

Nineteen

The day after her unsuccessful visit to the Aura Cove Police Department, Yuli put her Plan B in motion. At Kandied Karma, Beckett ran a hand through his hair and then fished out a clean apron from the pile folded under the counter at the register. He stuck his head through it and tied the ties behind him.

"You look like a dork," Callie said, pulling his apron strings untied. Her ribbing didn't have its usual vigor. She cast her eyes downward then added, "I had a nightmare about Mom last night." Tears welled up in her eyes, and Beckett wrapped his arm around her and gave her half a hug.

"I did, too," he admitted, and he scratched at his jawline which was leaning hard into scruffy territory.

"It's just that the longer this goes on…" Callie trailed off.

"I know, Cal, but do yourself a favor and stop watching Cold Case Files until Mom comes home," Beckett instructed. "We've done absolutely everything we can.

We've searched every inch of land within a ten-mile radius of Mom's house. We've knocked on doors, plastered Aura Cove with flyers, and Lauren was interviewed by the news. All we can do now is wait and help out where we can."

Callie nodded. "I do feel a little closer to her here." She pointed to several handwritten Post-it notes of instructions near the register and credit card machine. "Seeing her handwriting, it's kind of comforting."

Beckett nodded as Yuli walked through the swinging door of the kitchen, holding trays filled with truffles. "Let me help you." Beckett rushed over to lend a hand, pulling the heavy trays from his great-grandmother.

"Thank you, sweetheart," Yuli said as she flexed her back that was sore from being hunched over for hours, cranking out truffle varieties for the store. "Katia would be so proud of you both," she said as she watched them stock the glass case to prepare for the shop to open.

"Thanks for coming in. I'm taking the red-eye to Chicago tomorrow morning," Yuli informed them as Callie pulled out a stack of golden boxes and folded them to dispel her anxious energy.

"What's in Chicago?" Beckett asked.

"I don't want to get your hopes up, but I'm meeting with someone who might be able to help bring your mother home."

"Who?"

"Let's not worry about the specifics now. I can fill you in later." She looked between her great-grandchildren. "Are you sure you can handle the shop while I'm gone?"

They nodded. "It's not rocket science," Beckett said

with a grin. "We won't be as good as Mom, but I think we can handle it."

"Of course, you can," she said to them, reaching out to gently pinch his sandpapery cheek. "There should be enough stock in the chiller. If you sell out, just close for the day and put a note on the door. I'll be back late tomorrow."

"With some answers?" Callie asked, her voice filled with hope and looking for reassurance.

"I hope so." She gave them both a hug and quickly left.

———

The day passed swiftly, and sales were steady enough to stop both of the kids from obsessing about Katie. During the last hour, a plump, older woman with a smattering of age spots on her forearms wheeled a younger version of herself into the shop. She was thin and frail, but her stomach was swollen and distended as if she were seven months pregnant. The younger woman was clearly in pain, but she didn't let it stop her from oohing and ahhing over the beautiful truffles.

Her mother was dressed plainly, her clothing worn and faded. Her hair was a salt-and-pepper gray trimmed close to her head like a helmet. The pair looked completely out of their element inside the high-end chocolate shop and glanced around self-consciously. They weren't the usual sophisticated clientele clamoring for Yuli's gourmet candies, but Callie walked right over to them with an engaging grin.

"I want that one." The wheelchair-bound woman said,

pointing to a white chocolate butterfly dusted with edible glitter.

Callie smiled again and pulled it from the display case. She nestled it into the tissue paper of the golden takeout box in her hand. "Great choice."

"And two caramels, and a dark chocolate orange cashew cluster." The woman smiled, and it lit up her pale face. "Mom and I have been dreaming about tasting these since they hit Oprah's Favorite Things List."

"You're in for a real treat," Callie said as she packaged the chocolates together and rang up the purchase on the register. "That's twenty-four dollars."

At the cash register, her mother was frantically digging through her enormous purse that yawned open, revealing old receipts and yellowed hospital discharge papers.

"It was right here," she mumbled, sweating, as red blotches of shame descended from her cheek to her neck. She continued to rifle through the contents of her handbag, getting more frustrated by the second. "I can't find my credit card," she admitted. Her shoulders dropped, and she bit her lip, glancing down at her sick daughter, afraid to disappoint her.

"It's our treat," Beckett offered, and the distressed woman burst into tears.

"That's so kind of you."

"Mom." The younger woman wheeled herself closer and reached out to squeeze her overwhelmed mother's hand. "See? Good things happen to good people."

She turned to Beckett and Callie and added, "You just helped me cross something off my bucket list!"

"Really?" Callie asked.

"Yep. Eating chocolates from Kandied Karma was

number eleven. Right under participating in a flash mob." She grinned. "Now that things have taken a turn," she waved one hand at the chair with a self-deprecating smile, "I need to start crossing off the most important items sooner rather than later."

Callie's forehead crisscrossed in concern. "I'm so sorry."

She patted her protruding belly, "Contrary to what you might be thinking, there's no baby in here. It's Polycystic Kidney Disease," she explained and hiked a thumb back toward her mom. "This one is a little weepy now that I'm officially at the top of the transplant list."

"We decided to stop in after her check-up while we wait to receive our test results to see if my husband or I can donate a kidney," the mother explained. "I'm a nervous wreck."

"That is totally understandable," Beckett said. Then he turned and flashed a grin at the woman in the wheelchair and asked, "What's your name?"

"Lorelei," she said with a wan smile, "and this is my mother, Liz. She is a huge *Gilmore Girls* fan."

"It's nice to meet you both," Beckett answered, then offered, "You officially have an open invitation to come to Kandied Karma after every check-up to take home a complimentary truffle sampler."

Liz gasped. "That's so generous."

"It will give you something sweet to look forward to on days you dread," he said with a smile. "It's something our mother would have offered without a doubt."

Callie teared up behind him as she nodded in agreement. Liz glanced at the flyer taped to the front of the register and then back up at Beckett and Callie.

"Katie Beaumont is your mother?"

Beckett nodded, his expression weary.

"I saw her face on the news." Liz reached out a hand and squeezed Beckett's forearm. "I hope they find her soon."

"Thank you." Beckett commiserated, then turned to Lorelei. "You only get one mother, so make sure you appreciate yours."

"Oh, I do," Lorelei gushed. "I've always been such a daddy's girl, but now that we spend so much time together at doctor's appointments, it's brought us closer together than ever. Right, Mom?"

Liz was distracted, her eyes focused on the flyer, and had checked out of the conversation.

"Mom?"

"Sorry, yes, honey." She hung the strap of her purse on the back of the wheelchair. "Thank you both again. So much."

"Make sure to stop in after your next appointment," Callie called to them. "You'll be able to meet mom."

Beckett didn't have the fight in him to contradict her words. He followed them to the front door and held it open, watching Liz push Lorelei through it, then down the sidewalk. Praying Callie's desperate declaration would prove true.

TWENTY

Yuli clutched the paper airline boarding pass to Chicago in her hand. Refusing to rely on technology, she'd never owned a cell phone and, at ninety-seven, wasn't about to start now. In her estimation, Smartphones actually made society dumber. Transforming people into veritable zombies, staring down at the device in their hands and missing out on the life that was unfolding right in front of them. Yuli spent decades honing her powers doing the exact opposite. By paying attention, relying on her intuition, and seeing what the ordins were too distracted to see.

She waited at her gate in the Tampa Airport for the clerk to call her boarding row. First on the aircraft, she settled into the larger seat in first class after the flight attendant stowed her carry-on in the overhead compartment. Sure, the extra wide seat and legroom made the flight more comfortable, but the real reason she booked the extravagant ticket was because it meant she could exit the plane first. She glanced out the portal window at the darkened sky as a feeling of melancholy settled deep into her bones. Chicago held a lifetime of memories, many of them traumatic, and returning to the city often felt like a sting, like when a rubber band is pulled taut and then snaps back into place.

When the plane landed a few hours later, dragging her sensible carry-on behind her, she located the driver she'd hired to take her the rest of the journey. Her mind swirled forward and back as they sped toward the address she'd been given. The estate was in the Chicago suburb of Oak Park. After a long drive up curving blacktop streets, the driver stopped in front of an enormous black wrought-iron gate. He reached out to buzz the intercom and, after an exchange of information, the gate slowly swung open. Yuli glanced out the window, her nerves unsettled, and the tension stuck in her shoulders. It was a last-ditch effort, and she wore the desperation like a shawl.

The car came to a stop in front of a circular driveway. Two armed security guards met the car and swept it with a metal detector. They patted down the driver, who was instructed to wait in the car, and Yuli was hauled to the side for a more thorough security inspection. The men who performed it were gruff foot soldiers that didn't pay the old woman any attention.

She was eventually escorted into a dark wood-paneled library and offered a seat in front of a roaring fire that raged in a stone fireplace. Outside the window, snow fell in a horizontal pattern across the barren trees, and a gusty wind battered the branches that surrounded them. The first wisps of sunrise made the banks of snow sparkle like cut diamonds.

A few moments later, she heard a craggy voice behind her she barely recognized.

"Yuli! What has it been? A hundred years?" Dominic Lombardo called out as he shuffled into the library. His suit was a flashy maroon three-piece number with a yellow pocket square and a yellow carnation at the lapel. On his feet, he wore black and white wingtip shoes. His hair was a shock of close-cropped white that brushed back from his wrinkled forehead, and a pair of thick black boxy framed glasses perched on his bulbous nose. He was flanked by two much younger men wearing mostly leather and packing heat from the intimidating glimpse of steel she was afforded when they unzipped their jackets.

"Not quite, but it feels like it some days," she said warmly as she rose and pulled him into her arms for a long hug. He kissed both her cheeks and then pulled back with a hint of a boyish smile, then offered her his arm and walked her to the other end of the room where his dark walnut desk sat. "I appreciate you making the trip to Chicago. Maybe I'm old-fashioned and paranoid, but telephones and wiretaps historically haven't been kind to my family. I only conduct business face-to-face."

Yuli nodded. "I'm sure you can't be too careful."

"Have a seat," he offered as the bodyguards settled on either side of him, looking like bored gargoyles.

"How is it you look so robust and healthy, even at our age?" He smiled. The heavy lines on his face mirrored her own, but his eyes still held a mischievous twinkle. "To be honest, I never thought I'd live long enough to have Al Roker put my ugly mug on the back of a Smucker's jar," he shrugged, "but here we are."

Yuli smiled at the sentiment. Her earliest memories

included Dominic. They were only a year apart and had been thrust together since they were toddlers when Zoya shacked up with Salvatore. It was an unconventional living situation for the time, but Zoya was never one to play by the rules of polite society.

"You still a card shark?" he asked.

"Card sharks cheat." She made the distinction with a good-natured, competitive grin. "I *never* cheated."

Dom returned her smile. "Not gonna lie. I was livid when Dad gave you a twenty for beating me. That was serious moolah back in the day."

The memory of that moment rushed through her, unpacking all the trauma that came with it.

"You were like a sister to me," he confided, acknowledging how close they'd become when they were children. "How could you leave without so much as a goodbye after Dad died?"

"I've always felt terrible we left you alone. I'm sorry, Dom, but you have to know it wasn't up to me," Yuli answered with a heavy sigh. "I was thirteen and learned the hard way that, when Zoya makes a decision, you don't fight her on it."

He nodded. "They broke the mold when they made that dame."

"They did," Yuli agreed.

"That day," Dominic said as his lips turned down and sorrow crossed his face. "Some moments imprint on your nightmares forever."

Yuli shuddered. "I'll never forget it, either. I'd never seen so much blood."

She pushed away their painful past as a warm memory of Sally surfaced. Her voice softened. "Did you know he secretly brought home books and hid them in the house where I'd find them? I think Sally felt sorry for me."

"Of course he did! Your grandmother could be the Wicked Witch of the West."

"You have no idea," Yuli agreed. "Remember what she was like right after Sally died?" Zoya was inconsolable, a shell of her former self. The light behind her eyes had been extinguished by heartbreak.

He admitted, "Those weeks are honestly a blur for me."

"Of course they were. You were consumed with grief. We all were." Her eyes moistened. "But Zoya was never the same again. She went off the deep end. For weeks, she never left her bed, and then the next thing I know, we're boarding a plane heading to some property she'd inherited in the middle of the sea." Looking deep into his eyes, she said, "If I'd known it was the last time we'd see each other, I would have done so many things differently."

"It was a fork in the road for both of us," Dominic said with a sad smile.

They sat in silence, acknowledging the weight of his statement and the years that spooled out while they were apart. Dominic went on to live his life in Chicago, and by all looks of it had followed closely in his father's footsteps. Yuli was dragged to the island with Zoya, where her life took its own dramatic turn.

"Sally was good to me. I miss him," Yuli admitted.

"Well, it won't be long before I'll be joining him, so I'll be sure to pass along your sentiment." He gave a wry smile, then stood and walked over to the bar cart in the room and poured two glasses of whiskey, handing one to Yuli before knocking his back.

"It was a shock when you reached out. I honestly planned to come by Kandied Karma when you had your store downtown at the loop, but I was reluctant to open that door again," Dominic admitted. "It was easier to stay away, but I have a confession to make."

Confused, Yuli was taken aback. "What kind of confession?"

He pointed to the man on his right side. "I used to send Johnny to your store once a week. Your amaretto creams and tiramisu caramels are…" He clasped his fingers together and gave them a chef's kiss.

Yuli laughed. "I'll be sure to send some to you when I get back to the shop." If she cocked her head to the side and squinted her eyes almost closed, she could still see the little boy she'd spent hours playing checkers with when they were children.

"You've done well for yourself," Yuli said, taking in the oriental rug underfoot and the heavy antique furniture that smelled faintly of lemon polish and cigar smoke.

"So have you," he offered with a smile and a wink. "I might have helped grease the wheels for you over the years."

"You did?" Yuli was shocked.

"Yeah. Your rent never increased for an entire decade. In Chicago, that is unheard of. It wasn't a coincidence, Yuli. I was proud of your success and wanted to help, even if I didn't have the balls to see you."

"I had no idea." Yuli was touched. His confession stunned her speechless.

Dominic was the don of the Chicago Outfit. He had come up through the ranks over the years, and Yuli sized him up without judgment. He was a product of his circumstances. What would his life have looked like if he'd been born halfway across the world to a British aristocrat? Or to a potato farmer in Idaho?

You became what you knew. As much as Yuli tried to fight her lineage, and tried to make her own way free of Zoya's manipulation, it was a battle she'd lost, too. The invisible thread that connected them all had tugged her right back to her origins.

Turning her attention to a silver leaf frame holding a family photo on top of his desk, Yuli asked, "Are these your people?"

"Yes," he said proudly. "It's the one thing I did right." He gave a small smile as he pulled out a cigar from the humidor on his desk, clipped the end, and then puffed on it. He offered it to Yuli, who surprised him by taking a long drag on it before handing it back.

"What do you mean?"

"I got my son out. He went to college, became a doctor, and lives in a little town in Rhode Island. It was a bit of a reverse WITSEC situation, but he got to start over without all this weighing him down." He waved his hands around at his opulent surroundings. Then Dominic picked up the frame and glanced down at it with tenderness. "I have ten great-grandchildren I've never met who will never know this life."

Yuli swiped at a tear in the corner of her eye. "That is quite a sacrifice," she remarked. "If I was in your shoes, I don't think I would have been able to do the same."

"Call me a bleeding heart, but I'm convinced it's the only reason I'm still alive. I let Karma guide my decisions. Only evil deeds deserve punishment."

"Still, it was not an easy decision, I'm sure." Yuli felt a

flicker of hope that he would extend the same effort to keep her family safe, even if it was only out of his long-lost sense of childhood loyalty.

"I made peace with my decisions long ago. It's all over but the shouting." He sized her up. "I know you didn't come all this way just to reminisce with an old man from your past."

"That is true." She steadied her nerves as he set the frame back down on his desk. "I need your help."

He leaned in. "I'm listening."

"Rocco Gabriano has kidnapped my granddaughter," she explained. "I'm hoping you can help hasten her release."

The warm look evaporated from his face. He bit on the side of his lip and rocked in the chair. "That one is a hothead. We're trying to be legitimate businessmen, but that *cazzone* thinks he's Al Capone."

"Legitimate businessmen?" Yuli asked.

Dominic rewarded her with a self-deprecating smile. "I mean, for the most part." He shrugged. "We're just trying to get by, providing protection, and giving our customers an outlet to indulge in their vices: gambling, women, you know, the usual."

Yuli nodded, and he continued to explain, "The violence that used to define us brought more trouble than it was worth. Now, we're just trying to stay under the radar of law enforcement. The *Good Fellas* and *Godfather* heyday has been over since RICO." After a long pause, he asked, "What does he want with your granddaughter?"

"I believe she was helping his wife escape a domestic abuse situation."

"Ooof!" He steepled his fingertips together, placing

them under his sagging jowls. "I've never condoned violence against women or children."

"Then you will be interested to learn his wife, Marisa, is pregnant."

He leaned his head back into his tufted leather chair, deep in thought. She saw a shadow pass, and the surrounding air chilled. "Unfortunately, the Gabriano crew doesn't share the same sentiment." He was silent for several long moments, then asked, "Did you hear about a car fire that burned for twenty-four hours and shut down Marina Cove Road in Tampa last week?"

"Yeah, I *do* remember hearing about that incident in the news. Didn't a three-year-old and his mother die when the battery of their electric car caught fire? Such a tragedy."

"That's the white-washed version that made the six o'clock news," he answered. "I'm not sure you want to know the truth."

Yuli shuddered. "I should probably know who I am dealing with." She steeled herself for his next admission.

"Rocco was sending a message. The father was a soldier who went state's evidence on him," Dominic said. "He withdrew his statements after the Gabriano crew pulled that stunt last week." He shook his head. "A baby. God, I'm getting soft in my old age." Dominic poured more whiskey into his crystal glass.

"You call it getting soft. I call it having some basic value for human life. A three-year-old should never be sacrificed for the sins of his father."

"The bad blood between the Lombardos and the Gabrianos goes back a century, all the way to Sicily." He studied her. "Sally got caught with his hand in their cookie jar one too many times, and they made an example of him. He always thought he was smarter than they were. It was his ultimate downfall."

Yuli was riveted. She never knew why he was gunned down in the street.

"The crash of 1929 destroyed the resources of both families. Sally was trying to make us whole after the Great Depression and had been cutting corners and encroaching on the Gabrianos' territory for years. He got away with it for a long time, but eventually, it was time to pay the piper."

"Zoya probably thought she was next," Yuli offered, thinking out loud, discovering the missing pieces of her past.

"That's my guess." He nodded, swallowing the last of his whiskey.

"I know I am putting you at risk," Yuli admitted. "I wouldn't be here if there was another way."

He nodded thoughtfully and considered her request. "I can call a sit-down with Big Tony and see if we can come to a gentleman's agreement."

"I would deeply appreciate it." Yuli felt the rush of hope fill her heart. This was the first good news she'd heard since Katia was taken.

"I'll see what I can find out for you. I can't make any promises, though."

Yuli nodded. "I understand. If you can't persuade him to release her, even a location would help."

His thick brows wrinkled up in confusion. "The police will not want to get involved."

"I know," Yuli said. "I have other plans."

TWENTY-ONE

Two days after their stakeout, Frankie was driving home from work, with the windows of her Honda wide open and the breeze rushing in. She reached down to crank up the radio where "Right Round" by Flo Rida was blasting through the speakers. Her impromptu concert performance increased in both speed and volume when she hit the chorus.

She shot through a yellow light at an intersection on the second verse when she saw a police cruiser change lanes and pick up speed just behind her.

"Shit!" she said to herself and slammed on the brakes, already knowing it was too late. In her rear view mirror, blue lights flashed, and a siren wailed. She sighed as she signaled and then turned off onto a side street, finally coming to a stop.

A few moments later, she stole a quick glance in her mirror and saw an officer making his way to her window.

"I'm so sorry!" she declared, apologizing before the officer even had a chance to speak. "But you can't be expected to drive the speed limit when 'Flo Rida' comes on!" She laughed, trying to win him over.

"Ma'am, breaking the law is breaking the law." His mirrored sunglasses hid his eyes, but she could already tell this cop was a hard ass and would not fall for her usual schtick. "License and registration, please," he said. Frankie leaned over the console and opened the glove compartment to dig through its contents and produce the documents the officer requested. When she pulled the compartment open, a flutter of unpaid parking tickets drifted to the ground. She grabbed the rest in her fist and tugged them out when a white plastic-wrapped brick shape fell out onto the floor. Frankie leaned over to pick it up, completely confused.

"What in the world?" she said aloud as she scooped it up then turned back toward the officer, still holding it in her hands. Seeing it was crudely wrapped, she quipped. "If I didn't know any better, I'd think this was a kilo of cocaine! You know, I binged *Narcos* last month, and that Pablo Escobar? *He* was a real character." She was chattering to fill the void and felt nervous laughter bubble up and escape. Frankie flipped it over in her hands and dread filled her. She'd been joking, but the longer she held it, the more convinced she was that something was terribly wrong. The officer pulled his sunglasses off, and she felt his eyes lock on hers. "I don't know where this came from. It isn't mine."

"Ma'am, do you have any weapons in the vehicle?"

"What?" Frankie felt the shift in the officer's demeanor. "Of course not."

"Please exit the vehicle and place your hands behind your back," he ordered, and the first wave of panic crushed her. "I'm going to put you in the back of the cruiser while I search the car."

Frankie was speechless as the officer led her to the squad car and secured her inside. Observing the officer through the window, she saw him pull on rubber gloves and then run a swab over the outside of the package and place it in a vial. Several long minutes ticked by while he waited for the results. Then he pulled off the rubber gloves and disposed of them and spoke into the radio perched high on his shoulder.

Frankie didn't fully give in to the panic until a second cruiser pulled up behind her. Calling for backup indicated this wasn't a routine traffic stop anymore, but relief rushed in when a familiar face got out of it. Seeing Harry, she slammed her hands against the window, trying to get his attention. He kept walking toward the other officer and turned on his flashlight to search the interior of the vehicle. Seeing the air freshener and the hula lady on the dashboard, his head whipped over to the cruiser. After speaking to the other officer, she saw him make his way to the car.

Her heart leapt in her chest as the door opened and she got her first few breaths of fresh air. Being locked inside the cruiser, she didn't realize how easily a new claustrophobia fear could take hold. She wanted to jump into Harry's arms, but his intense stare immobilized her.

"Do not move." His stern voice silenced the objections on the tip of her tongue, and his next words were barely above a whisper, "It's Ludlow. I'm sure of it."

"How?"

"The delivery guy, he must have reported the incident to Ludlow, who ran the plate. Then it's just a matter of helping himself into the evidence room and planting

incriminating evidence in your vehicle." Harry's eyes
crawled over the objects in front of him as the gears in his
head spun. "We were getting too close to finding Katie.
Ludlow led us to Rocco, so he had to make a big play to
take the heat off him."

"Am I going to jail?" Frankie was panicked.

"I'm afraid so, Frankie. We don't have much time, but
this is how we need to play it. Pretend you don't know me.
After the search is over, you will be placed under arrest
and taken to the station for questioning."

"But, it wasn't…" Frankie felt the fear rising in her
throat, choking off the rest of her response.

"Listen." Harry's eyes locked on hers. "Do not offer
any information and immediately ask for a lawyer when
they begin to question you. I will straighten this out, I
promise you."

"What about Katie?"

"He's trying to distract us, but don't worry. I am not
easily intimidated. You have to trust me." He pulled out
his handcuffs and said, "I'm sorry, but I have to do this."

She gulped, then made a crude attempt at humor. "I
always hoped you'd put me in handcuffs one day, but I
never thought we'd have an audience." She barely got to
the punchline before she felt herself crumble and her body
quiver.

"Remember the plan," he whispered as he pulled her
out of the car. "Turn around, please." His request was
louder and more official, and she forced her wooden limbs
to comply. He gently pulled her arms together and pinched
the cuffs closed to secure them. The metal was cold on her
wrists as he led her back to her car where the other officer
had popped her trunk.

"Sit on the curb while we complete the vehicle search," Harry instructed, and she followed his directions to the letter.

Wedged inside the trunk were all the boxes leftover from her investment in a long-abandoned, multi-level marketing dream, Pure Seduction. One by one, the officer pulled box after box out of the trunk and set them down on the concrete. Then he tore into them and exposed massage oils, lubricants, and vibrators in every shape and size.

"Looks like we have a drug trafficking *pervert* on our hands," the officer declared as he continued to root through the contents.

"I am a sexual health and wellness consultant," Frankie emphasized while she watched the officer pull a twelve-inch long purple dildo and anal plug out of their boxes. Frankie didn't even flinch. One of the other boxes started vibrating when it hit the ground. Harry's eyebrows shot up, and he pinched his lips together to keep a grin from escaping, but he kept the rest of his expression stoic.

"You might want to get one of those for your wife," Frankie offered, noticing his silicone wedding band. "It's the only way a robot like you would be capable of bringing a woman to orgasm."

"You're pretty mouthy for a woman who's looking at spending the next fifteen years of her life behind bars for drug trafficking. And I hope you have an extra quarter mil lying around for the fines." He chomped on a wad of gum while a puzzled look filled his face. "I wonder, how many dildos will you need to sell to pay that off?"

"It's not mine!" She cried, "Why would I joke with you about Escobar if I were trafficking an actual kilo of cocaine? It doesn't make any sense. No one is that stupid!"

"Criminals typically aren't the sharpest tools in the shed," the officer commented gruffly. His tone was so condescending it silenced the rest of her snappy comebacks.

Still focused on the trunk, he continued to pull out the contents and empty them onto the ground while cars sped by and rubbernecked the interaction. "Well, well, well, what do we have here?" He pulled a pistol from the under the spare tire, holding it by the trigger with one black latex-covered finger.

"What in the hell?" Frankie cried. "I wouldn't even know what to do with that thing!"

"So, you don't have a permit for it?"

"Of course not. Why would I have a permit for a gun that isn't mine?"

The officer leaned down and pulled out one more box. This time, it was a rectangular brick of hundred-dollar bills. When Frankie saw it, she gasped and shook her head, completely dumbfounded.

"Come on!" she said, astonished. "You've got to be kidding me. Do you really think I'd be out hocking dildos and vibrators to housewives and divorcees if I had that kind of cash sitting around?"

The officer grunted and continued to search the rest of her trunk. If she wasn't in such a predicament, she'd laugh at the absurdity of the situation. At this point, anything was possible. If they pulled the Ark of the Covenant or JFK's brain swimming in formaldehyde out of her trunk, she'd just smile and nod.

With the search now complete, Frankie hung her head as the officer yanked her to her feet. She knew what was coming next.

"You're under arrest for possession of cocaine with the intent to distribute and carrying a concealed weapon without a permit. You have the right to remain silent…" He proceeded to read the rest of her Miranda rights and she tuned him out. She always knew she had the right to remain silent, but she lacked the ability. Frankie glanced over at Harry in a daze. He gave her the briefest nod of support, then the other officer opened the squad car, pushed her head down, and she folded herself down into the back seat.

The officer shut the door with finality. It didn't look good. She knew enough about how the prison system worked, thanks to Netflix. It was filled with corruption and the twisting of facts by sadistic men who often sought out a career in law enforcement to lord their power over others. It wasn't about the truth; it was about what could be proven in a court of law.

She watched Harry get into his car and drive away, reminding herself that he was one of the good guys and certain he was going to find a way to exonerate her. But when he disappeared from sight carrying all her hope with him, she'd never felt more alone.

TWENTY-TWO

Zoya stood on her veranda at the Castanova Compound listening to the sound of the pounding surf, a relaxing soundtrack that always soothed her calculating mind. Hanging high in the sky, the marbled white orb was a magnificent sight the evening before the full moon. Its bright light outlined the passing storm clouds that floated by. Lifting her arms to the sky, Zoya felt the same surge of gathering strength and power she always did on the eve of the full moon.

Terrance jumped at the patio door, clamoring for her attention. She crossed to open it and he tumbled out, his chocolate-colored paws clumsy on the slippery, mildewed surface. He shook for a solid minute and then yawned and sat at attention. Annoyed, Zoya snapped at him, "Get to the point, Terrance. My time is valuable, and I don't look kindly on those who waste it."

Terrance hung his head and tucked his tail between his legs. He barked once to clear his throat, then told her, "The items you've requested are waiting in your meditation chamber."

"Very good," Zoya said, reaching down to tug on one of his velvety ears. His right leg shot out and began to jiggle in blissed-out satisfaction. She left him on the patio and strode into the mediation chamber where a small wooden altar had been erected. A bank of black candles ringed the outside, and she struck a long wooden match and lit them one by one. A sultry red wine had been uncorked and was breathing in a decanter. She slowly poured it into a golden goblet as she chanted, then struck another match and lit the ends of four wands of incense resting in a golden dish. They began to smoke and fill the enclosed area with the musky scents of sandalwood, jasmine, and cinnamon. Walking around the perimeter of the room, she chanted again, "Lilith. First Wife of Adam, Mother of Demons. Insatiable Unyielding Creature. I am in need of your feminine light. Appear now and show me the path."

The amulet at her throat hummed, and the purple light that spilled from it spread across the room. She returned to the altar and dropped to her knees, her tone begging as she repeated the incantations. "Open my eyes, wise mother, show me the way."

She cupped the goblet in her hands and raised it up in offering and then took a sip from it when a thunderous noise and the jarring sound of the tuning fork sliced through the silence. Returning the cup to the altar, she reached to shield her ears and then felt herself melt into a cresting sound wave as it carried her deeper into her center. Then the sensation abruptly forced her face down onto the ground, prostrated in front of the altar. A swell of warmth rushed over her body, and beads of sweat broke out all over and rolled down her limbs.

"How dare you drink from the chalice you've offered me!" Lilith's voice was sultry and filled with husky desire. "Rise now, child, and look me in the eye."

Zoya rolled her head up from the floor, still kneeling as the most stunning red-haired woman appeared in a portal of flames. Voluptuous with enormous violet eyes, she appeared nude, and a wall of flame licked at her curvaceous form. Zoya's eyes tracked up her long legs, rippled with muscles, then to her waist and up to her plump bosom. Peach-colored nipples poked out from between long lengths of curly red hair. She was mesmerizing. Zoya couldn't tear her eyes away and reached out a hand. The portal of flames warmed her fingertips and traversed down her wrist to her forearm, finally making a pilgrimage to her heart, and she felt wetness track down the hollows of her cheeks. Confused, she brushed her fingers across her cheekbones and was shocked to discover they were tears.

"Who are you to summon me?" Lilith scoffed. Her eyes drilled into Zoya's, who felt herself shrink in the presence of pure, unadulterated feminine power.

"My Queen." Zoya was starstruck in her presence and once again bowed at her flame-engulfed feet. "As a woman who has the utmost respect for you, I offer my devotion."

"I do not want it," Lilith said. "The only reason I am appearing to you at all is due to my fondness for Salvatore."

At the mention of his name, Zoya expected jealousy to rear up, but instead, she felt favor and kinship with Lilith that they were united in seeing his value.

"Thank you for answering my call. I am in need of your blessed favor."

"What do you require?" Her words were razor sharp, with a harsh edge.

"A man is threatening my family's triad of power," Zoya explained. "He is holding my great-great-grand-daughter hostage."

Lilith's eyes bored into Zoya's, and the intense scrutiny made her shift uncomfortably. "Women are taught to be lambs," she explained. "But lambs get slaughtered. It is far better to become a tigress. You must rise to the challenge and fight for yourself."

"I *am* prepared to fight," Zoya explained. "I simply ask that you instill me with your strength and sovereign power. This destruction has been going on for generations, and it is time to end it once and for all. Our Salvatore was a victim of their deceit."

Through the flames, Zoya saw Lilith consider her request. Unwilling to irritate her further, Zoya remained silent, awaiting her response.

"Rise, daughter," Lilith declared, and Zoya scrambled to her feet. She reached out a flaming hand that burned into Zoya's shoulder. "You have earned my favor. I instill in you my determination and desire for justice against the sub-servitude of this man that has wronged you. I decree his ancestors feel the full brunt of your retribution. At the height of tomorrow's full moon, you will be at your most powerful. Do not waste this opportunity."

Relief flooded into Zoya, and her heart was filled with admiration. "Thank you, Dark Goddess." She bowed deeply. "I will not squander this gift."

"There is one more detail I wish to discuss. There is a child." Lilith continued.

"A child?" Zoya was confused.

"The subject of your vengeance has fathered a son that is now in the confines of his wife's womb."

Thinking quickly, Zoya made a bold offer, "If I bring you the child as my sacrifice, would you be willing to release Salvatore from his eternal damnation and allow his soul to transmigrate to the next dimension?"

Lilith licked her full lips in anticipation, considering Zoya's proposal. "That is the kind of devotion I savor." A cunning smile slithered over her features. "Yes." The word drifted from her lips like a reptilian hiss. "If the child is sacrificed to me, I will release Salvatore to the other realm." The flame grew hotter as her hatred grew. "You will be my vessel. I will fill you with my dark energy so you can avenge every child that was taken from me. You must destroy their family tree, branch by branch, and burn it down to the ground until it is merely ashes under my feet."

The room was flooded with red light so bright Zoya had to squint, and her skin sizzled from her proximity to the scorching flames. Overheating, Zoya passed out, and when she awoke, just minutes later, she was filled with a robust energy. A beguiling smile spread across her features and she ran down the marble stairs. She pulled a skeleton key from the pocket of her black jumpsuit and swiftly unlocked a door, striding to the bank of appliances ringing the secondary kitchen. Lights crackled on, and from the icy depths of her deep freeze, Zoya pulled out two blood-red truffles.

Glassy and decadent, with swirled designs, they were

painstakingly re-created from the ancient recipes that were included with the deed to the compound. Zoya closed her eyes and rubbed her hands together rapidly. Small blood-red sparks tingled between her fingers as the friction gathered heat then transformed into bigger sparks crackling from her palms. A red glow circulated through her on a track starting from her head, running down her arms and legs, and back again to her heart. She went deeper into the spell, chanting undecipherable words in an exact combination that hastened the quickening energy that seared through her, igniting her entire being. Reaching a fevered pitch, her eyes popped open.

Under the spell, her irises glowed with bright white light, and the plate of truffles began to quiver and sparkle. They jiggled on the plate, shuddering with purpose and power. Zoya picked up the first one and popped it into her mouth. A burst of intense sour cherry was followed by an astringent aftertaste and made the truffle hard to swallow. The bitterness lingered long after it left her tongue.

She picked up the second one, knowing she was pushing her luck, but ate it anyway. The tang of the tart cherry puckered her lips and made her salivate, and the acidity that followed was so off-putting she had to fight the urge to spit it out. Zoya forced it down, swallowing hard, and then was rocketed back into the wall where every cell in her body was lit up and tingling.

She staggered to her feet and over to a red glass orb. Ten inches in circumference, it crackled to life when she touched it. Zoya closed her eyes and envisioned Katia's face in her mind, meditating in an attempt to connect with her. She focused on Katia's green eyes and warm smile while she stretched her palms wide on either side of the gazing ball. The red glow intensified and cloaked every surface around her. Her eyes snapped open, and she saw the first scene flicker in the orb. At first, the picture was fuzzy like an old black-and-white TV with rabbit ears. But the more she focused her energy, the clearer the image became. She intensified the vision of Katia in her mind until the picture glowed with vibrant color.

Like watching a silent movie play out, she witnessed the scene unfold in front of her. Zoya observed Katia speaking to someone just out of her view. She even witnessed Katia smile and then laugh as she watched her great-great-granddaughter toil away, carving the letters of her name into brick. Zoya found her sunny resilience fascinating, much like a scientist would after injecting an animal with a toxic substance and documenting their struggle to survive despite it.

Returning her attention to the glass ball, she inventoried the scene in front of her. The vision reflected in the ball was too close up. She couldn't pick up any clues that would definitively mark Katia's exact location. Then she saw a man enter the room and begin talking to Katia, and rage infiltrated her vision. Her hatred was palpable. Locking eyes on Rocco Gabriano, her focus was consumed by destroying him, and Katia became an afterthought.

He set a box down on the floor and then kicked it to the center of the room. Katia raced over to the box, pulled out food and bottles of water, and walked them to a beautiful blonde woman who was leaning against the wall with her eyes closed. She watched Katia coax her awake and cajole the woman into taking bites of the food. Only then did Katia return to the box to pull out a sandwich for herself.

Zoya took a deep breath and then gritted her teeth together, focusing on Rocco's form. Her hands trembled as the electric current gathered strength. The room around her brightened and hummed, and a screeching sound intensified. Zoya's whole body contracted with effort, the surrounding noises so intense the din was mind-splitting. An instant migraine headache surged into the back of her skull and through her frontal lobe. The pressure was intense, but she fought her way through it, second by second, as the agony from the effort intensified.

Around her, the windows shattered and sent glass falling to the floor with a loud crash. She continued to concentrate, forcing all of her pain into her palms as lightning bolts raced from her hands to the crystal ball. The scene wavered, then blew back, rocketing her vision to a wider view. She got a glimpse of a sign, Port Tampa Bay, then a lightning bolt destroyed it. Close, she was so close.

She dug deeper and harnessed every ounce of her life-force and the additional power Lilith instilled in her, and the number 1110 flashed into her subconscious, then floated in a sea of lightning inside the crystal ball. A loud crack rang out. Zoya screamed as her eardrum burst and her head dropped forward onto the table. The glazing ball shattered, pieces of it becoming shrapnel as she felt them cut into her skin. Completely destroyed, it was now a pile of smoking ash. Zoya felt herself slip away into darkness. She tried to fight it, but her resources were so compromised she simply faded away.

TWENTY-THREE

"It's a full moon tomorrow," Katie mumbled to herself. Even without visual evidence, since her awakening, she was perfectly in-tune with the monthly moon phases. There was a stirring inside her and a quickening of energy as her strength ebbed and flowed during the course of a lunar cycle.

"Someone's coming," Katie insisted.

"How do you know?" Marisa asked.

"I can hear it." The steps were heavy and sure as they trudged closer. The air thinned, and she felt a weighty shift. She heard the metallic scrape of the key in the lock, and then the metal door screeched on its tracks. Katie ran to the opposite side of the room to protect Marisa, who sat cross-legged, leaning against the wall for support. They clung to each other as the scent of sweat and urine tinged the air, co-mingling with the metallic taste of fear on Katie's tongue. Her fight-or-flight mechanism fully engaged, and she felt her heart thundering in her chest. She whispered into Marisa's ear,

"The baby. Remind him about the baby. It's the only way we stay alive."

Rocco stood in the doorway and stared them down with an intensity so fierce it made Katie tremble. He walked over to the grocery sacks that had contained the food and water from Carmine's last delivery and noticed they were empty. Bending over, he scooped up the bags, crumpling them into balls with his powerful fists. Then he shot Marisa a warning glare. "Just because I gave in to your demands and put you in the same room together doesn't mean you get to call the shots from now on. You answer to me," Rocco stated. "Let's get that straight right now."

Katie could feel Marisa's body tense next to hers. Then a rhythmic thumping began that intensified with every step Rocco took closer.

"I've done what you've asked. I'm eating. I'm taking the vitamins," Marisa said then asked, "When are you going to let us go?"

Never.

The word appeared in Katie's subconscious mind like it was carved into a stone tablet. Rocco's eyes bore into Marisa, and she saw his jaw tighten and his Adam's apple move up and down after a hard swallow.

She's only valuable to me while she's pregnant. And that other bitch? She'll end up gator bait at our house in the Everglades, where she will completely disappear without a trace unless you count the alligator scat. An evil smile quirked the corners of his mouth upward.

Katie's body quaked with fear as his thoughts invaded her mind. They were the darkest she'd experienced, and she had to steel herself to absorb them. She studied

Rocco's face, stealing glimpses of it from the corners of her eyes. The voice in her head was a low growl and made her shiver. Far more lucid than the thoughts she'd intercepted from Marisa, the messages coming from Rocco were crystal clear and chilling. The pure hatred radiating from his gaze to hers could be felt in every cell of her body. Katie observed the black aura that ringed him was enlarging and blurring his physical body. He moved deliberately toward them, and the thumping intensified in Katie's ears.

"This is it," Katie whispered to Marisa, who blinked and forced her lips to curve upwards into a smile.

"Come closer, baby," Marisa cooed to him as Katie slid away, making room for the approaching man. His eyes locked on Marisa, consumed with his desire for her. She reached out for him, squeezing her fingers together to draw him closer, and as he drifted nearer, his stoney expression softened.

"I am sorry, my love," she whispered. "You were right, as you always are." Marisa continued, "Sometimes I just need a reminder."

He muttered in agreement, knelt down on the concrete, and pulled her into his arms. Marisa trembled, then encircled her arms around him, tucking her chin over his shoulder. Her eyes were wide and flashing at Katie, who was creeping away slowly, trying not to bring attention to herself. Inch by inch, each tread closer made adrenaline rush through her body.

The pipe was only nine feet away, and Katie took another step toward it. Marisa reached up and wrapped her palm around the back of Rocco's head and began to scratch the back of his neck with her long fingernails.

Seeing him enthralled with her, Katie seized the opportunity to shuffle closer.

Seven feet.

"You know I love it when you do that," Rocco murmured, his eyes half-closed and his voice warmer as he settled into the delight of the physical sensation that had a hypnotic effect on him.

"I want to do all the things you love, baby," Marisa purred. He was quickly becoming putty in her hands, and an emboldened Katie sprung another step closer.

Five feet.

He pulled back for a moment, and Katie froze. Marisa quickly grabbed his hand and pressed it against her stomach. "He's moving." She beamed at him. "He loves having you close. Can you feel your son?" She flashed him a huge, winning smile.

Katie dared to close the distance to two feet, and the movement caught the corner of Rocco's eye. He whipped around and shot Katie a glare.

"Where do you think you're going?" he growled and Katie had to tear her eyes away from the pipe, heartsick at her failure. So close, yet so far away.

"I thought you two would want some privacy," she offered in explanation.

Rocco's bliss melted into suspicion, and no one felt the abrupt shift more than Marisa. "I see what you're doing. You're manipulating me. Telling me whatever I need to hear to get what you want," Rocco claimed.

Sensing the jig was up, Marisa quickly changed tactics and pleaded, "Our baby needs *both* of his parents —his mom *and* his dad—in order to be happy. If you let us go right now, I promise I won't poison him against you. I will take your temporary lapse in judgment to my grave."

He paused to consider her plea and then seemed to dismiss it quickly while he strode over to Katie and yanked her over to where Marisa rested.

"This is between you and me," Marisa cried. "Let Katie go."

"Not anymore," Rocco grumbled. "When someone pokes their nose in my business, I need to teach them a lesson."

I'm going to savor the moment I get to cut her tongue out and shut her up once and for all.

The thought sent Katie reeling for a long moment before she gathered her wits enough to reason. "This won't end well if you don't release us both. There is no way a judge will grant you custody of this child."

"Is that right?" He folded his arms across his formidable chest and stared her down.

I'll get custody if, God rest her soul, his beautiful mother is deceased.

The unspoken message was chilling, and Katie fought the fear that was close to crisscrossing her features. She shivered in response, desperate to remain calm instead of letting panic overtake her.

Ludlow is worthless. Now that her ugly face has been plastered on every telephone pole from Aura Cove to Tampa Bay, she's a liability.

"My family and friends are looking for me," Katie insisted, playing on the tiny measure of doubt she heard in his thoughts. "They will not stop until we are reunited."

"People disappear all the time," he answered. "They go out for a gallon of milk and," he snapped his fingers for impact, "just like that, they are wiped off the face of the earth." His eyes darkened and leveled on Katie's before she deciphered one last terrifying truth.

Tomorrow night. I'm going to solve this problem forever.

Katie's body went rigid. Internally, she felt a wave of fright crash over her that left her breathless as a countdown clock began ticking. Knowing the waiting game was almost over, she had to steel herself for the battle they needed to wage to survive. Bored with her, Rocco walked over to the box he'd kicked to the corner when he first entered the room. He ripped it open and dropped it on the floor next to the women, and Marisa flinched. Katie's eyes drifted over to the box. Inside were two more liters of water and two sandwiches. The reduction in supplies got Marisa's attention, and her wide eyes locked on Katie's.

"Eat up, sweetheart, my son is a growing boy." He kneeled down and reached his thick palm out to stroke Marisa's cheek. She spit in his face and was rewarded with a swift backhand for her defiance. Katie watched Marisa press her lips together to prevent a painful whimper from escaping as a trickle of blood appeared in the corner of her mouth.

Rocco stood to his full height and then turned on his heel and left, locking the door behind him. The heaviness in the air dissipated the further he retreated. Katie pulled Marisa closer, desperate to protect the woman who, day by day, was feeling more like a daughter. She pressed her palms to Marisa's cheeks, looking deep into her eyes.

"Are you okay?"

"Yep," Marisa murmured, pressing her thumb to her bloodied lip.

"I have a feeling he's coming back tomorrow night," Katie offered, "and when he does, it will be our only chance to walk out of here alive."

Marisa nodded in agreement and then burst into tears. "I tried so hard."

"You did great."

"But it didn't work. I'm just an incubator for his child. We're disposable to him," she fretted. "I'm scared, Katie."

"I'd be lying if I said I wasn't, too," she admitted as she reached to squeeze Marisa's hand. "It's okay to be afraid, but we can't let it paralyze us." She looked around at the warehouse they'd been locked in. Now, her full name was carved into the wall, alongside Marisa's. There was a chance their escape attempt would fail, and the carved message would be the only proof left. Katie squared her shoulders, shaking off the fear, and declared, "We are getting out of here tomorrow night. I am going to hug my kids again or die trying."

TWENTY-FOUR

The same evening and twenty-four hours after her arrest, Frankie paced the constraints of the holding cell that detained her. "This is hell. I am in hell." Every minute ticked by more slowly than the one before it. In the windowless room, she thought, being in jail was like being inside a casino in Vegas. Without a clock on the wall, there was no concept of time. The stakes were high, and the potential to lose it all was definitely on the table.

She ran a hand through her hair, wanting to gather it up into a ponytail with the elastic that was perpetually on her wrist, then remembered she'd had to surrender it when she'd been processed. It was chilly in the holding cell, and she cursed the tank top and black work pants she'd been wearing when she'd gotten pulled over. They were too snug and cut in at her waist, and coupled with shivering uncontrollably for hours, had made for a long night.

"Francesca Stapleton?" She heard a guard bellow out her name. Another indication her life was going off the rails. The only other person who had called her Francesca was her mother before she'd passed, and the only time she'd used her full name was when Frankie had committed a serious offense.

"That's me." She rushed over to the officer, grateful for a change of scenery, desperate to escape the claustrophobic confines of the cell.

There was a loud buzz, and then the door unlocked, and the officer pulled it open.

"Turn around," he demanded.

"Oh, is it time for the Hokey Pokey already?" she joked, unable to stop herself. The guard didn't even crack a grin. He was like stone, and it eroded her confidence and usual carefree demeanor. "Tough crowd," she muttered under her breath.

Frankie clamped her lips together and obeyed his directions. A moment later, she heard the cuffs click as they fastened securely behind her and she was led down a long hallway. Once inside the interrogation room, the guard removed her handcuffs, and she took in her new surroundings. It was a stagnant box containing only an empty table and two chairs, giving off an institutional vibe that gave Frankie the willies.

She took a seat at one of the molded plastic chairs and crossed her ankle over her knee. Hugging her arms close to her body, she glanced around the room. Up in one corner was a closed-circuit video camera. A pane of glass she couldn't see through formed a window across from her, and the green on the walls was made even more sickly by the ugly fluorescent bulbs that illuminated it.

A door opened, and she gasped as a smug Detective Ludlow settled himself in the chair across from her, clasping a folder in his hands. His hair was thinning on top of his head that was bent toward Frankie, and she spotted bright pink, oily patches of his scalp through wispy hairs.

He closed the folder, then glanced up. "You've been read your Miranda rights. This is Officer Jerry Ludlow of the Aura Cove Police Department, and I am interviewing suspected drug trafficker, Francesca Stapleton." He rattled off the date and time and then continued. "We've got a kilo of cocaine, an unregistered firearm, and about thirty G's in cash that was recovered from your vehicle. Why don't we start there?"

Frankie was incensed and focused on his thumb that drummed on the table. He was jittery. "You know as well as I do, they aren't mine." She leaned in. "Although I *do* have some rather interesting theories as to how they were discovered in my car."

His reptilian eyes narrowed. "You're looking at spending the next dime behind bars. The best thing you can do right now is cooperate with law enforcement."

Remembering Harry's advice, she said, "I want a lawyer." Then she leaned back in her chair and folded her arms across her chest.

"That's your right," he said, adding, "But he'll probably encourage you to cooperate so you can get a reduced sentence."

"What do you think he'll advise me to do when I tell him about the moonlighting you're doing at ANO Deliveries?" In her mind, she heard Harry telling her to keep her mouth shut, but she couldn't make herself comply. "What do you think your *sergeant* would say if he knew you and Rocco Gabriano meet each other for cannolis at Diangelo's?" She spat the accusation out and it hung in the stale air between them. "You're awfully chummy with a known gangster. Not to mention, more than one person has reported him as a person of interest in the kidnapping of my best friend."

"Tread carefully, Ms. Stapleton," he advised, his voice oozing with intimidation.

Frankie was undeterred. "*Two* days after spending an evening witnessing your extra-curricular activities, I land in here?" Frankie waved her arms around the interrogation room. "It's not a coincidence, and anyone with half a brain can see the correlation."

Ludlow's lips tightened, and Frankie knew she'd hit a nerve. "We'll see about that," he muttered.

"I want my phone call and a lawyer," she demanded, refusing to back down from this snake even one iota.

"So, you want to do this the hard way? I get it." Then he leaned in, and his voice lowered to a barely audible tone. "Suit yourself, but if I were you, I'd get used to prison orange. I know it's not the most flattering color for a ginger, but them's the breaks." He shrugged unapologeti-cally, then stood and knocked on the door. The door buzzed, then unlocked. When he was gone, Frankie could finally exhale. She stood up and paced the small interroga-tion room.

"Police corruption is alive and well here at ACPD. Detective Ludlow should be the one in here. Not me!" she shouted up at the closed-circuit camera. Circling like a caged animal, Frankie fumed.

A few moments later, the door opened to a friendly face.

"Don't react," Harry whispered, his lips immobile. He removed his handcuffs from his belt loop and demanded in a gruff tone, "Turn around." Frankie followed his order, ducked her head, and let her hair fall forward to cover her mouth.

"I asked for a lawyer."

"Good. I've been collecting surveillance footage from our stakeout night," he offered. "It's a needle in a haystack kind of thing, but if we can find footage of someone tampering with your vehicle, they will drop the charges."

"Check my house. There's a key in the fake rock next to the door. Katie forced me to put in a security camera six months ago when our neighborhood was hit by teenagers going through unlocked vehicles at night. Maybe we'll get lucky. My passwords are written on a piece of paper on the fridge. Log in to my account and access the footage."

"Will do." Harry walked her down the hallway, away from the camera and back toward the holding cell. "I'm going to get you out on bail."

"But I don't have the money to pay you back," she admitted, feeling shame crawling up her torso.

"It's my fault you're in here," he admitted. "Don't worry, it's all going to work out."

Frankie's shoulders drooped, and she stifled back a sob. "How do you know?"

"I know NTM is one of the guiding principles in your life, but you're going to have to trust me."

A solitary tear escaped from the corner of her eye and tracked down the laugh lines on her face. "Okay," she conceded weakly, acknowledging she didn't have any other options.

The door to the cell buzzed open, and Frankie froze outside it, hesitating, paralyzed with fear at the thought of being trapped inside again. Being locked in a cage made her free spirit throat close and she couldn't budge.

"I'm going to fix this," Harry whispered. "I promise you."

"Please do." She let the air out in a rush between her gritted teeth, rubbing her wrists that were sore from their restriction in the handcuffs. She clung to the bars of the cell, resting her forehead on their cold metal surface, and watched Harry walk away, praying he was a promise keeper.

———

Six hours later, Harry came through and Frankie was let out on bail. She stepped outside into the bright Florida sunshine and shielded her eyes from the blazing heat of the afternoon. Inside her purse, her phone was dead.

"Shit," she said, looking at the dead black screen. "Can't even call an Uber." She heard a wolf whistle and her eyes darted around, looking for the source. Leaning against the front of a fully-restored El Camino, Harry's arms were folded across his chest. Frankie wanted to run to him but was afraid they were being watched. Instead, she walked in his general direction and, after locking eyes with him, continued past the car and down the sidewalk, out of the view of every prying eye inside the station. Picking up on her cue, Harry climbed into the car and started the ignition, and the El Camino sped by her and parked out of sight, next to the curb on a side street.

She ran over and hopped into Harry's car. "You paid my bail?"

"I told you I would, and I am a man of my word."

Frankie was stunned. "Wow. Truthful men *do* exist. I thought all of them died out in the last ice age. You could seriously knock me over with a feather right now."

"Happy to blow your mind, Ms. Stapleton."

"I'd be happy to blow…" Frankie's eyebrows shot up and a wicked grin spread across her face. Sexual innuendo was her super power and a harmless coping mechanism she found irresistible.

"While I am a huge fan of the sentiment and it ranks incredibly high on my list of favorite things, it seems a tad transactional," he said. "Let's at least get you home and wash the stink of prison off you first." He pulled his glasses off and winked at her. "Besides, you haven't heard the good news yet."

Frankie clapped her hands together. "It's been a hot minute since anything good has happened. Hit me with it, Willey!"

"I checked all the evidence logs at the station, and Ludlow seems to be in and out of it a lot, like it's his own private candy store."

"Really?"

"I wouldn't lie to you." He said, "Several items are missing or incorrectly logged. It appears that the very items recovered from the trunk of your car are on that list."

She victory punched him hard in the arm, appreciating how solid his bicep was and that he didn't even flinch. "That *is* good news."

"It's something," he acknowledged. "I'm still combing through surveillance footage. I got access to yours, but it is going to take some time to sort through it all."

Frankie felt the tickle of nerves in her belly. "I can't afford a lawyer. Hell, I can barely afford my mortgage. It's the hot mess express over here." She looked down at her grimy pants and lifted her arm, tucking her head into her armpit, and then sharply inhaled. "And, I'm pretty ripe." She folded her arms across her chest to contain the sharp, musky scent she emitted.

Harry glanced over at her and shot her a supportive smile. "I, for one, find your brutal honesty refreshing."

"Katie always loved that about me, too. God, I want my best friend," Frankie whimpered, looking out the window as a forlorn expression settled on her features. She turned back to ask, "Are there any new developments in her case?" Frankie's voice was wistful.

"I'm sorry, nothing yet," he answered with another quick glance over at her, his lips pursed. "It's becoming a two birds one stone situation. If we can exonerate you, then we can get Ludlow kicked off her case."

"*And* if we get Ludlow off the case, we might actually find Katie!" Frankie leaned forward, feeling the first burst of hope she'd felt since her arrest.

"Exactly!" Frankie stole glances at him as he drove the rest of the way to her house. Depending on a man never came second nature to her, but she was starting to think the idea sounded like a good one.

TWENTY-FIVE

L
ate the next afternoon at Kandied Karma, the bell at the door jingled, and Yuli glanced over to see a group of four intimidating men entering the store with Dominic in tow. One of the leather-clad body guards flipped the lock and turned the sign to closed. Yuli rushed over to Dominic, desperate for an update, and another guard penned her in with his arms.

"Johnny, it's okay," Dominic said. "I can take it from here." The burly man nodded, released his hold on Yuli, and then retreated to the wall of windows. Standing shoulder to shoulder with the other three men, they formed an impenetrable wall.

Dominic cleared his throat, then got right to the point. "I had to pull a few strings, but I think I've got some solid intel for you." He leaned in, "Check down by the docks at Port Tampa Bay. There are a series of steel buildings and warehouses by the shipping yard. Big Tony confirmed he's holding her in one of those."

A location. Yuli heaved a sigh of relief. "Thank you,"

she breathed out in reply, and a long, awkward silence followed. Dom was the one to break it.

"So many memories of you and me and my dad came flooding back after your last visit. Isn't it bittersweet how the passage of time softens the rough edges?" He looked deep into her eyes. "We were something to each other for a long time, family, you might even say." He paused and his voice deepened. "Closure—that lily-livered, weak-minded word all the snowflakes won't shut up about. I always thought it was overrated." He pursed his lips together. "Turns out, it might not be."

His sentiment choked Yuli up. The tenderness she felt for him and his father came rushing back, opening a chamber of her heart that had been locked for decades. "How can I repay you?"

"There is no need." His voice was steady and sure. "But I wouldn't turn down a few of your caramel macchiato truffles."

"Of course." Yuli folded a box and quickly filled it with truffles until it was bursting.

"Yuli?" Dominic asked as she was folding the lid closed. "You need to be careful," he warned. "Rocco's family called him a loose cannon. A man like that is capable of anything, especially when he is pushed into a corner."

"I understand." Yuli swallowed the fear that reared up, knowing she would have to push past it. She handed the golden box over to him, and his warm fingers brushed against hers.

A funeral parlor flashed into her subconscious, and she saw Dominic in a casket. A calendar came next, and she saw December twenty-ninth circled in red.

She gasped and her hands flew to her mouth.

"Are you okay?" Dom asked, his wary eyes settling on hers. She felt a single tear break away, and she quickly turned to hide her face and brush it off with her fingers.

"I'll never forget you," Yuli whispered. How could you forget a friend who protected and shared the secrets of your adolescence? There were so many things she yearned to say, but she held back, knowing it would arouse his suspicion. Yuli's eyes drank him in, fully understanding this was the last time she would ever lay eyes on Dominic Lombardo. He would be gone before the New Year, and it would lock the door to their tortured past, leaving only her and Zoya to remain.

She opened her arms and pulled him close, inhaling the scent of tobacco and cedar. "Sally would have been proud to see the man you turned out to be."

He pulled back and cleared his throat, his eyes red and watery. Then he offered her a wry smile and turned to follow his bodyguards out of the shop.

She stared at the door for a long while. The older you got, the more frequent the goodbyes. Nearing one hundred years old, if you were still alive, you were one of a handful of lucky folks. This goodbye gutted her, the enormity of it engulfing her in silence. She watched his town car pull away through the front window as the last warm rays of the sun filtered in. Then Yuli untied her apron, balling it up into the pile that was sent to the laundry service, and smoothed the flyaway hairs that gathered around the crown of her head.

Now that she had answers, she quickened her pace and opened the blast chiller to dig out a special truffle she'd made. It was flat and shaped like a compass with an arm on it formed from white chocolate. Dom had given her a general location, but she was sure the port was filled with buildings that would match his description. Time was of the essence. Eating it would reveal Katia's location, but it would also weaken her.

On the plate, the truffle jiggled and quivered with anticipation, glowing with a bright golden light. She chanted under her breath, taking a deep inhale. Then Yuli picked up the truffle and bit into it. The blood orange flavor squirted its bitterness onto her tongue. She swallowed the first bite with great difficulty. It felt like razor blades slicing her throat on the way down. The second bite was easier to swallow, and by the third, her throat was numb and she didn't feel it at all. She fell back into her chair, her body going limp for one long second before it convulsed forward, and the intensity of the auditory stimulation jolted her. Yuli pressed her hands against her ears to stop the sensory overload. She heard a screeching noise and then three long whistle blasts. Shutting out the sounds, she focused more intently on the warm timbre of Katia's voice that was being overpowered by the cracking sound of chains weighed down from shipping containers being unloaded from cargo ships. At first, Katia's voice was like a whisper. She took a deep breath and fixated harder, flinching from the stronger assault on her senses.

"We have one chance to escape." She heard Katia's voice speaking to another woman in the room. "It has to be tonight."

Yuli braced for the pain she knew was coming next, but she was ill-prepared for it. She cried out as the clattering of a locomotive resounded in her ears, followed by the screeching of the wheels against the rails as it shuddered to a complete stop. The intensity of the cornucopia of sound made her eardrums throb, and a small trickle of blood seeped out. There was a tearing sensation as her physical body pulled away from her spirit. Blissful silence followed, and she shot straight up into the sky where she had a bird's eye view of a map of Florida. She stared down at it from her perch in the clouds and reached out to tap Port Tampa Bay.

"Recalculating," a robotic female voice said, and a closer map appeared of the port. There was still too much ground to cover. The port was near an industrial area and filled with shipping containers and huge metal buildings, one of which Dom had confirmed held Katia. Yuli took two deep breaths to center her thoughts and envisioned Katia's face in her mind. She visualized her granddaughter's coal-black hair and beautiful green eyes. In an altered state, she harnessed the love in her heart for Katia and felt her heart expanding in her chest. A warm glow radiated there, and then a beacon of light shot from her chest to the map and illuminated a cluster of industrial buildings across from the train tracks. Yuli tapped on the map again.

"Recalculating," the voice repeated, and this time, it narrowed in on a single city block in the industrial park that was emitting light, revealing Katia's location with better accuracy.

Trembling, she felt her consciousness fall back to the earth and sew itself back into her immobile body that remained at the store. Time was an incongruent concept in the astral plane. Hours slipped past at an astonishing rate, and when she awoke, Yuli discovered she'd lost hours. The clock on the wall revealed it was nearly midnight. Quickly, she gathered up her keys and steered her car toward the location in Port Tampa Bay she'd seen from the air.

The full moon hung high in the sky, and she felt the tremors of its power vibrating through her. Grateful for its strength and the recharge she felt in its presence, she slammed her foot on the gas pedal, using the energy of the moon to guide her. Its pull and tug toward any location was infinitely more accurate than Google maps. She connected with her divine energy and let it light the way.

Eager to get to Katia, she whipped the dark sedan through traffic lights that curiously turned green as she approached. Finally, she abandoned the car on the side of the road and walked the rest of the way to the industrial park. It was deserted and Yuli was grateful for the cloak of darkness that would make it harder for Rocco to detect her presence. Her vision hazed over, as she stood in the street in front of the buildings she'd seen from the air. There were three contenders. She took a step and the warehouse across the street began to hum. She took another step, and it adopted a faint glow. Testing the accuracy, she side-stepped in the opposite direction, and the glow disappeared. Grateful for the confirmation, she quickened her pace faster toward the illuminated building, and as she drew nearer, the glow intensified.

Once inside, she hid in the shadows, getting acclimated to the darkness. Down a long hallway, she heard a deep male voice. A sense of panic filled her center, and she strained to make out his words.

Tiptoeing in the darkness, she stepped closer, using one of her hands on the wall to guide her down the dark passageway. "Stand up!" She heard the man bark out orders from maybe twenty feet in front of her. A wooziness crept in, and the lightheaded feeling grayed everything down around her and dampened the noises. Yuli leaned against the wall for support, suddenly feeling the entirety of her ninety-seven years crashing down on her. She took three calming breaths, trying to summon the courage and the burst of energy she would need to save Katia.

A tug at her heartstrings distracted her and, deep in her soul, an alarm bell rang. She felt a shift in the air and a magnetic pull stronger than any full moon she'd ever experienced. Confused by the sensation, she tried to shake it off and counted to twenty, still hidden in the darkness. Each number flooded her with the adrenaline she would need to rescue Katia.

Behind her, a tuning fork tingled, and the ringing sound it emitted was deeply disturbing. Powerful sound waves crashed over her body and made Yuli dizzy. The sensation grew, worming its way through her memories, winding through her fears, looking for a permanent place to settle. Yuli tried to calm her mind and regroup, but a foreboding sense of danger filled her. Bewildered, she tried to focus on its origin. A powerful magnetic field was approaching, and the closer it got, the more vulnerable she felt. Then, in a gush of wisdom, she became enlightened to the truth.

Zoya.

It had to be Zoya.

She was coming to claim Katia. Apprehensive, Yuli steeled herself for a battle she'd long known would be waged. It was a war she couldn't afford to lose.

TWENTY-SIX

Hours earlier, inside the locked cell of the warehouse, every second that passed filled Katie with more trepidation. Jittery, she paced the perimeter of the room, thinking through potential escape scenarios that would have them both walking away alive.

"You're making me nervous," Marisa admitted. She wrung her hands together and then dragged her dirty fingers through her greasy hair. "I'm filthy. God, I can't wait to take a shower."

"The way I see it, we'll both be taking one very soon," Katie offered, trying to soothe Marisa's frayed nerves.

"What do you mean?" Marisa was confused.

"We have one chance to escape. Rocco is coming back tonight, and one way or the other, this nightmare is going to be over," Katie answered.

"How do you know?"

"I just do," Katie answered, and an exhausted Marisa blindly accepted her admission.

Katie's fingernails were caked with grime, and her yoga pants hung loosely on her frame. She sat down next to Marisa. "We need a plan."

"What do you have in mind?"

"It will not be easy, but we can do this," Katie encouraged, reaching out to squeeze her shoulder. "One of us needs to distract him, and the other…" She couldn't bring herself to say the words.

"Needs to grab the pipe and swing for the fences," Marisa finished without batting an eyelash, a sad smile tugging up the corners of her mouth.

Katie nodded. She'd never engaged in a physical altercation before. The very idea of it would have cued up panic in her years ago, but now, she knew brute force was necessary. "We have to be willing to do whatever it takes to get out of here." It was a bold blanket statement she uttered to instill confidence, but immediately after the words left her lips, she wondered if she'd be able to make good on her promise.

They passed the next few hours eating the rest of the food, drinking the water, and trying to rest. Katie never relaxed enough to fall asleep; she was too keyed up. Instead, she closed her eyes and visualized the faces of Beckett, Lauren, and Callie, her parents and Yuli, Arlo the wonder dog, and her best friend, Frankie. Those were people worth fighting for, and the dream of reuniting with them fortified her resolve.

Daylight faded into the darkness of night, and from the windows high in the concrete room, light poured in from the full moon. Katie walked over to the window, craning her neck to bring the glowing orb into view. It was beautiful. She felt a tug and a tightening sensation, and all of her senses became more astute the longer she looked at it.

Her zodiac sign was Cancer—the moon child—and in that moment, the sign never felt more fitting. During her entire existence, the moon phases always affected her physically. Years ago, she'd crashed a car during a full moon and had gone into pre-term labor with Lauren during another. But ever since her awakening, full moons made her feel energized and more intuitive. Her senses delivered more intense sensations, scents were stronger, colors were brighter, and sounds were louder. It was like living in a technicolor dream world.

She breathed deeply and tried to center herself. Stilling her frantic mind and slowing it down to a dreamlike state that encouraged creative problem-solving. Her eyes fluttered as a wave of strong audio sensation cued up around her. Katie heard a car pull up and then footsteps echoed in her head as he walked closer.

"He's here. Are you ready?" Katie stood on the balls of her feet, shuffling from side to side as adrenaline gave her a burst of energy.

Across the room, Marisa slowly staggered to her feet and faced the door. A few minutes later, they heard the key turn in the lock and Rocco appeared dressed in a black hoodie and jeans, blending into the darkness that engulfed him. Katie could barely make him out. The intensity of his black aura covered the little skin that was exposed.

She eyed the hiding place for the pipe, waiting for her chance to grab it. Marisa was silent, leaning against the wall for support, her skin ghostly white.

Rocco pulled out a handgun that had been tucked in the back of the waistband of his jeans. A wave of panic swept through Katie, and she held up her hands defensively as he leveled the weapon at her.

He pulled back the hammer, and Katie whimpered and closed her eyes, bracing for a blast.

"NO!" she shouted. Rocco squeezed the trigger, and reflexively, Katie flinched and squeezed her eyes shut again. Next to her, Marisa's scream shattered the quiet of the night.

"Shit," he cursed under his breath, and Katie's eyes popped open as a wave of relief crashed over her. The gun jammed, and he fiddled with it, yanking the cocking mechanism back as a never-ending flow of obscenities flowed from his mouth. Katie darted out of the way as he released the cartridge, and it clattered to the floor. He reached inside his pocket and produced another one, swiftly loading it into the butt of the gun with one heavy smack delivered from the palm of his hand. It clicked into place and he leveled it back on Katie.

"Wait," Katie begged.

"For what?" A pompous chuckle escaped his lips. "Your fairy godmother?"

As if on cue, Yuli burst through the open door. All eyes in the room flew over to her. Confused, Rocco asked, "Who the hell are you?"

"Yuli!" Katie whimpered in relief at the sight of her grandmother. Yuli's eyes locked on Katie's for one long second, assessing the dire situation. Then she hurried to place herself as a human shield between Katia and the gun. Katie's heart leapt with joy, then crashed with fear. She reached out to touch Yuli. For a split second, she wondered if Yuli was a hallucination or a mirage of her terrified subconscious, but her hand connected with the strong, warm presence of her grandmother and confirmed with joy that her eyes were not playing tricks on her. She felt herself breaking down, realizing for the first time how hard she had been working to project a brave front for Marisa. Trying to instill complete confidence had been emotionally draining, but now that Yuli was involved, Katie felt her reserves strengthen. She felt the capable energy of Yuli ground her and give her a second wind.

"You don't want to do this," Yuli said, positioning her ample body in front of Katie's.

"This is rich," Rocco snarled back at her. "Granny to the rescue?" Seizing the opportunity presented by his distraction, Katie's eyes darted to Marisa's, giving her a subtle nod to spring into action. Marisa quietly tiptoed the few feet to where the pipe lay.

Yuli shrugged off his condescending question and distracted him by challenging his intelligence. "Ladies, this is why you never engage in a battle of wits with an unarmed man."

A deep laugh bubbled from him as he waved the firearm around. "Unarmed? Looks like Granny needs an eye exam." Gathering the handgun between his palms, he fully extended his arms, his finger on the trigger. A burst of pulsating light shot from Yuli's palm. There was another click and then silence before an enraged Rocco roared in frustration.

"Son-of-a-bitch!" He focused on the firearm, desperate to dislodge the ammo that had jammed a second time.

Hiding behind Yuli, Katie mouthed to Marisa, NOW!

Marisa bent down and retrieved the long length of black pipe from the hiding place and rushed toward him. Her eyes were wild and her face stark white. She swung it behind her and hollered, "I hate you!" With a loud shriek, she swung the pipe like a baseball bat and connected with his gut in a blow that sent him and the malfunctioning firearm reeling to the floor. Marisa stood over him, swinging the pipe again, but he was too quick and scrambled to his feet. She brought the pipe back over her head. He tackled her into the concrete wall and they wrestled with it. Fighting for her life, Marisa kicked and screamed, refusing to let go. Overpowering her, he yanked the pipe away, and it clattered onto the floor.

Marisa's arms and legs flailed around, connecting with different parts of her husband, who became incensed, emitting a rumbling growl. His aura shifted from red to black, and his eyes became two inky black holes. On his forehead, a thick vein bulged with fury, and a sneer distorted his features into an ugly mask.

He roared and wailed at her, shoving her into the wall roughly with both hands. When she connected with the concrete, she let out a yelp and crumpled to the ground like a rag doll, clutching her stomach.

"Marisa!" Katie screamed and lunged at him, jumping on his back and clawing at his eyes. Rocco stumbled backward and crashed into the wall. Yuli heard a crack as Katie let go and slid down to the ground. Still thinking it was the answer, Rocco raced to the gun. Yuli got there first and kicked it away.

Dazed from the hit, Katie struggled to her feet and swayed, locking eyes with Yuli. She groaned, pressing her hand to her temple where a dull ache formed. "I don't feel right. There's so much pressure." In her field of vision, the room wavered and began to swim, and she wasn't sure if it was the result of a possible concussion or if there was another reason.

"In your chest?" Yuli asked as she clutched at her own, the tightness spreading deeper and seeping through her torso.

Katie nodded and struck her chest with a balled-up fist. "Here," she indicated, fighting for oxygen.

"I feel it, too," Yuli admitted.

Across from them, Rocco swayed on his feet, seemingly under the influence as well.

Katie took a deep breath. "I can't breathe. My chest is tight." She stumbled over to Marisa to assess her injuries. "She's hurt. I'm worried about the baby." Katie gasped with effort, then dropped to her knees, placing one protective hand over Marisa. The young woman was curled into the fetal position, moaning, when a thunderous sound descended upon them. Rocco dropped to his knees with a howl and covered his ears.

Terrified and immobilized, all their eyes slid to the open door, waiting in anticipation for what was to come through it.

TWENTY-SEVEN

Several minutes earlier, Zoya's driver, Higgins, pulled up to 1110 Pixel Bay Drive and held the door open wide for her while she slid out. Dressed in a flowing black robe and black combat boots laced up to her knees, she was ready for battle. She rushed forward and let the energy pull her in its path. In a trancelike state, she followed where it led, fully engrossed in the flow. She heard a warm, sultry soundtrack cue up in her mind, and her skin tingled.

"Burn it down. Destroy every branch of that misogynistic tree and bring the infant to me." It was Lilith. Her voice was tantalizing and hypnotic, calling to her like the sirens of centuries-old that lured sailors into a certain death.

"Yes, My Queen," she answered, feeling power surge into her as if she were a vessel being filled. Electricity crackled and Zoya felt it ripple throughout her body and zing up and down her limbs. The steel building in front of her radiated red light. Thunder rolled and lightning struck, then raced between her palms and back up into the sky. The first raindrops of a tropical storm brushed down her cheeks, and she glanced up at the black clouds gathering above, whipping by the glorious full moon.

She balled her fists tight together and circled her clenched hands, gathering the electric power and harnessing it. Circling and circling, the charge built in intensity and raw power. The pleasure of her impending revenge sent shockwaves through her system. The pool of feminine power overflowed, and she laughed in astonishment and relished the sensation as pleasurable as any orgasm she'd ever had. Drunk on it, she flung her open palms to the doors of the glowing warehouse, and they blew off the hinges, ripped open by her pure, unadulterated control. They crashed to the ground and settled in the rain that raced down in sheets. Rage gathered in her center, then flooded her limbs. It was a red-hot burning sensation that propelled her forward into the building.

Every one of her senses was heightened and charged as Zoya marched through the doors, moving deeper into the warehouse, following the sound of voices. Waves of fury rippled through her, honing in on the animosity that grew with each step she took toward a deep male voice.

Each inch she traveled closer to him whipped her into a frenzy. When she crossed the threshold, her entire being was on fire and radiating red-hot rage. Sparks and flames crawled up her sides from the floor to the ceiling. Every person in the room was enraptured for several long moments, observing the magnificent spectacle of a fully empowered Zoya. Then the terror set in and they began to scramble for cover.

Katia hovered near a young blonde woman and was

helping her to her feet. The blonde woman was sobbing, clutching her stomach. Yuli's muscular body bridged the divide between Zoya and Katia. A look of disgust infiltrated Zoya's features as she regarded Yuli's futile attempts to protect Katia. Yuli's arms shot out to her sides and her stance widened. She was a brick house, her golden energy crackling in response to the threat. Behind her, Zoya's eyes fixated on her obsession, Rocco Gabriano, who stood paralyzed by the radiant sight of a glowing female figure vibrating with rage.

Zoya opened her mouth, and one loud roar reverberated through the night. It was a sound so loud and fierce it made Rocco stumble backward. The windows shattered and glass rained down on them. On all sides, the concrete bricks started to crack as fissures ran down the lengths of the crumbling mortar. Then the roof ripped off the building, torn away by hurricane-force wind gusts. Now uncovered and exposed to the elements, cold rain pelted down on everyone inside the demolished building.

"YOU!" Zoya leveled one finger at Rocco, who scampered back to his feet while his eyes darted around for an escape route. She crossed her arms in front of her chest, and the fire brightened and recharged. Behind Zoya, a redhaired female figure appeared, and from across the room, Katia felt the warm flash of nuclear heat sear her cheeks. Yuli rushed to Katia's side, and their eyes were locked on Zoya. She shielded Katia from the assault of Zoya's power and wavered, absorbing the brunt of the oppressive heat.

"I avenge thee, Salvatore Lombardo!" The tropical storm howled and a deluge of rain dropped from the sky, sizzling and crackling when it came in contact with the forcefield of flames that now obscured Zoya from head to toe. "I curse the blood of the Gabriano Family. The entire ancestral line from the smallest babe in the womb to the oldest living devil. My Dark Queen, Lilith, condemns you all to burn in everlasting punishment."

She pressed her palms out toward Rocco and began to chant in long, low syllables. Yuli stood paralyzed, concentrating on the words, struggling for understanding. The spell made Zoya surge with more heat, and more rubble fell at their feet. The warehouse was disintegrating around them in the storm consumed by Zoya's fury.

Zoya let out a loud, strangled cry, and then two massive bolts of lightning radiated out from her palms. Both of them initially focused on Rocco when one jolted over to Marisa, who dropped to the ground with a strangled sob.

Rocco grabbed his chest and let out a primal scream.

Yuli shouted to Katia over the shrieking wind. "It's dark magic!"

Katia's eyes were huge and unblinking, frozen by fear.

"She's summoned Lilith, and by channeling her strength has become more powerful!" Yuli shouted against the roar of the storm. "Quick! Circle Marisa and take my hands!" Katia obeyed, and when their hands connected, a golden orb of beautiful light centered on a writhing Marisa and radiated out in a perfect circle.

"Look at me!" Yuli directed Katia, whose horrified gaze kept darting back toward Zoya. Her wide eyes locked on Yuli's. "Repeat after me. Karma appear. Let no one innocent perish here." Yuli shouted. "Again!"

"Karma appear. Let no one innocent perish here." Their voices joined together, getting louder as they repeated the phrase. The glow of golden light sparkled and shimmered as it encased Marisa, who lay on the floor clutching at her chest.

A deep thumping sound joined the howling of the wind, and it sped faster and faster. Rocco and Marisa let out groans of tandem agony afflicted by the same pain as their heartbeats quickened.

"Karma appear. Let no one innocent perish here." Katia closed her eyes, focusing every ounce of her intention on the phrase, screaming out into the storm that wailed like a banshee. The golden field whirred and spun, encircling the three women, growing stronger with each repeat of the spell.

The thumping sped faster, and the space between each heartbeat decreased until the overpowering thumping became one long, single tone. Then Rocco lurched forward and hit the floor, settling into unconsciousness.

Yuli and Katia shouted louder and louder, their voices melding together and protecting Marisa with an aura of bright golden light.

"Release her. The unborn child is mine!" Zoya screamed at them, her eyes wild and glowing a bright silver hue. Her hair was an electrified white halo that circled her head.

"You can't have her!" Katia hollered over the wind. "Leave us alone."

"My demon queen requires a sacrifice. The Gabriano child is simply collateral damage. It's a soul for a soul. I will trade Sally's for that evil seed."

"We will not allow you to hurt this child!" Yuli barked.

"Allow me?" Zoya's eyes snapped to Yuli's. "*You* do not allow me anything." Her face was twisted in a sneer of contempt. Hatred radiated from her in a wave.

"On the count of three, do what I do!" Yuli advised Katia, who nodded, fear coating her features, with her unequivocal trust in her grandmother.

"One." Zoya shook with fury as she rebuilt her reserves.

"Two." Deep thunder rolled through and startled Katia.

"Three." A lightning bolt crashed down. Yuli clung to Katia's right hand and whipped her body around to face Zoya's, her palm extended fully. The bolt of lightning jolted Katia and Yuli in tandem, then raced from their palms and shot out at Zoya. Her eyes bugged out of her head, and the veins raised in her neck as her body contorted under the strain of their combined effort.

The bolts connected to her sphere of energy and exploded on contact. The wave of power sent Katia and Yuli reeling back as it collided with their own.

"Argh!" Zoya let out one final primal scream before she was silenced and frozen in place. Crystalized ice raced up her legs and consumed her entire body.

Instantly, the storm quieted and the heaviness that had engulfed them all disappeared.

———

Katie staggered to the wall and leaned against it, gasping for breath. The mutual effort expended to freeze Zoya had depleted her. Several moments of complete silence later, she pushed away from the wall and over to where Zoya remained immobile.

"Why?" Katie asked her as if she would respond. Stepping closer with trepidation, Katie was afraid she'd come roaring back to life, but her curiosity got the best of her.

She studied her great-great-grandmother and felt tears well up. Zoya's limbs were spread wide and her open mouth stuck in a permanent howl, pure hatred engraved on every feature of her face. Every muscle in her body was rigid and veiny. Katie could plainly see she was a stunningly beautiful woman, but filled with so much unconcealed hate and ugliness, it rendered her hideous.

"You were right," Katie mumbled to Yuli, who was coming out of a stupor and stumbling forward, trying to find her feet. "About Zoya. I'm sorry I doubted you. How did we…" Katie trailed off, pointing to Zoya's immovable form.

"We're stronger together," Yuli answered. "She's the most powerful witch in our bloodline. The only way to battle against the decades she's spent strengthening and honing her abilities was to join forces." Yuli exhaled a hot and heavy breath and clawed her way up the crumbling wall to a standing position. "Summoning Lilith is dangerous. There is always a debt to pay." She glanced over at Zoya's frozen form, which was nearly unrecognizable when she heard the first crack. "We need to hurry. I don't know how long she'll remain frozen."

Marisa mewled in pain, and their focus shifted. Katie brushed the remaining tears from her cheeks and rushed over to Marisa.

"Lilith is coming for the child," Yuli said.

"What?" Katie was panicked.

"Dark magic always requires a sacrifice," Yuli explained, "and can only be defeated by light magic."

"Help me get her to her feet." Katie wrapped her arm around the young woman and pulled her up from the ground.

"Yuli, look." She pointed at the puddling blood on the floor where Marisa previously rested. "She needs a hospital," Katie said.

Half-carrying, half-dragging Marisa, they wedged her body between them and raced out of the ruins of the warehouse and to Yuli's parked car.

TWENTY-EIGHT

A few moments later, at the warehouse, the second crack was heard. Then a series of several more hairline cracks and small fissures could be seen running up Zoya's frozen arms and legs. The sound was reminiscent of ice on a lake during an early springtime thaw.

Zoya's form wobbled, and then the sheet of ice that had been covering her crashed down to the concrete and rubble underfoot. She cracked her neck and stretched her arms behind her, her muscles strained from the effort. Still on the ground, Rocco was lying on his back. His eyes remained closed and he was unresponsive. Zoya stalked over to him like a cat with a mouse. She knelt down next to him as a scowl lit up her features.

The warehouse was silent, destroyed by the tropical storm that had battered it and torn the roof from the rafters. The ceiling was bare, opened up like a can of sardines. In the sky above, the view of the stunning full moon was unobscured by the missing roof. Shafts of moonlight illuminated Rocco's peaceful face, and the sight of it filled her with seething hatred.

"Dark Queen, I am in need of your wisdom." She meditated, and a spark of flame lit up the night then grew into a wall of fire. Through it, she got a glimpse of Lilith seated on a royal throne, being fanned and fed grapes by two muscular men. Salvatore stood behind her, dragging a golden comb through her long locks.

Zoya's heart leaped at the sight of him. Their eyes locked on each other for a long moment, and she was speechless.

"Because you've pleased me," Lilith praised. "I am going to allow you to sentence Rocco Gabriano and carry out his punishment."

Zoya felt a surge of delight at Lilith's recognition. "Yes, my Dark Goddess."

"But there is still the matter of the child and the covenant we made." Lilith turned and curled her finger toward Sally, beckoning him closer, and Zoya felt jealousy sear her heart when Sally came forward and took Lilith in his arms. His lips locked on hers as she pulled him closer and kissed him hungrily, her eyes locked on Zoya's.

It was a brazen display of affection that propelled a possessive Zoya into action. She bent down and snapped her fingers in front of the incapacitated Rocco, then shook his shoulder when he remained listless. Eventually, Rocco moaned and started to stir.

"Wake up!" she snarled at him. Staring down at the face of Rocco Gabriano, her thirst for vengeance consumed her. She could do anything she wanted to him in his weakened state and she considered her options while she roused him. Finally, his eyes fluttered open.

"Who the hell are you?" Rocco asked, his words slurring, still becoming aware of his surroundings.

"Your worst nightmare," Zoya spat at him.

"Isn't that cute?" he dared to ask as he pulled himself up to a sitting position. He rubbed his hands over his face and then palmed the back of his head with one hand.

"Cute?" she sneered back at him with narrowed eyes.

"What happened?" he asked her, and Zoya's anger welled up anew. His ordin brain had buckled under the weight of her power and, in order to survive, had removed every trace of their altercation.

"Your heart was erratic and beating too fast," Zoya answered. "You almost had a stroke."

Her confession stirred something deep within his memory, and his eyes bugged out as fear walked its way across his face. He slid away, trying to get onto his feet, desperate to run.

"Where do you think you're going?" she asked as she rubbed her hands together, and small jolts of electricity coursed back and forth between them again. She circled her hands faster and faster, spinning up the inner light into a frenzy. It was a fraction of what she'd unleashed moments ago, but it would do.

She muttered under her breath as Rocco pitched forward, landing hard on his hands, his legs not functioning properly. Dropping to the ground, he started crawling to the door on all fours. With glee, Zoya shot her palms at the retreating figure. The blast hit him like a wave, and then a tornado of red light surrounded him, pulling him off the ground and swirling around in front of her rapidly. He spun so fast, his figure blurred and shifted until it was unrecognizable, and then it shrank and contracted together, slowing down as a tiny, indistinct shape dropped onto the ground. When Zoya opened her eyes, his clothing lay in a pile of tattered rags. A blade peeked out from the holster that had been on his leg. Curled up in the middle of the pile of clothing was a tiny teacup Yorkie. Groomed impeccably, with a bowtie at his collar, the diminutive canine yipped and growled. He bared his teeth at her, and this time Zoya laughed.

"Hush now," Zoya commanded, and with a snap of her fingers, the dog whined, then laid down and began to lick himself. Then he growled at her, baring his teeth, and she reached down to pick him up by the scruff of his neck. The dog focused his dark brown eyes on Zoya, his entire body quivering and his adorable ears standing up.

"How's that for cute?" she asked, pleased with herself. She carried him out of the warehouse by the scruff of his neck as he gnashed his teeth at her and continued to growl. It was a ridiculous sound he emitted that was meant to be intimidating but, coming from a four-pound dog, just sounded pathetic.

Zoya rushed out of the wreckage as the first sirens from police and emergency vehicles could be heard in the distance. All around her was destruction. Downed trees needed chainsaws, and flash flooding left water deep in the streets.

Seagulls circled ahead, crying out, now that the storm had passed. They were back in the business of hunting down scraps of French fries and dive-bombing for the occasional fish. Zoya brought the miniature dog closer to her face, and he nipped at her nose. To teach him a lesson, Zoya let him drop to the ground where he whined, then ran off. A bald eagle joined the seagulls and circled above him as Rocco's tiny paws scampered away, unable to cover very much ground. Seeing prey, the eagle dove and scooped him up with its beak. Zoya laughed at the entertainment playing out in front of her. The eagle spread its wings, flying farther away, still grasping the dog by the collar in his mouth. She snapped her fingers, and a second later, the eagle swooped by again, dropping the terrified dog onto the street below. It reduced the tiny Yorkie to a trembling wreck who urinated the second he landed.

Zoya gathered up the wayward canine and handed him off to Higgins, who opened the door of the town car for her. Exhausted, she crashed into the back of the car, her energy waning. There was still one loose thread to tie up.

"Head east on Biscayne Road," she demanded and then closed her eyes, grateful the yipping dog was up front with her driver. Leaning back into the plush leather of the town car as it headed to the nearest hospital, she plotted her next move. She would have to be strategic. Though there was little left in her reserves, she was fueled by exacting her revenge and her desire to set Sally's soul free. The car sped down the street, and she relished each mile that passed as they closed in on Marisa. She would not rest until the baby was found. She owed that much to Sally.

Then there was the matter of Katia's defiance and her alignment with Yuli. They'd bested her by joining forces. She had to admit to herself their reaction surprised her. It was obvious Yuli would not stand idly by, and the old woman was intent on standing on principles.

Fine. She'd deal with her later.

TWENTY-NINE

Marissa was doubled over in pain, clinging to Yuli and Katie's shoulders as they rushed her to Yuli's sedan. A fresh round of cramps gripped her belly, and the pain made her cry out, "It hurts!" She whimpered, "God, it hurts so much." She bent over, bracing her hands on her thighs as Katie opened the door. Slowly, Marisa crawled into the back seat and tightened up into a ball of shrieking agony.

"You drive," Yuli instructed as she got into the back seat and passed the keys to Katie. Marisa's eyes were closed, and she rocked forward and back, keening. Her body tightened in response to the cramps that wracked her abdomen. "Argh!" she cried out, as another round of cramps began its full-on assault. Katie started the car and hit the gas, the urgency to get medical attention now reaching emergency status.

From the back seat, Marisa whimpered and looked down with a gasp at the red pool that was growing between her legs. She touched it and brought her hand to her face. Seeing the crimson stains, she started to cry. Katie drove faster, casting glances back over her shoulder as they barreled down the dark streets toward the hospital. Hitting a few potholes in the dark, the car lurched, and Marisa cried out as Yuli whispered in the back seat. She pressed her hand to the woman's belly. Tiny golden sparks flitted from Yuli's hands to Marisa's abdomen. Katie caught glimpses in the rear-view mirror, fascinated by the sight of her grandmother's magic in action.

"Drive faster, Katia!" Yuli instructed and then chanted louder. In a tone that reminded Katie of monks she'd once seen in a monastery when she was a child, her incantations filled the car, spilling out of her mouth in a constant stream.

Katie forced herself to turn away and focused on the road. She pressed the gas pedal to the floor and ran through a red light.

Yuli stopped chanting and made a grave announcement. "We need a doctor. I am not strong enough right now to help the child."

"What do you mean?" She yanked her head back, confused.

"Healing is my gift," Yuli admitted. "All witches have their one true power. A supernatural ability that comes to them as naturally as breathing. Healing is mine, but containing Zoya and protecting this unborn child weakened me."

"Keep trying," Katie said as she careened down the deserted street, rushing down the road and rumbling over railroad tracks. Then the steering wheel jerked to the right and a loud cha-chunk noise was heard. In the rear-view mirror, she gasped when she saw a large piece of rubber fly up, illuminated by her brake lights, then disappear into the darkness behind them. The car was pulling hard to the right, and she was forced to slow down, considering her next move. Then a metal screeching sound accompanied a shower of sparks.

"Oh no! I think we have a flat!" Katie slowed to a stop and yanked open the door. The front tire was ripped into shreds, and the rim rested on the concrete. Chunks of black rubber were strewn out behind the car for several feet.

The streets were barren in the industrial park in the middle of the night. There was an eerie quality that surrounded them. Panicked, Katie reached for her cell phone on instinct and felt her heart drop when she remembered it was gone. She knew Yuli loathed modern technology and refused to bend to the will of it. Exhausting that option, she drew a blank.

"What are we going to do? The tire is shot. We're down to the rim," Katie admitted as she got back into the car. From the back seat, Marisa's cries could be heard over Yuli's soothing voice. More sparks flew as Yuli worked feverishly to gather energy, then lost it just as fast. In a panic, Yuli's head jerked up as a tingling sensation gathered in her chest.

"Do you feel that?" Yuli closed her eyes to focus. The barometric pressure dropped, and her limbs were plagued with a heaviness she fought to shake off.

"Is it Zoya?" Katie dared to ask. There was an oppressive strain gathering she couldn't deny either, a magnetic swell of energy that made her uneasy.

"She's close," Yuli answered as Marisa cried out. Sheer panic spurred Katie into action.

"I'm going to find help!" Katie exited the vehicle again

and ran down the road for a block. The street was a ghost town in the middle of the night. Engulfed in darkness and isolated, there were no houses around. At the end of the next block, a few ancient cottages were tucked in between the businesses that made up the industrial park.

"Help!" she screamed. "Fire!" FIRE!!!" She ran down the middle of the street, hollering until she was hoarse. She raced to the cottages and banged on the front doors of two of them. Not a soul stirred, not a single light came on. Energized by adrenaline, she kept going. Marisa needed help. After all they had been through, Katie would not fail her now. Gasping for breath, she gripped her knees, trying to calm her hammering heart in the middle of the darkened road. Then blessedly, headlights appeared, turning onto the street where Yuli's car was stranded. The lone vehicle was several blocks away, and she turned back toward it, waving her arms up and down, racing toward it as she howled. With each step she took closer, her feet flew faster and the oppressive energy swelled in her chest, but she continued to run toward it, anyway.

Seeing the car slowing down as it got closer to Yuli and Marisa, relief flooded in. In the distance, the after-shocks of thunder from the tropical storm rumbled. Katie felt bricks on her chest and struggled to take a full breath. Mentally and physically exhausted from the ordeal, she had to dig deep to find the energy to sprint the rest of the way to the approaching vehicle.

On the driver's side of the stopped car, Katie's fists pounded on the black tinted glass. Slowly, the window mechanically rolled down and Katie leaned in. Sitting in the seat next to the driver, a tiny teacup Yorkie scrambled over the driver's lap and growled at Katie. He nipped at her face, baring his teeth and clawing at the door. Dismissing the annoying dog, she shouted, "Can I use your phone? It's an emergency."

With a sneer of disgust, the driver picked up the dog by the scruff of his neck and banished him back to the passenger seat with obvious disdain. The little dog continued to bark and carry on but was easily ignored. The driver was unaffected by her plea and refused to make eye contact, but Katie continued to beg anyway.

"Please. My friend, she needs an ambulance!" The driver ignored her, then got out of the car and slammed the door shut. Desperate, Katie lurched closer to him and begged, "A baby's life is at stake!" She grabbed his jacket by the lapels and shook him. "Can you hear me? I need help now!" Katie shouted.

Without a word, the driver gripped her wrists and promptly pulled her away in the same dismissive way he'd just handled the dog. He straightened his jacket and dusted himself off before bending down to open the back door.

Dumbfounded by his response, Katie continued to plead. "Just one phone call. I'm begging you." He pulled the door open with a flourish, and one curvy leg emerged. A second later, Katie's belly filled with lead and her heart dropped to the floor when her great-great-grandmother, Zoya Castanova, emerged from the vehicle with a self-satisfied grin on her face.

"Never beg for anything, darling. It's beneath you."

THIRTY

Katie gasped. Standing in front of Zoya again, her adrenaline surged and her eyes darted over to Marisa and Yuli in a panic. She heard two thumping heartbeats that throbbed in unison. Marisa and the baby were in danger.

"That was quite the coup you and Yuli almost pulled off." Zoya's green eyes glittered in anger, boring deeply into Katie's. "Such a shame to see Yuli waste her supernatural energy. She might have been able to help save the baby if she hadn't used all her life force subduing me."

"Zoya, this feud is between you and me. Leave them out of it," Katie heard over her shoulder as Yuli advanced closer, and she breathed a sigh of relief.

"I will not leave here without the child." Zoya stepped closer, hearing Marisa cry out. "The infant is already in peril. You must release the mother to me immediately," she demanded.

"The important fact you seem to forget, dear grandmother, is that we are not gods among the ordins. We do not get to choose who lives or who dies," Yuli answered, her jaw set in determination.

"Hmm." Zoya considered Yuli's answer. "We do not play by the same set of rules. We never have and we never will."

Marisa let out a long screech of pain. Yuli circled her palms, gathering energy to protect her. Sparks flew but quickly fizzled out.

A loud peal of self-important laughter rang out from Zoya. "You might want to pay attention. This is how it's done." She circled her hands together until they began to emit a red glow. A wave of warmth surged toward Katie, who rushed to put herself in front of the car door. Yuli blasted Zoya with one last jolt of electricity that she shook off, and the effort sent Yuli reeling to her knees on the street. Katie opened the car door and wrapped her arms around Marisa, who was soaked in sweat and writhing in the back seat. The pool of blood grew underneath her.

"No," Katie whispered to the terrified girl. "I won't let her take you."

Marisa slumped forward and then passed out as another flood of blood thickened between her legs.

Zoya stepped closer, and Katie saw flames lick up Zoya's legs and arms. She opened the door and the wall of heat radiated out as she reached one desperate, clawing hand toward Marisa's womb. In Katie's ears, the stereo throbbing quickened before the thumping stilled to one weakened rhythm. A single heartbeat. Aware of the shift immediately, Zoya's glowing eyes swallowed Marisa's frail form, and then she seethed with rage, threw her head back, and shrieked into the wind.

"You're too late. He's gone," Yuli mumbled from the

shadows, struggling to find her feet. "His soul is now free."

"What?" Katie cried, "No!"

Zoya shrieked a primal scream that shattered the silence. "Salvatore. NO!" Rage made her form burn brighter, and then Yuli clutched her chest and collapsed to the ground.

In the distance, the wail of a siren intensified. Katie sat up in the car, watching the flashing lights of an approaching ambulance speed closer. Relieved to see emergency services closing in, she was torn between staying with Marisa and rushing over to Yuli. Afraid the ambulance would speed by, she gently extracted herself from Marisa to flag it down. "I'll be right back," she said.

Zoya dropped to the ground on her hands and knees, becoming an inconsolable puddle. The fire that had consumed her and burned so brightly was now extinguished, and she was flooded with grief. Higgins got out of the town car and rushed over. "My Queen, the ordins are close. We need to leave unless you want your identity revealed."

Katie's heart leapt as the ambulance slowed its approach, and she ran toward it, waving both her hands in the air to get their attention. The flashing lights on top of the rig bounced around the metal buildings for several blocks.

Higgins pulled Zoya reluctantly to her feet and back to the town car. "We have to go now!" Katie glanced back in time to see the driver shut her inside the car and then reverse and speed away in the opposite direction. Relieved she was gone, Katie quickened her pace toward the approaching emergency vehicle.

A few seconds later, the ambulance came to a complete stop in front of an unconscious Yuli, who was lying on the street.

"There's a pregnant woman inside my car who's lost a significant amount of blood," She said to one of the paramedics. He followed close at her heels, and she opened the door to let him in. "We were headed to the hospital but got a flat tire."

"Grab the gurney," he shouted to his partner, who ran back to the rig to pull it out.

Katie rushed over to Yuli's side, followed by the other paramedic, who knelt and assessed Yuli's vitals.

"This is my grandmother. She collapsed a few minutes ago."

After a few long minutes assessing Yuli, the attendant said, "Her vitals are strong and she's breathing, but we should take her in to be sure, in case she hit her head when she landed on the concrete."

Yuli's eyes fluttered open, and Katie felt relief rush in.

"Can you help me to my feet?' Yuli asked Katie.

"I'm not sure that is a good idea."

A stubborn Yuli fumbled on the ground, struggling to rise. Katie wrapped her arm around her grandmother and helped her stand. A few moments later, the attendants pushed a pale Marisa back to the rig on the gurney and loaded her into the back of the ambulance. One of the men hung a bag of fluids while the other extended a hand and easily pulled Yuli up the steps. Then he glanced down at Katie, offering her a hand up, and pulled the doors shut behind them. The siren blared, and the driver slammed his foot on the gas to hasten their return to the hospital.

After a flurry of activity, Marisa's blood pressure stabilized, and the attendant finally looked over at Katie. "You look familiar." A puzzled look appeared on his face before the truth set in. "Wait a minute, you're Katie Beaumont. I saw your photo on Bay News 9!"

Katie was crouched next to Yuli, both of her hands locked around her grandmother's, who was breathing deeply from an oxygen mask placed over her nose and mouth. She reached over to brush her thumb across Katie's cheek, unable to tear her eyes away.

"It's a miracle," Yuli said, leaning closer to Katie, cradling her granddaughter's face in her well-worn hands. "We found you." Katie burst into tears now that the threat had passed. Sobbing, she released all the tension and stress she'd been holding in. A few minutes later, they pulled into the bay at the hospital and Marisa was whisked away.

Yuli refused a wheelchair at first. "Please, just let them check you out and make sure you're okay," Katie begged.

"All this fuss, Katia, it's unnecessary," she said. "I promise you, I *am* fine."

"You're also ninety-seven years old, so I'd appreciate it if you'd humor your granddaughter."

Yuli nodded with a somber smile and allowed them to wheel her into the emergency room, with Katie following closely behind. An hour later, Yuli was given a clean bill of health. They were both sitting in the waiting room, desperate for news about Marisa, when the sliding glass door opened, and Callie, Beckett, and Lauren rushed through it.

"Mom?" Callie cried and hurried over. The sight of her children made Katie choke back a sob and her knees wobble. She lurched forward, and Beckett caught her, cradling her to his chest. Callie and Lauren wrapped their arms around her, and she breathed in their familiar scent. The fabric softener from Beckett, the body spray Lauren preferred, and the cinnamon of Callie's favorite gum and her joy bubbled over, unable to be contained. Katie sobbed in relief. They clung to each other for several long moments, unable to let go. When Katie finally pulled back, she laid eyes on them all, letting her gaze linger. She brushed her thumbs across Beckett's sandpapery cheeks, then stepped up on her tiptoes to deliver a peck on his cheek. Lauren squeezed her arms around Katie. "Are you sure you're okay?"

"Yes, sweetheart, and the doctor checked Yuli out. She's the one you need to watch like a hawk."

Then Callie let out a little cry and flung herself into Katie's arms. She cupped the back of Callie's head and pulled her in tight. "I'm right here and I'm not going anywhere."

The sliding door opened again, and Frankie rushed through it with a police officer in tow. Letting out a shriek of joy, she raced over to her best friend.

"Oh my God," Frankie cried. "I never want to let you go." She squeezed Katie tighter, and over Frankie's shoulder, her eyes met the officer's.

"Who's that?" she murmured into the warmth of Frankie's neck.

"It's Harry Willey," Frankie whispered into Katie's shoulder.

"Excuse me?" Katie asked, sure her ears were playing tricks on her. "Did you just say Harry Willey?"

"It's a long story," Frankie said, finally pulling back and leading her over to the officer. "I'd like you to meet Officer Willey. He was assigned to your case."

"It's nice to meet you, Katie." All around them, the excited voices of the kids talking over each other made three a.m. at the emergency room seem like a party. "I want to let you get settled and reunited with your family, but I will need you to come by the station so I can take a statement while the events are still fresh."

"Of course," Katie said, glancing around the now-crowded waiting room. Her heart swelled with love for every person in it. Katie smiled, then her nose wrinkled when she caught an offensive whiff of herself.

"Whew! I stink. You might want to forgo future hugs until I've showered," she admitted to her kids with a grin.

"Don't tell us what to do, woman!" Beckett joked and swept Katie up in his arms again. "You stink so good to me!" They spent the next hour catching up and eating vending machine snacks while Katie waited for an update about Marisa.

"Katie Beaumont?" A nurse dressed in green scrubs was holding a clipboard. "Marisa would like to see you. Please, follow me."

"Just give me a few minutes, kids," Katie said. "I'll explain everything later."

She brushed away the happy tears on her cheeks and followed the nurse into a darkened exam room. Marisa was awake and white-faced, tears coursing down her own cheeks. Katie rushed over to her and gathered up her cool hand in her warm ones.

"I'm so confused. The last thing I remember is laying down in the back of a car. Before that…there's nothing."

"Shhh." Katie whispered, secretly relieved. "You were in shock. It's probably for the best you don't remember all the gory details."

Marisa held one hand over her womb and whispered, "The baby. He's gone." Her voice was one tone, flattened by shock. Tears washed down her cheeks, and she stared at the ceiling.

"Oh, honey." At the head of the bed, she wrapped her other arm around Marisa's head to comfort her.

"There was no heartbeat. I'll pass him, like a..." She dissolved into tears again, and Katie pulled her closer. "I am being punished. My ambivalence about this pregnancy made me miscarry," she whispered.

"I can't imagine how much your heart is hurting," Katie murmured. "What can I do for you right now to help you feel better?"

"Nothing," Marisa stated woodenly. "It's over. I guess, on some level, I should feel relieved. Seeing what Rocco was capable of doing to the mother of his child, it's obvious he was not ready to be a father. As cruel as it sounds, I should look at it as a tender mercy, but it still crushes me," she sobbed, gasping for air.

"You suffered a significant loss at the hands of a man you thought you loved," Katie said. "I'm so deeply sorry. Can I call someone for you?"

She sighed. "I don't have anywhere to go."

"Come stay with me," Katie offered. "I can keep an eye on you while you say goodbye to your son." She brushed Marisa's hair away from her teary eyes. "I've always believed that salt water is the cure for everything. I know it's saved me a time or two."

"Are you sure?" Marisa was wary.

"Absolutely. I wouldn't have it any other way."

Thirty-One

The next afternoon, Katie was awakened by the doorbell and Arlo's reaction to it. He jumped off the bed onto the floor and trotted out to the front door.

Glancing at the clock on her bedside table, she was surprised to see it was already after two p.m. She stood and stretched for a minute before forcing her feet into her yellow slides, and padded out to the door. Opening it, Katie found a crowd of her people gathered outside.

"Sorry, guys, I changed the code when I got home last night." She smiled at Beckett, carrying a breakfast pizza. He stopped to deposit a rough kiss on her cheek. Then Lauren crossed the threshold, carrying a Pyrex dish of cinnamon rolls. Callie brought up the rear, holding a potato casserole, with Frankie, who was double-fisting two bottles of champagne for mimosas.

"What is all this?" Katie asked, overwhelmed by their gesture. "You guys are spoiling me!"

The doorbell pealed again, and Arlo lost his mind,

breaking into another fit of barking. Katie opened the door to the smiling faces of Kristina, David, and Yuli. She opened her arms wide, gathering them all in close for a hug. Katie squeezed her eyes tight to stop the tears from escaping. "Everyone I love gathered in one room? My heart is bursting." She wrapped her arm around David and helped him to the sofa and then ringed one of each of her arms around her mother and grandmother.

"I'm just so grateful to be safe at home."

Hearing the commotion, a shy Marisa appeared in the hallway, hovering on the outskirts of the celebration. Seeing her, Katie walked over and asked, "Did we wake you up? My gang can be a little boisterous."

A small smile played peek-a-boo on Marisa's beautiful features. "I don't mind. I was actually getting a little hungry."

"How are you feeling today?"

"Better than last night," she admitted while pressing her palm to her abdomen, then pulled it away like she'd been burned and covered her mouth with her hand.

"Oh, sweet girl." Katie leaned in to give her a hug, and Marisa clung to her, bereft with grief. "I promise you, someday you will smile again, but today is not that day and it is okay." She pulled back and cradled Marisa's face with her hands. "Do you want to join us, or would you feel more comfortable if I made you a plate and brought it to your room?"

She considered it for a moment, then answered, "I think it might be good to be around people."

"Alright," Katie enthused with a bright smile. "Let me introduce you to everyone." She turned to meet the surprised eyes of her kids. "Guys, this is Marisa Gabriano. She's going to be staying with me for a while."

"Are you sure that's a good idea?" Lauren cautioned, her eyes wide, quickly latching on to the notorious last name.

"Honey, you haven't even been home for twenty-four hours. I'm sure Marisa is eager to get back to her own life," Kristina remarked.

"It's not up for discussion, my loves." She wrapped an arm around Marisa and led her to the island. "We kept each other sane in captivity. She's like an honorary sister to me now." Her serious tone silenced all their objections.

"It's a celebration!" Frankie didn't need to be encouraged. She broke the seal from the bottle in her hands, twisted off the metal fastener, and then popped the cork and everyone cheered. Making quick work of pulling out plates, silverware, and napkins, Katie let her kids cater to her. They forced her to sit down at the head of the table and kept her champagne glass filled to the brim. Frankie pulled out an eyedropper from her purse and squeezed a tiny amount of orange juice into her glass of champagne.

"What are you doing?" Katie laughed observing her odd behavior.

"It's just for color," she explained with a lopsided grin.

Katie chuckled at her friend. "God, I missed your quirks. I missed all of you so much. To be sitting here surrounded by your love is such a gift."

"Hear, hear!" David cheered.

Two hours later, while Frankie, Lauren, and Callie cleaned up the remnants of their late brunch, she said, "Hey! Clean-up is not solely women's work. Where's Beckett?"

Callie's eyebrows shot up, and her head nodded toward the patio door. Through the glass, she saw him seated on a chair by the pool next to Marisa. Katie's eyes settled on them. He was grinning from ear to ear, clearly smitten with Marisa's captivating beauty. Even without makeup on and pale from their ordeal, she was stunning. He said something, and she saw Marisa break into a genuine smile. The first one she'd seen on her face since their nightmare began.

Katie grimaced and shrugged. "It's just puppy love. A harmless crush that will fizzle out." Then she turned away and glanced over at Yuli. "I have to give my statement tomorrow morning, but then I'll be able to work the rest of my shift at the shop." Yuli nodded, gathered up Kristina and David, and after long hugs goodbye, went home.

Callie walked to the patio door, swung it open, and hollered out, "B! Climb out of the thirst trap that is our new honorary aunt and take me home. I have to work tonight."

A few minutes later, a red-faced Beckett slid the door open. His sheepish expression reminded Katie of when he got his hand caught in the cookie jar when he was five.

Lauren said to him, "You've got a little something here." She tapped a finger to the corner of her mouth.

Embarrassed, Beckett swiped his hand over his chin and looked down at it. Seeing nothing there, he asked, "What is it?"

"Drool."

"Shut it." Beckett grinned, his ears pinking up. "I was just trying to make her feel comfortable."

"Oh, she looks comfortable," Callie teased him. "I don't think a woman could *be* more comfortable. "

He rolled his eyes and gathered his keys, then brushed a kiss on Katie's cheek. "Bye, Mom. I'll call you later."

Callie and Lauren gave her a quick hug and continued to razz him as they walked out the door.

"Your kids crack me up," Frankie said as she folded the damp dish towel and took a seat at the island. Katie yawned. "I can leave if you need to take a nap."

"Not yet." Katie shook her head. "But can we continue this discussion horizontally?"

"Of course," Frankie answered.

"Let me check on Marisa first." Katie made her way out onto the sun-drenched patio and over to her. Arlo heeled in close, never leaving her side, even following her into the bathroom and back out of it all day long. She bent down to scratch under his chin. "I'm not going anywhere, silly boy. You can relax, too." His warm eyes looked deeply into hers. It was obvious Katie had imprinted on his soul from day one. "We'll take a walk on the beach tomorrow," she promised, "when I'm a little more rested."

She pulled up the chair next to Marisa, giving her a grin. "I think I'm going to hang out in the bedroom and chat with my best friend. Now that I'm full and happy, the chances of having a nap-cident are off the charts."

"A nap-cident?" Marisa asked, confused.

"An accidental nap," Katie informed her. "It's a rite of passage when you hit middle age." She looked down at the woman, who had a little more color in her cheeks. "Did you get enough to eat?"

"More than enough," Marisa answered. "Thank you for opening up your home to me and letting me invade your family reunion. You're lucky to have so many people in your life who love you."

"I am," Katie agreed.

"Your son," Marisa began. "He's exactly the way I'd have wanted mine to turn out." Her voice cracked, and Katie reached out a hand to squeeze her trembling one.

"I'm sorry you did not get the chance to meet yours," Katie offered and sat for a long moment with Marisa, listening to the fountain burble. "Some lucky baby is going to hit the jackpot one day when you become a mother."

"You think so?"

"I know so," Katie said and stood. "I'm here for you. If you need anything, please ask, and help yourself to anything in the house. I want you to be completely selfish and prioritize your own healing right now."

Marisa nodded, and with an encouraging smile, Katie walked back into the house, sliding the door behind her closed. When she got to her bedroom, Frankie was already in her bed. Arlo lay next to her, and she was engrossed in giving him serious belly rubs. As Katie crawled into the bed next to Frankie, he stood and vigorously shook out his coat and then circled and plopped down on her thigh.

"God, I missed that," Katie told Frankie with a smile. "There is something oddly comforting about a creature choosing to cuddle you."

"He was a distraught mess while you were gone. We all were," Frankie admitted.

"Tell me everything I missed," Katie insisted, stifling a yawn with the back of her hand. "Especially all the good parts about Officer Willey." She smiled at Frankie, then asked, "Is his name seriously Harry Willey?"

Frankie chuckled. "Technically, it's Harrison, but you know I'll never be able to call him that."

"That poor, poor man." Katie grinned. "He has no idea what he's getting into with you."

"I can't give him too much grief because he paid my bail."

"Bail?"

"Yeah. It was a rip-roaring good time around here while you were gone. I convinced him to let me join him on a stakeout, and we exposed a corrupt cop who tried to bust me for drug trafficking."

Katie reeled, shaking her head in shock. "Wait... What?"

"It's a long story," Frankie answered and then proceeded to fill Katie in on the grim tale. Words spilled from her tongue in a flood, punctuated by Katie's yawns. Frankie got up to go use the bathroom, and when she returned, Katie was fast asleep. Frankie pulled the blanket from the end of the bed, tugged it up and over her best friend, and then tiptoed out of the bedroom, shutting the light off while Katie snored.

THIRTY-TWO

The next day, Katie drove herself to the police station where she was pulled into a room to be interviewed. A tough-looking woman strode in and offered one thick hand that crushed Katie's.

"I'm Detective Raine." Her features were plain and unassuming, the kind of woman who never spent a moment at a makeup counter and was unapologetic about it. "I'm new to your case. It's been reassigned to me while Detective Ludlow is on extended leave." She glanced down at the thick folder in front of her and then closed it and brought her eyes to Katie's.

"I've already spoken to Mrs. Gabriano, so I am looking to corroborate her account. Can you fill me in on the events as you saw them?"

Katie nodded. "I met Marisa at our divorce lawyer's office and we became acquaintances. It was obvious she was in fear for her life and the life of her unborn child. I gave her my phone number and offered to help her escape an abusive relationship."

"With whom?'

"Her husband, Rocco Gabriano."

"Did you witness the abuse firsthand?" Detective Raine asked. "Marisa refused to file charges against him. Unfortunately, since there isn't an established pattern of abuse documented in hospital records or police reports, it becomes a 'he said, she said' situation."

Katie thought for a long moment, frustrated with the system and the lack of protections for women in it. "We were the victims of a home invasion, Detective Raine. We were assaulted, drugged, and then imprisoned and feared for our lives every day. Rocco was going to do whatever he had to do to keep Marisa in his life. He's a violent man with a long history of criminal behavior that has gone unpunished by law enforcement." Katie stood. "My grandmother identified him as the prime suspect to Officer Ludlow just a few days after we were taken. This department turned a blind eye to a viable lead and should be held culpable in the loss of life that resulted from their inaction."

"I understand you are frustrated," she said, trying to regain control of the conversation. "Would you please take a seat so I can fill you in on what disciplinary actions we've taken?"

"Sure." Katie sat down again and folded her arms across her chest.

"We've launched an internal investigation into Detective Ludlow, and I would like to express the sincere apologies of the Aura Cove Police Department for the mismanagement of your case. Rest assured, there will be a thorough investigation with appropriate measures of accountability."

"What about the ludicrous charges against my best friend?"

"As of this morning, Francesca Stapleton has been cleared of any wrongdoing, thanks to the solid police work of Officer Willey. He found video footage of Ludlow gaining access to Ms. Stapleton's car, and I am confident her case will be closed once the appropriate paperwork is filed."

"What about Rocco Gabriano?"

"We have a warrant out for his arrest, but he seems to be missing." Detective Raine continued, "We've just brought in Carmine DeBreccio for questioning. He's been charged with unlawful entry, assault and battery, and unlawful imprisonment. I don't expect us to get too far as his loyalty runs deep, but we'll keep you posted on any advancements in the case. Can you tell me what you remember about the last time you saw Mr. Gabriano?"

Katie mulled her request over, then answered, "Marisa hit him in the stomach with a pipe we dislodged, and he fell to the ground. We were terrified she was going to lose her baby, so we got the hell out of there to get her to a hospital."

"There was a small pool of blood and other physical evidence at the warehouse, but no sign of Rocco. He's probably at a safe house by now, waiting for the heat to settle down."

She was wrong. Katie's intuition tingled. Zoya. He had to be with Zoya. It was the only logical explanation. But then doubt began to bloom in her belly. There had been no man in the car, only a tiny, yipping dog. Remembering when Yuli explained how Zoya thought all men were dogs and frequently cast them into the body of a canine when they wronged her, the truth flooded in. A wide, knowing grin spread across her features. Wait. He *was* the dog.

Across from her, the detective's brows pinched together in confusion. "Is there something you're not telling me, Ms. Beaumont?"

She wiped the grin away and shook her head no. "Just looking forward to getting my life back. I will not live in fear."

"Well, that's all the questions I have for now." Detective Raine stood to signal the interview was over. "We'll be in touch." She opened the door, and Katie walked through it and out into the warm November air with a satisfied smile on her face.

———

An hour later, she reported to Kandied Karma for her regular shift, where Yuli was ladling a black liquid into small espresso cups.

"Let me guess? More poison?"

"It's the ultimate pick-me-up," Yuli admitted, handing a cup to her granddaughter.

Katie hoisted her cup up into the air and clinked it against Yuli's, then threw it back with one harsh swallow. She pressed her lips together to keep it down and broke out with beads of sweat near her hairline while Yuli watched her reaction. She recovered much more quickly this time, and Yuli opened her arms and pulled her in for a hug.

"Gosh, I missed your hugs," Katie said, savoring the enveloping softness of her grandmother's plump arms with her eyes tightly closed.

"How was the interview?"

"Pretty straightforward," Katie admitted. "We don't have to worry about any retaliation from the Gabrianos. I believe Rocco is Zoya's teacup Yorkie now."

Yuli muttered, "Of course, I bet he is. That woman will never change."

"At least Marisa can move forward with her divorce and walk away from the Gabrianos once and for all. I know it's a terrible thing to say, but having a baby together would have connected them for the next two decades. Maybe it was more merciful it worked out this way."

"I would agree," Yuli stated, then confessed, "I failed Marisa. If only I'd reserved some of my energy, I might have been able to intervene and give her time to seek medical treatment."

"You're not being fair to yourself," Katie reasoned. "You had no idea what you were up against and had to play the cards you were dealt." Her forehead knotted up in concern and she asked, "Do we need to worry about what Marisa and Rocco witnessed?"

"No." Yuli answered. "Their minds are too limited. Our supernatural acts dissolve in the presence of the ordins disbelief, leaving holes in their memories."

"Good." Katie relaxed. "I have to admit, Zoya was *not* what I expected."

Yuli shivered, remembering. "Zoya's power multiplied when she joined forces with Lilith. I'm not sure what will happen when she returns to the dark goddess empty-hand-ed." Yuli looked deep into Katie's eyes. "All magic comes with sacrifice, but dark magic always takes much more than it gives."

"Then why would she risk it?"

"Zoya has always had tunnel vision when it comes to

Salvatore. They were obsessed with each other, and nothing else in the world existed outside of the warm cocoon of their love. Not Dominic, and certainly not me. She always said she would burn the world down to avenge him someday, and it looks like she did." Yuli looked down and straightened her apron.

"Do you think she'll come back?"

"She's got to make things right with Lilith, but once the dust has settled, I don't know how she could stay away," Yuli admitted.

The doorbell jingled, and Oz walked in with Shasta on a leash. Seeing Katie, he burst into a huge smile. "It *is* true!" he said warmly. "Fact-checking has never been the strong suit of Channel 11. I didn't want to interrupt your homecoming with the kids, but I am thrilled to see you home safe and sound!"

"Oz!" she said warmly. "Your regular order, I presume?"

"You know me well."

"What's your next podcast episode about?" she asked and grinned at his eagerness to share.

"There's an old hotel down at St. Pete's Beach that opened in the 1920s, and shortly after, a young woman's body washed up on shore."

"You mean that lavender monstrosity right on the water? What's it called? The El Conquistador?"

"The very same," Oz confirmed. "I've booked a room there this weekend and am going to meet up with one of my paranormal investigator buddies. He's got all the latest equipment. We're going to see if we can make contact with her spirit."

"Whoa." Katie's eyes were wide. "That sounds

interesting."

"I think it will be." He offered Katie a quick smile as she handed him the box of truffles and his latte.

"You'll have to give us the inside scoop."

"Always."

Later that afternoon, she was surprised to see Beckett, Lauren, and Callie rolling in together. Beckett was clutching a wireless speaker in his hand. Katie rushed over to them and swept them all into her arms for a group hug. "To what do I owe this tremendous pleasure?"

"Someone special is coming in soon, and we've decided to help her cross one of the items off her bucket list."

"What?" Katie was instantly intrigued. "Who?"

"Just wait." Beckett went outside the shop and set up the wireless speaker while Lauren stayed inside.

"Mom, that streak in your hair is even more pronounced!" Lauren noticed, and she reached out to grasp it between her fingers with a smile. "I used to agree with Dad, but I have to admit, it's starting to grow on me."

"It is?" Katie asked, then explained, "I'm happy to hear that. It's part of who I am, and I've decided to embrace it."

Lauren considered her answer. "I never really thought of it that way." She looked down at her perfectly pressed suit and raked her fingers down the length of her smooth, straight hair. "I don't blame you. All the maintenance required to beautify yourself in a futile attempt to hold on to youth is exhausting."

"I refuse to do it anymore," Katie boldly declared.

"I like this new version of you."

"Aww. Come here, sweetheart." Katie wrapped her in another hug.

Ten minutes before closing, the door jingled again. This time, Lorelei was rolling into the shop with Liz. When they stopped in front of the case, the younger woman closed her eyes and deeply inhaled the mouthwatering scent of cocoa butter mingling with chocolate. "This is what heaven smells like!" There was such a sweetness to her reaction it made Katie's heart lift.

"Can I help you?" Katie walked over, offering Liz a bright smile as she pulled out a golden box and began to fold it.

Liz gasped, and a huge grin washed over her features. Seeing the pair, Beckett quickly re-entered the shop. "Mom, I want you to meet a couple of new friends we made while you were gone. This is Lorelei and Liz, and you'll be happy to know eating truffles from Kandied Karma was on their bucket list."

"That's awesome. We feel so honored!" Katie enthused. Through the plate-glass window, she saw a small crowd starting to gather outside, wearing black. Confused, she glanced at Beckett, who responded with a quick wink.

He bent down next to Lorelei's wheelchair and said, "There's something you need to see outside. Can I roll you out there?" Katie noticed Lorelei's forehead pucker with confusion, yet she nodded. It was hard to say no to her dashing son.

Lauren held the door open, and he pushed the wheelchair out to the square. When he got to the planter box that contained the speaker, he fiddled with his phone, and a few seconds later, the first few notes of Journey's "Don't Stop Believin'" drifted into the open mezzanine area.

"What is happening?" Lorelei's hand drifted to her mouth as the mob of people dressed in black lined up and began to dance to the music. Lorelei's eyes twinkled with glee as she belted out the lyrics. When the song started the chorus, the front man ran over to her wheelchair and grabbed the handlebars, pulling her into the mass of dancing people. Pure joy radiated from her and she laughed out loud. Within seconds, she was mimicking their movements, moving her arms in sync with theirs, fully engaged in the sea of dancers. Katie grinned from ear to ear, taking in the spectacle of dozens of people executing perfectly timed choreography with the sick woman in the middle of it.

Liz burst into tears, and Katie rushed over to wrap an arm around her. "Isn't this incredible?" She laughed as tears raced down her wrinkled cheeks. When Katie's finger brushed the woman's skin, she felt the first jolt. A visual flash of a gynecologist's stirrups confused her.

Katie pulled her arm away quickly as if she were scalded. Next to her and oblivious to what had just happened, Liz was swaying on the sidewalk as the song played the final chorus. Bowled over, she watched the woman laugh, witnessing the absolute joy on her daughter's face. Lorelei was flushed pink with excitement as she was pushed and pulled on the pavement in time with the song. At the climax, the group gathered close around her and hoisted her chair up into the air, letting her crowd surf the last few bars. When the song ended, she was delicately lowered to the ground, and the large group of people dispersed without an explanation or a single word.

Beckett pushed her back to Liz with a huge, satisfied grin on his face.

"I can't believe it!" Lorelei said. "I thought my crowd surfing days were over. Thank you!"

"Hey!" Callie interjected, "Believe it. You can't let *Journey* down!"

Beckett groaned and shook his head. "You're the worst." He pulled Callie in and balled a fist, rubbing it over the crown of her head while she tried to fight him off.

"That is unwanted physical contact!" Callie protested, and Katie laughed at their antics.

"God, I missed moments like this," she said.

They all gathered together out front on the sidewalk. Yuli turned the sign to closed and handed Liz and Lorelei an enormous golden box filled with truffles.

"I will never forget this moment," Lorelei said, and Katie saw Beckett's eyes fill. Her tender-hearted son offered her a flash of a grin and turned away to hide his tears.

"We'll see you after your next appointment," Callie told Lorelei. "Like it or not, you're a lifetime VIP customer now."

Liz grinned at first, and then Katie noticed the sadness well up in her eyes as she flinched at the word 'lifetime'. Katie offered her a sympathetic smile and reached out to squeeze her one more time. Her skin brushed against the crepe-like skin on Liz's forearm, and another flash of an image rocketed forward into her psyche. A white coffin draped in pink roses being lowered to the ground. Katie's stomach dropped and she fought to regain her composure.

"Well, we better get going. It's a long ride home," Liz said, then asked Beckett, Callie, and Lauren, "Can I give you a hug?"

"Of course." Beckett opened his arms, and she

squeezed him tight, small phrases of gratitude rushing from her in an embarrassed, grateful stream. After hugging them all, she gathered up her purse.

"Katie, it was wonderful to meet you! We're both thrilled about your safe return," Liz said.

"Thank you," Katie mumbled, lost in thought.

"This was the best day ever!" Lorelei called out over her shoulder and waved at them as Liz pushed the wheelchair down the sidewalk and crossed the street. As Katie watched them walk away and get into their minivan, she willingly accepted her next assignment with Karma. Her eyes darted over to Yuli, who was standing outside the candy shop watching the interaction with great interest. Her watchful gaze hadn't missed a thing. Katie tipped her head toward the retreating women, and Yuli gave her a small, almost imperceptible nod.

There was a honk, and Lorelei gave one last enthusiastic wave out the window as they drove past Kandied Karma on their way out of town. Lorelei was a vibrant woman who should be enjoying the prime of her life, and in that moment, Katie was more determined than ever to find a way to help her.

————

Thank you for reading "Flash Mob: Midlife in Aura Cove." Here's an exclusive sneak peek of the next thrilling installment of this hilarious and heartwarming series! Lunar Flash: Midlife in Aura Cove. Order here.

———

Zoya paced at the Castanova compound on the edge of the sea right until the last moment, rage seething from every pore in her body. She raked a brush through her long, white hair, roughly pressing the bristles of it into her scalp just short of drawing blood. Cursing under her breath, she gathered her hair, sweeping the brush upward in rhythmic strokes until all of it was gathered on top of her head in a high ponytail. In the pit of her stomach, a knot twisted. She'd come home empty-handed, and she knew Lilith would not react favorably. But most of all, she'd failed to set Sally's soul free and the defeat ate at her. When you're always a winner, you forget what it feels like to lose.

At her feet, Terrance, her chocolate Labrador Retriever, barked once. She'd promoted him to the head of the pack when she'd freed Magnum from his dog body after years of servitude. It was a jarring sound that snapped her out of her self-destructive spiral.

"What is it?" She snarled at him and he lowered his head and focused on a spot on the ground, delivering the update she'd forgotten she'd requested. "I've prepared the altar for you and the dog is waiting inside."

"Very good." Zoya said, "You may go." He jumped to his feet and the metal choke chain on his throat jingled like a bell as he departed. Not able to put off the meeting any longer, she exhaled and opened the door to her meditation chamber. Inside, Rocco yipped and snarled at her when she entered. Seeing the mafioso reduced to a teacup Yorkshire Terrier briefly slid a smug smile across her lips. It never got old, reducing a man drunk on his own power into a helpless creature trained to serve her every whim. Rocco growled and barked again and she rolled her eyes. This one would never learn his lesson.

With a scowl, she snapped her fingers, sending a little electric jolt through him like a shock collar. His resulting squeal was satisfying and she was slightly placated by her ever present lust for revenge.

"Use your words." She demanded when he circled the room, yipping non-stop for a solid minute after the jolt.

"Free me now or I will end you!" Rocco's speech distorted into a high pitched Munchkin style voice, like he'd deeply inhaled on a helium balloon. Zoya found it amusing as she roared with laughter. "What in the hell is happening to me?" The voice was even more ridiculous the more frustrated the tiny dog became.

"Do you hear how pathetic you sound?" Zoya mocked him. "With that intonation, your intimidation techniques have lost their usual fervor, darling. I can't even take you seriously at all when you sound like a chipmunk."

Rocco growled and then emitted two high-pitched whines.

"I suggest you calm down, because we've got a deal to make with the devil." Zoya said, appraising the tiny Yorkie, hoping Lilith would accept this paltry sacrifice. "Or should I say she-devil?" She mused, "As much fun as we have had together, and it *has* been a raucous good time, you're a necessary sacrifice I'll need to make to get back in Lilith's good graces."

"Lilith?" Rocco's head cocked like she'd asked him if he wanted to go for a ride.

"Oh! She's a hot one. You'll see."

Zoya struck the match on the slate and the flame lit up in the room's darkness. One by one, she lit the bank of black candles and the sticks of incense in the black obsidian dish. She waved the smoke toward her body and hummed one long note, and she circled her hands in front of her torso as she kneeled in front of the altar. Zoya chanted and the tines of a tuning fork created a sound wave that rippled into the air.

"What the hell is that noise?" Rocco cried and raced to Zoya's thigh, laid down next to her trembling, and covered his ears with his paws. A burst of warm light illuminated Zoya's face and as she chanted louder as the flames grew and transformed into a wall of light. Through the portal, a vision of Lilith's nude form emerged. She was seated on a golden throne where Sally was kneeling at her feet, massaging them with oil. Zoya's eyes lighted on him and she felt a tingle of jealousy. Feeling her eyes on his back, Sally turned and his sad eyes connected with hers. Her personal failure to set his soul free made it difficult to maintain eye contact.

"What is this?" Lilith spat with contempt. "You were to bring me a child, not a worthless dog." She stood to her full six-foot height and leaned forward, crossing her arms across her naked breasts.

"Who the hell do you think you are?" Rocco stood up on his haunches, his distorted voice taking all the power out of his words. "*You* are the one responsible for the death of my child?" He attempted ferocious barks at the wall of flames that only sounded wimpy.

Zoya huffed in outrage and reached out to grab the annoying dog by the scruff of his neck and placed him on his back in a submissive position. "Shut up! Where is your personal accountability? Your violence is as much to blame as mine was." She turned toward the vision, shutting down any further interaction. "The child is gone, My Dark Queen." Zoya waved one hand at the dog. "I was hoping to make a deal and offer the father of the child in his place."

Lilith leaned further out of the portal and, with one inflamed hand, plucked the tiny dog up by the scruff of his neck and looked him over. She extended her arm further through the portal, but each time she tried to claim him and pull him through it, the dog couldn't pass and fell to the floor.

"All dogs go to heaven." Lilith explained. "I guess we've proven the old adage true."

"There is a simple solution to this problem, mistress." Zoya offered. "I will return him to his human form."

Rocco tried to scamper away, but Lilith's hand came through the portal and clasped his neck. Zoya reached out one palm and focused all her energy on him. The wall of flames leapt from Lilith's hand through the dog, who howled on contact and then over to Zoya's wrist. The searing pain and scent of burning flesh and singed hair infiltrated her nostrils. Acrid smoke made Zoya's eyes water and sparks fly from her hand. In one surge of strength, Rocco burst into flames. Then he crossed over completely, landing naked on the granite rocks next to Sally, who was still seated at the foot of Lilith's throne.

Rocco stood up. Roaring and enraged, he charged at Lilith, clawing at her with his fingers. An amused expression slid across Lilith's features as he ricocheted off her body and fell to the ground with a loud yelp. When he gathered enough energy to stand on his feet, Lilith wrapped a thick metal choker around his muscular neck. In an instant, he dropped to his knees in front of her. "I'm sorry, my queen, if I have not pleased you." The words came out of his mouth against his will. Confused by the apology he'd just made, he shook his head to clear it. Rocco yanked at the choker in desperation as his eyes darted around the cave of the hellish rocky landscape he was now contained in, looking for an exit.

"Shut up." Lilith told him. "From now on, you will only speak when you have been spoken to." A vein in his neck bulged and anger colored every feature on his face. He opened his mouth to defy her, and a metal ball gag shot from her hand to clamp down on his mouth. "Did you think I was playing games?" She rolled her violet eyes and shook her head. "Stupid creatures, the entire lot. Men never learn."

"I couldn't agree more, mistress." Zoya said, eager to prove to Lilith they were similarly minded.

Lilith stood and spread her legs wide, and rested her hands on her hips. Obediently, Sally scrambled to his feet and stood behind the glowing woman. His fingers encircled her tiny waist and made their way up her torso. Seeing the sensual display, Zoya shifted uncomfortably on the balls of her feet and averted her gaze. She couldn't bear to see what came next. "Zoya, my child, you must fix your gaze on me." Lilith grinned like a lioness on the hunt and tipped her head down as black horns emerged from the top of her head. Salvatore's shaking fingers dexterously wandered up to her breast, and he cupped one in each hand. Salvatore closed his eyes and Zoya saw tears break free from the corners of them and cascade down his face. Lilith moaned in delight as the tips of her peach colored nipples hardened with arousal. "This is your penance. To watch in bitter agony as the green monster of jealousy takes root in your soul." Zoya rankled and bit back her usual harsh retort. "Sally is a very skilled lover, but you already know this." She closed her eyes as her pleasure intensified and Zoya felt it like a sucker punch. Zoya watched in horror as Sally's fingers walked down her hip and tangled into her mound and she felt her heart break. She bit her lip to prevent a wounded cry from escaping. She would not show weakness. Breathing in through her nose and out her mouth, tears blurred her vision until she couldn't see it at all. Lilith's breath came faster, and she cried out as an orgasm crashed over her. Afterward, the Dark Queen was glowing, her skin dewy and resplendent.

"You have served me well, Salvatore." Lilith detached the chain that was connected to Rocco from her wrist and clipped it to a metal handcuff already on Salvatore's wrist. "This is your reward for pleasing your mistress."

Salvatore's eyes darkened into black holes of hatred. He tugged on the chain and yanked Rocco to his feet, and then quickly disappeared into the blackness. Zoya swiped her eyes with her hands, grateful for the end of the Lilith's sexual gratification and Sally's participation.

When Lilith's eyes bored into hers, she curtsied and averted her gaze.

"Although I accept your sacrifice, it does not fulfill the terms of our agreement. I know it was difficult to witness my pleasure with your beloved, dark daughter, but that is why it is considered a punishment. It's the only way the impart the seriousness of your infraction."

Zoya compartmentalized the betrayal and tucked it away into the recesses of her mind. Intellectually she understood what transpired, but in her heart the jealousy burned. The only way to avoid repeating the act was to make a new deal. She bowed. "The infant died in utero, it could not be avoided. There must be another way I can garner your favor and earn the release of Sally's soul."

A fire ball burst into view and obliterated the entire vision. A cunning smile stretched across Lilith's features as her attention focused elsewhere for a few seconds. "Looks like the Gabriano and Lombardo reunion is hitting a few bumps, and I must intervene." She stood. "Testosterone is the downfall of mankind, but at least it always proves to be entertaining." Her eyes leveled on Zoya's as she considered her offer. "Bring me another worthy sacrifice and I will consider your request."

The flames shrunk, then sputtered out, and Zoya was alone in the meditation chamber again. Her skin was flushed, and she felt desperation sear through her soul. Her thoughts circled back to Lilith, writhing her hips against

Salvatore's hand. "No!" She shook her head to clear it, but the image returned over and over on her one track mind. She had to find a way to free him, because she could not bear the thought of his sexual servitude to Lilith for an eternity.

———

Order Lunar Flash Here.

Also Available on Amazon, BN Nook, Apple iBooks, Kobo, Google Play and many international booksellers. Or request it from your local library.

Like FREE Books? Enter to Win a Gift Card to My Bookstore https://tealbutterflypress.com/pages/join-our-email-list-and-win
There's a new winner every week!

READ MORE BY THIS AUTHOR

Use the QR code below to access my current catalogue. **Teal Butterfly Press is the only place to purchase autographed paperbacks and get early access.** Buying direct means you are supporting an artist instead of big business. I appreciate you.

https://tealbutterflypress.com/pages/books

Also available at Barnes and Noble, Kobo, Apple books, Amazon, and many other international book sellers.

Find My Books at your Favorite Bookseller Below.

Books by Ninya

Books By Blair Bryan

ABOUT THE AUTHOR

Under the pen names of Ninya and Blair Bryan, this creative powerhouse channels her passion into crafting stories that entertain and immerse readers of paranormal women's fiction, travel memoir, and contemporary women's fiction.

A risk-taker by nature, Blair Bryan fearlessly embarked on her author journey at the age of 44, bringing to life captivating tales that will leave you on the edge of your seat. She's a magnet for wild experiences, breathtaking locations, and fascinating individuals, seamlessly weaving their essence into her women's fiction novels. From unexpected encounters to daring escapades, she draws inspiration from the tapestry of her own life, ensuring an endless supply of captivating storylines that will leave you hungry for more.

If you love a good dirty joke, a cup of coffee so strong you can chew it, and have killed more cats with your curiosity than you can count, she might be your soulmate.

Visit her online www.tealbutterflypress.com

Join her exclusive facebook reader group: https://www.facebook.com/groups/tealbutterflypress

Made in the USA
Columbia, SC
24 June 2024

37590801R00171